# ON WHOM WILL THE CRIME BE PINNED?

**EVANGELINE FAIRFIELD**—The widow who probably would have nagged her husband to death if someone hadn't killed him first.

**ANDY McNASTER**—Sworn enemy of the Grub-and-Stakers who is suddenly acting like their friend...and whose ulterior motives will shock them—maybe to death.

**FREDERICK BROWN**—The roofer who left his ladder as a stairway to heaven for Fairfield...and who left his past and real name behind.

**HUNDING PAFFNAGEL**—Fairfield's former colleague, a woman who has terrible taste in clothes, a thirst for adventure—and a hunger for forbidden fruit.

Charlotte MacLeod
WRITING AS
# Alisa Craig

# THE GRUB-AND-STAKERS QUILT A BEE

**AVON**
PUBLISHERS OF BARD, CAMELOT, DISCUS AND FLARE BOOKS

Lobelia Falls, its people, and their doings are all fictitious. However the esprit de corps among the Grub-and-Stakers is typical of garden club members in general. Like Niagara Falls, they are a vast international source of natural energy, wondrous to behold in action, and adaptable to many useful purposes.

AVON BOOKS
A division of
The Hearst Corporation
105 Madison Avenue
New York, New York 10016

The Doubleday edition contains the following Library of Congress Cataloging in Publication Data:

MacLeod, Charlotte.
  The grub-and-stakers quilt a bee.

  I. Title.
PS3563.A31865G74        1985        813'.54

First Avon Printing: December 1987

*Affectionately dedicated to all the grubbers and stakers in the Sudbury Garden Club*

# THE GRUB-AND-STAKERS  QUILT A BEE

# CHAPTER 1

"Well, fry me for a doughnut!" cried Hazel Munson.

Therese Boulanger whanged her gavel. "May we have that in the form of a motion?" Therese was a stickler for protocol.

"Stuff it, Therese," muttered Dittany Henbit Monk, who was not.

Her utterance was drowned in cries of "I don't believe it!" "My stars and garters," and similar outbursts including a "gadzooks" from Arethusa Monk, the famous author of roguish regency romances. How could their president drag in *Robert's Rules of Order* at a time like this? Never before in all its long and checkered history had the Grub-and-Stake Gardening and Roving Club of Lobelia Falls, Ontario, received a bequest of any magnitude at all, much less a whole dad-blanged museum.

The "dad-blanged" was contributed by the aforementioned Dittany Henbit Monk. Her vocabulary had taken strange new directions as a result of her recent marriage to Osbert Monk, better known to the sagebrush intelligentsia as Lex Laramie. Osbert would be back at the house on Applewood Avenue right now, throwing his literary lasso over the neck of some dreamed-up maverick and wondering if he'd meant to write "dogie" instead. Did he but know! Dittany could hardly wait to tell him.

She'd jolly well have to wait, though. Therese was no slouch with a gavel. The meeting was back to order.

"For the benefit of those who may not have grasped the details of the matter before us" (Therese meant everybody who'd been too busy gabbling to pay attention, but was too good a parliamentarian to say so) "I shall read the terms of the bequest again. The subject will then be thrown open for discussion. If you wish to speak, please raise your hand and wait to be recognized by the chair. Otherwise," she added, for Therese was human too, "we'll be here all night."

"Read on, Macduff," boomed Arethusa.

Therese cleared her throat. "Under the terms of the holograph will that was found in the files down at the water department after we'd all assumed John Architrave had died intestate, his house on Victoria Street, which we all know to be a fine though sadly run-down example of Early Lobelia Falls architecture, of which we have far too little left, thanks to what some people choose to call progress . . ."

"Is that all in the will, for Pete's sake?" Hazel Munson whispered to Dittany.

"Shh!" The shush was Samantha Burberry's. Being an elected town official and chairman of the club's legislative committee, she felt duty-bound to uphold the torch of parliamentarianism.

Therese got herself back in hand. "The gist of it is, John has left his house to the club free and clear, on condition that we maintain and operate it as a museum dedicated to the memory of John's wife, a former president and four-time winner of the Winona Pitcher Award, and that the museum be in fact known and designated by an appropriate sign or plaque as the Aralia Polyphema Architrave Museum. Before we begin our discussion, I'd like to ask our legislative chairman whether there's anything in the bylaws that might preclude our accepting such a bequest."

Samantha rose, poised and elegant as always. "Nothing whatever, to my knowledge. It would appear to fit nicely under Section A, Clause 3 which states that the club shall initiate and carry out projects for the general education and beautification of our community."

"Thank you, Samantha. Any objections?"

Hazel Munson's hand shot up. "I'm not objecting. I'd just like to know if that old meathead left us any funds to run the place with."

For one long, horrified moment, there was not a whisper in the room. Everyone knew John had left his life's savings to his one surviving relative, their own beloved Minerva Oakes, co-chairman of the landscape committee. They also knew how desperately Minerva needed the cash, and they'd rejoiced over the elderly widow's great windfall. Hazel, realizing too late what a brick she'd dropped, clapped her hand over her errant mouth.

Minerva looked stricken, but rose gamely. "I'm quite willing to . . ."

"Shut up," barked Zilla Trott, the other half of the landscape committee. "You're out of order. Madam Chairman," she waved her hand wildly, "I make a formal motion that the club refuse to accept one plugged nickel from Minerva Oakes."

"Second the motion," cried the members as one voice. Even Therese seconded before she remembered she wasn't supposed to, then called for a vote before Minerva could get another word in. The ayes had it so loudly the windows bulged.

"Now," said Zilla, "I move the chair appoint a ways and means committee."

"Objection," cried Arethusa. "First we elect a board of trustees, then they appoint their own committee."

"That's right," Therese agreed, clearly nonplussed to find Arethusa in possession of so mundane a fact.

"Then I nominate Arethusa chairman of the board of trustees," Zilla amended, nothing daunted. It took a lot to daunt Zilla.

Again there was a free-for-all to second the nomination. Arethusa was not only the club celebrity but the member with the most spare cash. Furthermore, she had Dittany to keep her in hand. While still a Henbit, Dittany had been Arethusa's typing service and voice of reason. As a niece-in-law she packed even more clout. Hence Dittany got nominated forthwith as secretary.

Therese would be a member ex officio, Dot Coskoff would be treasurer because she could both add and subtract. Hazel Munson had to be on the board because she could keep her head when all about her were losing theirs and blaming it on anybody who came handy. Minerva was named vice president as a matter of courtesy and a way of salving her conscience anent the money by giving her a reason to work her head off for the museum, which she'd have done anyway. Zilla Trott came next because nobody could envision a committee that Minerva was on and Zilla wasn't.

Mrs. MacVicar then moved the nominations be closed because six trustees were plenty. Nobody cared to contradict Mrs. MacVicar, whose husband was the law in Lobelia Falls, so they elected the board and broke up the meeting. Instead of staying to participate in the wild babble that followed, Dittany sped home to her husband.

"Osbert, listen!"

"Eh?" Osbert dragged his attention away from some distant arroyo or mesa and focused it on his wife. "Darling, it's you!"

"And whom were you expecting?"

"Well, you see, Harold the Headless Horse Thief was galloping

into the haunted canyon and for just a second there I wondered if
—if we mightn't have some of those big molasses cookies with the
crinkly edges hanging around anywhere handy?"

"Let's go look," said Dittany, for she loved Osbert dearly.

They went, Osbert nuzzling gently at the back of his bride's
neck as the faithful Appaloosa of his hero was wont to do. To the
hero's neck, of course. Dittany's was a neck just right for nuzzling,
whereas the cowboy's must perforce be tanned to leather and
perhaps not very recently washed. Osbert was feeling pleasantly
one-up on the Appaloosa as he buckled down to his tea and cookies. The mood was dispelled by his Aunt Arethusa's barging
through the back door in full cry as was her lamentable habit.

"Osbert, go away" was her greeting. "We have to hold a trustees'
meeting."

"Stuff it, Arethusa," said Dittany, Osbert's mouth being full of
cookie at the moment. "A man is king in his own castle."

"What castle, prithee? This house is yours, not his."

It was in fact the ancestral residence of the Henbits, but Dittany
refused to yield her point. "It's ours. Osbert's spent more getting
the place glued back together than it was worth before he started.
Sit down and have a cookie. We can't hold a meeting without the
rest of the trustees."

"Why not, egad? We haven't drawn up any bylaws yet, so how
can we be in violation of them?"

"I'd have to clear that point with Therese. Anyway, I don't want
to hold a trustees' meeting. I want to—"

"I know what you want to and I think it's perfectly disgusting.
Can't you wait till bedtime, forsooth?"

"Arethusa, that was not what I meant," said Dittany with quiet
dignity.

"Why not? Aha! A rift i' the lute. What's that beastly nephew of
mine been up to now?"

"Osbert is not beastly. Osbert is a lambie pie with fur-lined
booties on. What I intended to say was that I want to start supper
because we horsed around at the meeting this afternoon far too
long and I'm practicing to be a perfect wife."

"Darling, you already are," cried Osbert, having coped with the
cookie.

"I haven't ironed your shirts yet."

"A bagatelle. I'll wear this same one tomorrow."

"You will not. What would the neighbors think?"

"Figo for the neighbors," said Arethusa. "Could we get on with the meeting? The gist or nub of the matter is that we've got to appoint a curator forthwith."

"Why forthwith?" said Dittany.

"Because I've already been approached by seventeen people who want to donate priceless artifacts to the museum, that's why."

"What priceless artifacts?"

"A hand-embroidered corset cover worn by Samantha Burberry's husband's great-grandmother on the occasion of her presentation to Queen Victoria at the Court of St. James, a set of hand-carved false teeth once owned by a certain Sam Small, the first wagon driver who came to Lobelia Falls, later hanged for cattle rustling in Alberta—"

Osbert brightened. "Now, there's an item of genuine historical interest."

"To whom, prithee? If you think I'm going to accept any bogus bicuspids in my capacity as chairman of the board of trustees of the whatever-her-name-was museum, you can think again, eh. The trouble is, I can't come straight out and say so, because Zilla Trott's the one who wants to donate the teeth."

"I see," said Dittany.

"I don't," said Osbert.

"You wouldn't," snarled Arethusa.

"It's quite simple, darling," Dittany explained. "We need somebody who can winnow out the junk from the good stuff without making everybody hate him."

"Him?"

"Or her. I used the pronoun abstractly. You remember about abstract pronouns, dear?"

"Certainly I remember about abstract pronouns. Aunt Arethusa wouldn't know an abstract pronoun if it walked up and tipped its hat to her."

"I would so," said Arethusa.

"You would not. You only know words like stap my garters."

"Garters. Egad, yes. A pair of red silk arm garters won by old Mr. Busch in a poker game when he was a telegraph operator up in Yellowknife in 1909. You see what we're up against?"

Dittany nodded gloomily. By nightfall they'd have been offered a wealth of hand-crocheted chamber pot covers, secondhand beehives, wooden legs, Moody & Sankey hymnals, autographed photos of Ivor Novello, moth-eaten army uniforms, and that umbrella stand made from interwoven buffalo horns Dot Coskoff's mother had been trying to unload on somebody for the past forty-three years. Would anybody in town have the guts to explain that none of these things was precisely what the Aralia Polyphema Architrave Museum happened to be in urgent need of at the moment? Sighing, she reached for the telephone.

"Whom are you calling, forsooth?" Arethusa demanded.

"Hazel, Dot, Minerva, and Zilla, of course. Much as I hate to admit it, Arethusa, you're right."

# CHAPTER 2

Many years had passed since Aralia Polyphema laid down her bow and gavel for the last time. After her death, John Architrave had lived alone. He'd managed his housekeeping much as he'd managed the water department, and that was as ill as anybody in Lobelia Falls cared to speak of the dead. Before they could start putting things into the museum, an awful lot would have to be taken out.

Osbert donated part of the advance on his latest Western, whose heroine had blue-green eyes, blondish brown hair with highlights the color of dawn on the mesa, and cheeks like the bloom on the yucca, or Spanish bayonet; and happened, by apt coincidence, to be named Dittany. That paid for the hiring of a dump truck to cart away enough trash so that the peeling wallpaper and cobwebbed ceilings could be got at.

Before restoration could begin, though, the problem of what to restore it to had to be resolved. After considerable wrangling, the trustees decided to do what everybody then claimed to have been in favor of all along: namely, to plan the museum as a typical Canadian home of the Early Lobelia Falls period. Only genuine antiques or accurate reproductions would be used, and decisions of the curator would be final. The curator would be kept firmly enthumbed by the trustees, but the general public wasn't to know that. By this stratagem or ruse they hoped to keep out the carved coconuts and art deco smoking stands without antagonizing friends and neighbors who'd been kidding themselves that they'd at last found a place to park the family relics without upsetting the in-laws.

Finding a curator turned out to be a piece of cake. Dot Coskoff's sister's brother-in-law had an uncle who had a cousin who'd just been retired as assistant curator from a museum down in Boston or Chicago or some other benighted outpost of civilization. He wasn't finding retirement to his liking. Since he was already collecting a pension, he'd be willing to accept the meager stipend they could afford, provided the Architrave—that was the first time they'd heard it called that—threw in living quarters for himself and his wife.

That was no problem, either. Old John, in his infinite chuckleheadedness, had installed the one bathroom in a former woodshed off the back entry, as far away as possible from the upstairs bedrooms. Some said it was this inconvenience that had vexed the late Aralia into an early grave, but now John's thoughtlessness worked to the museum's advantage. The bathroom could stay where it was, the big old kitchen be turned into a sitting room, the pantry into a kitchenette, and what had been called the birthing room become a smallish but adequate bedroom. It was doubtful if a pair of retirees would be doing much birthing.

Mr. and Mrs. Fairfield, such being their name, appeared charmed by these plans and set to move in right away, but of course they'd have to wait until the transformation was accomplished. Meanwhile, Minerva Oakes offered them free room and board.

Before coming into John's money, Minerva had eked out her widow's mite by taking in boarders, most of them spectacular duds. Undaunted by disastrous experience, she remained a hospitable soul, didn't mind strangers at her breakfast table, and was still having qualms about her inheritance. Hence nobody tried to talk her out of having the Fairfields, and thus it came to pass.

Once they'd got to meet the newcomers, the trustees saw why Mr. Fairfield had remained an assistant all those years in his old job. He couldn't have given orders to the museum cat, let alone the staff. Nevertheless, he seemed to know his artifacts and to have sound, though diffidently expressed, ideas about what the Architrave ought and ought not to contain.

Mrs. Fairfield was a different matter. Hazel Munson summed up the consensus best. "You sure can tell which of that pair never has to starch her undershirts." The new curator's wife was pleasant-spoken enough, but she did show an awful lot of gum when she smiled. She wasn't lazy, though. Despite a broken wrist sustained, she told them, on moving day by falling over a box, she insisted on pitching right in with the clean-up crew.

Lobelia Falls folk were born pitchers-in, by and large. If you wanted the ghastly old wallpaper stripped, for instance, you had but to drop a hint to Mr. Peavey at the hardware store. Before you could turn around, he'd be on deck with his wallpaper steamer, his four stalwart sons, and their four stalwart girlfriends. If you wanted spiderwebs swept down, you could summon whole platoons of broom wielders who gave neither jot nor tittle for the most fearsome arachnid ever hatched; at least never hatched in Lobelia Falls, where spiders aren't usually very fearsome anyway. If you had mice to be caught, and you did because old John had been an awful slob, you called in a few of the neighborhood cats.

Even Andrew McNaster, who owned the local construction company as well as the inn next door to the Architrave, sent a couple of busboys over one hot afternoon to help with the cleaning up. Everybody's natural reaction was "What's he up to this time?"

"He figures we're all dying of thirst over here from the dust" was Dittany's theory. "He's trying to get us to quit boycotting his lousy den of iniquity and start dropping over for cold beers. Then he'll get us drunk and pull another of his cute tricks."

"Such as what?" Hazel Munson asked, wiping a cobweb off her nose.

"I don't know, but don't try to tell me he's doing this out of the goodness of his heart. He hasn't got one. You know McNaster was hoping to get his mitts on this property so he could turn John's house into a disco bar. We'd better search the place for incendiary devices after those kids leave."

They duly searched, but found no sign of malfeasance. As the days wore on and McNaster workmen kept showing up with offers of free carpentry, free electrical wiring, free washers for the dripping faucets in the Fairfields' new kitchenette and a free plumber to put them in, their wonder grew.

"Can you beat that, eh?" Hazel marveled. "He's either got religion or gone soft in the head."

"In a pig's eye he has." Dittany insisted. "He's up to something, you mark my words."

"Oh, Dittany, don't be paranoid," said Dot Coskoff. "Those workmen are on McNaster's regular payroll. If he doesn't happen to have a full day's work for them, he packs them over to us so he can build up a reputation for philanthropy at no extra cost to himself. I wonder if we might finagle a few more feet of free shelving out of him before he gets tired of being Mr. Nice Guy."

Dittany scowled. "Don't we have enough money to buy the lumber ourselves?"

"Yes, but why should we if we can get it for nothing? We've got to think of the future, you know."

So they did. Thus far, the trustees hadn't been plagued by fiscal woes, thanks to Osbert's handsome donation and Arethusa's determination not to let a mere nephew head her off at the pass. Still, there was a long, cold winter coming. Therese Boulanger talked of bake sales but it would take an awful lot of brandy snaps to keep the boiler running. Dot Coskoff came up with the truly brilliant plan of accepting everything everybody was hell-bent on donating, with the proviso that whatever proved inappropriate for exhibition could be peddled at an ongoing flea market, or *marché aux puces*. Donors' names would, she stipulated, go down regardless in the handsome book provided for that purpose by Mr. Gumpert of Ye Village Stationer. Being a donor wouldn't exempt anyone from having to pay membership fees, but it would keep the egos buttered.

This was all very well but, as Zilla Trott pointed out, they weren't going to get rich in a hurry peddling secondhand arm garters and cracked shaving mugs. Nor were people going to flock to join the museum until they had something tangible to flock to.

Be that as it might, things were moving along well enough at the moment. Mr. Fairfield was finding a reasonable amount of wheat among the chaff. Mrs. Fairfield was cleaning and refurbishing what he found. By the first of August, the front parlor was actually painted, papered, and ready to go on view.

To be sure, they'd zeroed in on the front parlor first because it was the easiest. No Architrave had ever been known to enter the room except for weddings, funerals, tea with the minister, or ritual cleaning back in the days when there was still a housewife to clean it. The furniture, of the carved grapes and horsehair period, was mostly salvageable. There was a square rosewood piano whose ivories required only to be glued back on and whose finish responded nicely to lemon oil and elbow grease. It wouldn't play anything except a thunk, but it did look elegant under a gorgeously shirred and tasseled silk piano scarf Samantha Burberry's mother-in-law donated. As to ornaments for the whatnot and mantelpiece, Mr. Fairfield had but to choose among a plethora of hair wreaths, wax fruit, souvenirs from Lake Louise, and bone china mustache cups.

The rest of the house hadn't been such a happy hunting ground. Once the place had been built and furnished, succeeding generations of Architraves had made do with what was already there. As tables and chairs wore out or collapsed, they'd been thrown down cellar or up attic and left to molder away. Thanks to Osbert's dump truck, the cellar had now been cleaned out and was temporarily being used to hold the overflow of donations for Dot Coskoff's flea market. Even the most zealous among the clean-up crew shied away from tackling the attic, though, until one day when Osbert Monk was off in Toronto seeing his publishers and Dittany was feeling specially bereft. To take her mind off the pain of separation, she wandered up and began poking around. Less than three minutes later, Mrs. Fairfield joined her.

"Found anything interesting, Mrs. Monk?"

Dittany would have preferred to be alone in her bereavement, but good breeding prevailed. "I just got here," she answered. "Horrible, isn't it? I'm going to fight my way over to a window and see if I can't get a breath of fresh air in here."

"That would be a great help. Do you think you could?"

There were few things Dittany wasn't willing to have a shot at, especially with Mrs. Fairfield standing there flashing those shiny pink gums in challenge. She squirmed a path through the debris and managed after several attempts to wrestle open a window that had perhaps never been opened before. The window promptly fell shut again because the cords had either rotted out or never been put in, so she reopened it and propped up the sash with a bit of wreckage that lay close to hand.

The window was not very big, hardly more than dollhouse size, and recessed into the mansard roof to render it even less efficient at catching what breeze there was, but it did help a little. After a few refreshing whiffs and a brief rest, Dittany managed to reach and open a couple more. Gradually the air became almost breathable. Sneezing a good deal, for the dust lay half an inch thick everywhere, she and Mrs. Fairfield got down to business.

Moths and mice, allowed to chew unchecked for half a century or so, can do a remarkable lot of damage. Most of the articles touched by the searchers crumbled to bits in their hands. Dittany did find a wrought iron trivet no predator had found palatable, and Mrs. Fairfield unearthed a flowered slop jar with only a minor crack in it. Spurred on by these small triumphs, they persisted.

There is a fascination about hunting for hidden treasure, even in places like John Architrave's attic. Dittany got filthy and sweaty, and knew she was doing dreadful things to the hands Osbert loved to touch; nevertheless, she kept going.

Mrs. Fairfield put up a valiant effort, but she really couldn't do much with that cast on her wrist. It was Dittany who forged ahead to where the dust lay thickest, Dittany who found the trunkful of old clothes, Dittany who almost had a heart attack when sixteen mice jumped out at her from among the shreds, and ultimately Dittany who came upon a package wrapped in brown paper, tucked between the remains of a redingote and a corset cover.

"That trunk might do for one of the bedrooms," Mrs. Fairfield was musing when Dittany hauled out her find. "The clothes are hopeless, I'm afraid, but—what have you there, Mrs. Monk?"

"I don't know. I'm scared to open it."

Mrs. Fairfield took the package out of Dittany's hands. "It doesn't look as if it's been gnawed. Feels like a box of some sort. Perhaps it's photographs or letters. Mr. Fairfield always gets excited over letters."

Very carefully, Mrs. Fairfield eased off the wrapping without tearing the paper or breaking the string. That was important, it seemed, although Dittany couldn't imagine why. She was rooting for a Bible or a family album herself, for the perverse reason that she didn't want Mrs. Fairfield to have guessed right about the box. A box, however, it was; and not just any box but a well-made little walnut chest with a neat hook-and-eye fastening. Mrs. Fairfield slipped the hook and opened the lid. The box was full of silk and satin scraps.

"Why, it's a bride's quilt," she exclaimed. "Or rather the pieces for one. You've never heard of those, I don't suppose."

At least Dittany got to contradict her. "As a matter of fact, I have my own great-grandmother's at home. She got it for a wedding present. All her girl friends took pieces of their best Sunday go-to-meeting gowns and embroidered pretty little doodads and whatnots on them. Then they featherboned them together into a crazy quilt for the nuptial couch."

The nuptial couch rather slipped out. Perhaps she'd typed one too many of Arethusa's roguish regency romances before Osbert lured her off to the wide-open spaces where men were men and didn't go around stapping their garters. It didn't matter, though, because Mrs. Fairfield wasn't paying attention. She was turning over the charmingly embroidered patches, rubbing the satins and velvets between her fingers.

"I wonder why the quilt never got put together. Perhaps the bride-to-be died. No, it was more likely the groom. That's why she'd have treasured the pieces even though it had become pointless to complete the quilt. We'll have to do some research on who she might have been. What a pity the quilt never got finished. I can't think how we're going to exhibit all these loose scraps, but it would be a dreadful pity not to."

"Then we'll hold a quilting bee," said Dittany. "That will attract more people to the museum, and we'll hit 'em up for donations. While we're about it, we can make up a modern copy of this one, and raffle it off."

"But Mrs. Monk, that's an extremely ambitious project. It would require a crew of expert needlewomen."

Dittany opened wide the eyes which Osbert had compared favorably to the azure-tinted skies which o'erspread the western deserts when gentle rains of spring awake the cactus buds to bloom. After the rains had done their thing, he'd meant, and gone away and let the sun come out, but that had been on their honeymoon when he'd been filled with too great a euphoria to boggle at meteorological detail. Nor had Dittany been in any mood to carp. Right now, her mood was less yielding.

"Mrs. Fairfield, there isn't a woman in Lobelia Falls who can't embroider. Minerva Oakes featherbones like a house afire. My mother does, too, when she puts her mind to it. She's at an optical convention with my stepfather just now, but they may stop over for a while on their way back to Vancouver. Then again," for Dittany knew the nomadic habits of Mum and Bert, "they may not. But anyway, I'm sure we can manage a quilting. We even have a bee to quilt. Look."

She pointed a grubby index finger at one of the scraps Mrs. Fairfield was still fingering. "Two bees, in fact. There's another on that piece of blue velvet stuck to the inside of the lid. I wonder why."

Mrs. Fairfield flashed her gums. "Why the bees, you mean? I should venture to say it was because the bride's name happened to

be Beatrice and people nicknamed her Bea. Or else she had several friends called Betsy and Bertha and so forth, and they called
their sewing circle the Busy Bees. This really is a nice find. I'm sure
Mr. Fairfield will be pleased."

She shut the lid and tucked the box under her cast. "Now don't
you think we've earned the right to get out of this filthy old attic?
I'm longing for a bath and a change, myself. We can leave the
windows open to air out the dust we've stirred up. I'll leave word
for somebody to close them before nightfall. Don't you think?"

The "don't you thinks" were rhetorical. Dittany knew perfectly
well that Mrs. Fairfield didn't give a hoot what she thought. Dittany was to take it for granted Mrs. Fairfield knew best. Dittany
reached over and took the small wooden chest gently but firmly
into her own hands.

"I'm quite ready to quit, and I'll take this with me. I want the
other trustees to see the quilt pieces."

"But Mr. Fairfield should look them over first, surely? They may
need special treatment to preserve them."

"I don't see why. That can't be all that old, and they've been
well protected. Anyway, Arethusa will know. She's a shark on this
sort of thing because her heroes wear satin waistcoats and velvet
knee breeches. Or vice versa, as the case may be."

Dittany made sure all the scraps were safe inside, shut the lid
with a businesslike snap, fastened the hook, and tucked the box
under her own arm. It was high time she got home anyway. Osbert
was due back at suppertime and she wasn't about to welcome him
in the guise of a chimney sweep who'd had a rough day among the
cinders.

Mrs. Fairfield looked a bit sniffy when they parted, but Dittany
merely gave her another wide-eyed smile and went home. She'd
got herself prettied up and had supper on the table when Osbert
came in eager for their joyous reunion. They were still reuniting
two hours later, when Arethusa rushed in with a message of doom.

# CHAPTER 3

"Arethusa, you're bonkers" was Dittany's reaction.

"And why, prithee?"

"You just told us Mr. Fairfield fell out an attic window at the museum and killed himself."

" 'Demised' seemed a bit literary, and 'met his end' had overtones of flippancy, considering that he landed on his head."

"Arethusa, stuff it. How could he? Those attic windows aren't big enough to swing a cat through. Besides, they're set into the roof. There's a ledge outside he'd have had to crawl over, for Pete's sake."

"You're mighty cocksure, forsooth."

"I ought to be. I opened the windows myself, this afternoon. Mrs. Fairfield and I were up there scrounging around. We found a box of quilt pieces."

Dittany's lip quivered. She wished now she hadn't been so mean about letting Mr. Fairfield see them. Osbert rushed to comfort her.

"Darling, you're not feeling guilty about opening the windows?"

"Will you two cease canoodling?" snarled Arethusa.

"Why the heck should we? Those idiotic characters of yours are always hurling themselves at each other in fervent embrace and all that garbage," her nephew argued, juggling his wife into a yet more fervently embraceable position to illustrate his point.

"Unhand me, sirrah," Dittany told him absentmindedly, though making no effort to be unhanded. "Why should I feel guilty? If I hadn't opened the windows, we'd have been stifled. I'd have shut them myself when we left, but Mrs. Fairfield said we should leave them open to air the place out. I suppose she sent him up to shut them before they left. I cannot for the life of me imagine how he managed to fall out."

"I suppose he was struggling with a sticky sash."

"Struggling, my left eyeball! I had to prop the silly things open with bits of old chair rungs. All he had to do was snatch away the props and mind his fingers. Besides, the openings would have been down around his waist and only about a foot square. He'd have had to double up and wiggle out on his belly. In so doing, he'd have knocked out the prop, eh, and the window would have come crashing down and pinned him to the ledge. I think we ought to go and talk to Sergeant MacVicar."

Osbert repressed a sigh. The homecoming that had begun so auspiciously was not turning out in the way he'd envisioned. However, he knew his Dittany. When duty whispered low, "Thou must," she was constitutionally incapable of murmuring back, "Sorry, I had something else on the agenda." He contented himself with tucking her into a cardigan to assert his role as manly protector, but missed out on the fun of fastening the buttons because his Aunt Arethusa kept her eye on him and something of the old terror still remained.

Arethusa was not wearing her purple cape on so warm a night, merely a Spanish shawl some six feet square with a pattern of exotic flora done in reds and pinks and a black silk fringe nine and a half inches long. As an act of defiance, Osbert put on his buckskin vest with the Indian beadwork. Thus accoutred, they set off for the museum.

They found Sergeant MacVicar standing like the stag at eve on Monan's rill, two points north-northeast of a recently pruned viburnum on what had erst been John Architrave's front yard. He vouchsafed a greeting with stately affability.

"Ah, Dittany."

The wee, fatherless bairn, as he still tended to think of her, was a special favorite of Sergeant MacVicar's. Osbert, who had served as his special deputy on an earlier occasion*, rated a comradely nod and Arethusa a gallant though far from subservient bow.

"This is indeed a direful and inauspicious beginning to your new venture."

Sergeant MacVicar intoned the words through his impressive Highland nose in a way that not only gave due emphasis to the awfulness of the event but conveyed to Dittany a hint that Sergeant MacVicar knew pretty well what it was she'd come to tell him, and why. She gave him the briefest possible glance, and he

* *The Grub-and-Stakers Move a Mountain.*

replied with the merest hint of a nod. Since a fair-sized crowd had by now gathered on the sidewalk around the museum, no more overt communication would have been politic, nor was it needed.

"I was the one who opened the windows in the first place," Dittany decided it would be safe enough to say. "I thought I'd better come and tell you."

"And rightly so. You did not, I gather, shut the windows again before you left the attic?"

This was purely for the benefit of the assembled multitudes. Sergeant MacVicar knew when to dispense a few loaves and fishes.

"No," Dittany replied in a good, clear voice so nobody would miss anything. "Mrs. Fairfield was with me. We were just hunting around. We found the pieces for a bride's quilt," she threw in because naturally people would want to know.

"Anyway, the air was pretty bad up there as you can imagine, so I opened some windows. When we decided to call it quits, Mrs. Fairfield said to leave them open and she'd have somebody shut them later."

So that was what the husband had been doing in the attic. No question who'd worn the trousers in that family, eh. A comfortable buzzing went through the crowd. Now was the strategic moment for Sergeant MacVicar to suggest ever so casually, "Ah, yes. Suppose we step inside so you can show me just how you left the windows."

Leaving the spectators well entertained, with Sergeant MacVicar's two henchmen Bob and Ray keeping them under benign surveillance, Dittany and her entourage followed the leader into the museum. Nobody else was inside the place now. Earlier on, Dittany recalled, the Munson boys had still been painting woodwork in the bedroom Mr. Fairfield was to have occupied with his spouse, and a plumber she'd recognized as one of McNaster's men had been gazing despondently into some piece of equipment he'd removed from the kitchen piping.

It was surprising, the amount of interest McNaster had been showing in the museum all this time. Some were theorizing that he expected the place to be a drawing card for his restaurant. Others thought he was intending to stick the Grub-and-Stake Gardening and Roving Club for a hefty bill once work had been completed.

McNaster had been standing on the fringe of the crowd outside just now. Perhaps he'd strolled over from the inn. He often ate his supper there after he'd left his office out on the property he'd finagled from the town by one of his shady deals. Perhaps he'd come to brood over what might have been if John Architrave hadn't left that astonishing will. Perhaps he wasn't brooding.

"Did you notice McNaster out there just now?" Dittany murmured to Arethusa.

"Egad, yes. I wonder where he was when Fairfield took that header out the window," Arethusa muttered back.

Osbert gave his aunt a reproving look. Sergeant MacVicar, however, did not.

"Ladies, am I to infer you suspect yon McNaster of dark and perfidious deeds?" he inquired.

"Have you taken a good look at those attic windows?" Dittany replied.

"I have."

"You've noticed how small they are, and how wide the ledge is in front of them?"

"I have."

"Did you try getting them to stay up without being propped open?"

"I did."

"Then would you care to speculate, eh, on how the flaming heck Mr. Fairfield could have managed to fall out by accident?"

"I have speculated, Dittany. I have also remarked the absence of smudges, stains, or deposits of bird droppings on his garments despite the fact that yon aforementioned ledges have visibly served as roosting places for our feathered friends for, lo, these many decades. I have concluded that it would have taken a degree of ingenuity, agility, and persistence most remarkable in an elderly man of sedentary habit and scholarly inclination for Mr. Fairfield to have accomplished such a feat."

"But he is dead," said Osbert, who believed in facing facts even when he had to invent them himself.

"He is indeed defunct, Deputy Monk. I have seldom," Sergeant MacVicar amplified, "seen anybody deader, at least not on such short notice. There was a fracture of the occiput as well as of the cervical vertebrae."

"Meaning he landed smack on his head, bashed in his skull, and broke his neck, eh?"

"Correctly and succinctly stated."

"Ergo, he fell out the window belly-bumper, wearing an apron to keep his clothes clean, and then plummeted to earth as a feather is wafted downward from an eagle in its flight," said Arethusa. "Now that one sees the complete picture, it's all drearily commonplace, isn't it? Too bad."

"Except that this eagle you cite so glibly couldn't have just wafted a feather and flapped away," her nephew pointed out. "He'd have had to be hovering around ready to zero in on the apron and fly off with it."

"Don't be absurd, Osbert. The apron blew away, that's all."

"There is no wind tonight, Miss Monk," said Sergeant MacVicar. "Nor has any protective covering that might have been worn by the demised or spread over the ledge been found anywhere in the vicinity. I am inclined to the opinion that Mr. Fairfield fell not from the window, but off the roof."

"Poppycock! What would he have been doing up there?"

"That, Miss Monk, I have not as yet ascertained."

"Mr. Fairfield had no head for heights," said Dittany. "Last week, when they were fixing the ceilings, Hazel Munson's son asked him to climb the ladder and take a close look at the plaster doodad around the light fixture to see if it could be restored or ought to be taken down. He turned *eau de Nil* at the mere suggestion."

"He did what?" demanded Arethusa.

"He looked seasick," Dittany interpreted. "He claimed he wasn't supposed to climb ladders on account of his high blood pressure. In my considered opinion, he was plain chicken."

"An interesting observation." Sergeant MacVicar took out his notebook and made a neat memorandum. "I will elicit information as to her late husband's physical condition from Mrs. Fairfield."

"Speaking of Mrs. Fairfield, where is she now?"

"She is back at her temporary lodgings, being ministered to by Mrs. Oakes and Mrs. Trott."

"Was she around when her husband fell?"

"It would appear she was not. The sequence of events, according to testimony thus far received, is that Mrs. Fairfield left her husband still working here at about a quarter to five and went back to Minerva Oakes's house to get bathed and changed. She said she had been working in the attic all afternoon with young Mrs. Monk. You confirm this officially, Dittany?"

"Yes, we'd been at it since half past one and we were both filthy. I wanted to get cleaned up before Osbert got home for his supper, and she told me she was going to do the same."

"This was when she told you to leave the windows open?"

"Yes, as we were about to go."

"Did she stay in the attic after you left?"

"No, we went downstairs together, carrying a slop jar and a couple of other things we'd found in the attic. I did leave the museum before her, though. She said she was going to pop in and tell her husband about the bridal quilt."

"What bridal quilt is this, Dittany?"

"None, actually. It's just pieces for one that never got put together. We found them in an old trunk."

"Where are they now?"

"I took them home with me. I thought we might use them to organize a quilting bee as a fund-raiser. It seemed to me Arethusa ought to see them first because she's head trustee."

"Then why didn't you show them to me, addlepate?" Arethusa demanded.

"Because you didn't give me time, that's why. You galloped in and told us Mr. Fairfield had been killed and we galloped out and came here."

"A likely yarn, i' faith! You forgot because you were too busy being tumbled and tousled by that lecherous lout of a nephew of mine. You'd never catch Sir Percy carrying on like that with Lady Ermintrude."

"You'd never catch me carrying on like that with Lady Ermintrude, either," her nephew retorted. "She's got no more sex appeal than a bowl of tapioca pudding. Like the rest of your silly characters."

"May I interrupt this literary discussion before Miss Monk gets off on the subject of Appaloosas?" Sergeant MacVicar inquired mildly. "Dittany, would it not have been more consonant with the dignity of his position for you to have left these quilt pieces you found with Mr. Fairfield, instead of taking them straight home?"

"I suppose so. And I would have, if you want the truth, only Mrs. Fairfield was throwing her weight around. I thought I'd kindly and gently let her know she can't lord it over the trustees the way she does her husband. Did, I mean. No I don't. She couldn't have. Could she?"

Sergeant MacVicar turned his head from left to right, then from right to left. "Dinna fash yoursel' about that, Dittany. Not on the strength of the information we have at hand. Minerva Oakes avers that Mrs. Fairfield arrived at the house at approximately five o'clock in a state of dishevelment and went upstairs to tidy herself. She remained there for some while, having found it necessary, as she later explained, to shampoo her hair and rinse out the garments she had been wearing. She came downstairs at half past five or thereabout, hung the aforementioned garments on Minerva's clothesline to dry, then sat on the front porch and partook of some iced tea Minerva had ready in a pitcher.

"Zilla Trott stopped by and the three ladies chatted until they heard the church bell strike six. Thereupon, Zilla said she'd better get on home to fix her supper. Minerva Oakes also made some comment with regard to the evening meal. Mrs. Fairfield expressed mild vexation that her husband had not yet made his appearance. Mr. Fairfield did have a tendency to become absorbed in his work, but she had been endeavoring to instill in him a regard for punctuality out of courtesy toward their hostess.

"Minerva said his tardiness was of no moment, as supper was only going to be cold meat and salad, and she had everything ready in the fridge. The two remaining ladies sat on the porch a while longer. As time passed, Mrs. Fairfield grew increasingly restive. At last it was decided the pair of them would stroll down to the museum and wrest Mr. Fairfield away from his labors by brute force if necessary. This was said in jest, according to Minerva. Mrs. Fairfield seemed in no way concerned for Mr. Fairfield's safety or well-being, merely somewhat testy at his apparent lack of consideration."

"I can believe that," said Dittany.

Sergeant MacVicar gave her an indulgent nod and went on. "By this time, needless to say, they assumed Mr. Fairfield would be alone at the museum. Everybody else would have gone home to supper some time ago."

His hearers nodded. People in Lobelia Falls all ate breakfast, dinner, and supper pretty much at the same time as their neighbors. So many of them belonged to so many different committees, clubs, and whatnot that careful synchronizing of family habits was the only way to get members to their meetings on time.

"The two ladies entered the museum together," he went on. "Having found the door still unlocked, they naturally assumed Mr. Fairfield remembered that his wife had asked him to close the attic windows before he came away. Mrs. Fairfield wondered if he was still up there gloating over some serendipitous find. She expressed dismay at the prospect of climbing all those stairs again, whereupon Minerva, who as you know is a fount of boundless energy, volunteered to make the ascent."

"As Mrs. Fairfield knew darn well she would," said Dittany.

"Dittany, were I not so well acquent with the inherent sweetness of your nature, I should begin to entertain a wee suspeecion you have developed a certain animosity toward Mrs. Fairfield."

"I wouldn't call it a certain animosity, Sergeant MacVicar. More a chronic pain in the neck. Which I suppose I'd better try to hide or you'll be hauling me in as a suspect. Changing the subject back to where it was, what did Minerva find when she went up attic? Is that a more appropriate remark, eh?"

"Entirely suitable. Minerva found two of the windows still open and Mr. Fairfield not present. She closed the windows and went back to tell Mrs. Fairfield, who became somewhat alarmed at this report and suggested they search the grounds, such as they are. This, the ladies did, starting in opposite directions. It was Minerva who came upon the lifeless form of Mr. Fairfield."

"How ghastly!" This time, Dittany hadn't had to search for the appropriate rejoinder. "What did she do?"

"Let out a yelp, according to her own testimony. That fetched Mrs. Fairfield, eh, who burst quite understandably into sobs and outcries. Minerva pacified Mrs. Fairfield as best she could, then used the museum phone to call me away from a dish of tea and a portion of excellent grosset fool with which I was ending my evening repast," said the sergeant in a voice from which he was unable to keep a tinge of regret.

Arethusa noticed. "This was hardly the time to think of gooseberries," she chided.

"I could not, as my grandchildren say, agree with you more. That was why I asked Mrs. MacVicar to set the remainder of my grosset fool in the icebox and came here at once. To resume my narrative, Minerva Oakes then summoned Dr. Somervell, although there was no doubt Mr. Fairfield was already dead as a finnan haddie. The doctor arrived immediately after I did and confirmed that Mr. Fairfield had indeed shuffled off this mortal coil not long since."

"He was presumed to have gone up to shut the windows just before he left for supper?" said Osbert.

"That was the general assumption, yes. I have so far advanced no alternative theory, except among yourselves."

"And we're to keep it among ourselves, eh?"

"You are. That includes you, Miss Monk."

"I should hope so, egad," Arethusa replied. "I shall sit mumchance at the sideboard, like the twenty-ninth of February."

"Huh?" said her nephew.

"Don't make noises like an illiterate nincompoop, Osbert, though I suppose it's too late to hope you'll ever be anything else. Where did Dr. Somervell get to?"

"He took Minerva and Mrs. Fairfield back to the Oakes house in his car. It was his recommendation that Mrs. Fairfield be given a sedative and put to bed, since she was by then in what is commonly referred to as a state. I should assume she is now being ministered to, no doubt by Zilla Trott, with a nice cup of camomile tea."

"No doubt," said Osbert, to show he was unscathed by his aunt's disdain. "What happened to the body?"

"It was carried to Dr. Somervell's office for further examination, by willing volunteers using a stretcher provided by Roger Munson."

Dittany nodded. Hazel's husband was not the sort of man to be caught without a stretcher in time of need.

"When Dr. Somervell and I have completed more detailed observations," Sergeant MacVicar went on, "the corpus delicti will be sent along to the undertaker in Scottsbeck, pending Mrs. Fairfield's instructions as to its final resting place."

"It's rather awful to be thinking of Mr. Fairfield as remains." Dittany fastened the top button of her cardigan and snuggled closer to Osbert. "A few hours ago, he was crowing like a barnyard cock over a wooden potato basher Grandsire Coskoff's new wife brought in. Sergeant MacVicar, do you have any idea at all who did it?"

# CHAPTER 4

Arethusa stopped giving Osbert dirty looks and turned to Dittany with a gaze of wonderment. "Did what, forsooth?"

"Shoved Mr. Fairfield off the roof, of course. Surely you don't think he was up there by himself practicing swan dives?"

Sergeant MacVicar cleared his throat. "It ill becomes us to form conclusions before we have examined the evidence, Dittany. Deputy Monk, you are a far younger man than I, and one whose powers of observation and deduction have proved efficacious during your previous unpaid but far from unappreciated service to the police force. Perhaps you would be good enough to accompany me to the top of this somewhat overflossy stairwell, from which access to the roof can be gained via the skylight."

Osbert blushed and stammered that he'd be delighted. "Do we need to fetch a ladder?" he asked, ready to give his all for the cause.

"There's one up there," Dittany said. "The roofer left it. We've had to get the skylight repaired because it was leaking buckets and ruining all the plaster that hadn't been ruined already."

"You never told me, darling."

"I didn't want to burden you with trivia when you were trying so hard to finish your book before you went to Toronto, darling."

"Oh, darling, have I been neglecting you?"

"Unhand her, varlet," cried Arethusa. "Sergeant MacVicar, haven't we any town ordinances against public displays of wanton lust?"

Sergeant MacVicar rubbed his hand across his chin to hide a paternal smile. "Noo, Miss Monk, let us e'en be tolerant to the wee follies of those but newly wed. Dittany lass, do I take there has been much going up and coming down within the recent past?"

"I should jolly well hope so. The roofer's sent in a bill that would choke a walrus."

"Then if the work has been completed, why has the ladder not been taken away?"

"Because he hasn't got around to it, I suppose—or else because we've told him we're not paying the bill until we've had a good, soaking rain and made darn sure the leaks are really fixed."

"Cannily reasoned." Sergeant MacVicar craned his neck to look up through the high stairwell. "I doubt not this will make a handsome effect when the papering and painting are finished. Were you not concerned lest yon roofer might slop tar around the walls and woodwork? I observe that you allowed him to rig his hoist straight down through the skylight into the hall."

"And leave his woundy great ropes and buckets here where people can fall over them," said Arethusa crossly.

"Well, there's no sense in his taking them away till he knows whether he's going to need them again. And we certainly weren't going to let him drag stuff up over the side of the roof so he could whack us with another bill for replacing the slates he chipped," Dittany snapped back.

Sergeant MacVicar nodded. "The roofer would be Browns from Scottsbeck?"

"Who else is there? We'd have chiseled a free job out of somebody local if we could, but these old slate roofs are tricky to work on. If anyone was going to slip off and break his neck, we didn't want it to be anyone we knew. Oh dear, I wish I hadn't said that."

"The tongue is a treacherous instrument, Dittany. You were aware that Brown does much of Andrew McNaster's roofing work?"

"Why do you think we're waiting for the rainstorm before we pay the bill?"

"He finished the work some days ago, then? Assuming that it is indeed finished."

"A week ago last Thursday, I believe it was."

"And he has not been back since, eh?"

"Not to my knowledge. Mrs. Fairfield could probably tell you better than I. She's always around here. Keeping out from under Minerva's feet, I suppose," Dittany added quickly lest she be accused of all uncharitableness.

Osbert, who'd been fiddling with the heavy manila ropes of the hoist, reluctantly gave up the notion of playing Tarzan on them and started up the stairs. Dittany followed, wanting to beseech him to be careful on the ladder, but decided she'd better keep her mouth shut and just stand ready to faint if anything happened. Osbert made the ascent without incident, however, and opened the skylight with no visible effort. He then, to his wife's horror, climbed up and out.

At that, she could not resist calling to him. "Darling, are you all right?"

"Perfectly, darling," came the welcome reply. "The roof's quite flat on top, and there's a little iron railing. Oho!"

"Oho what?"

"Oho what sort of clothes was Mr. Fairfield wearing? There's a piece of gray fuzz caught on one of the spikes."

"Leave it," shouted Sergeant MacVicar. "I am preparing to ascend. Ladies, would you oblige me by steadying the ladder?"

"Egad," cried Arethusa. "The plot thickens."

"That is as may be," grunted Sergeant MacVicar, plodding cautiously but undauntedly from rung to rung.

A moment later, Dittany was relieved to see the loved though begrimed face of Osbert hovering above the skylight. He gave the sergeant a helping hand up to the roof. Then both men disappeared and the two women below could hear them treading overhead.

"What do you suppose they're up to?" Dittany fussed. "A person might just sneak up the ladder for a quick peek."

"And leave me here alone to pick up the arms and legs, forsooth?" cried Arethusa. "Obliterate the thought from your addled pate, wench. If anybody's going to come crashing through that skylight, let it be Osbert. At least he has no brains to knock out."

"I find that remark to be in decidedly poor taste."

"'Ods bodikins, you're a fine one to talk. Nattering away about what a pest Mrs. Fairfield is and sparing not so much as a passing sigh for the greater tragedy; namely and to wit, that we are again without a curator and I, forsooth, am stuck with the churl's task of supervising this misbegotten moth hatchery. Wherefore all this detective garbage, i' faith, when there can be but one explanation for the nefarious deed? Killing poor old Fairfield was an artful ruse of my arch rival, that caitiff knavess, Lydia E. Twinkham, to divert my attention from literary composition and give her the regency romance field all to herself."

"Barring the fact that Lydia E. Twinkham is eighty-three years old and residing in a nursing home at Lesser Gimbling-in-the-Wabe, I can't think of a likelier explanation. Quick, grab the ladder. They're coming down. Stop wiggling it, for Pete's sake."

Despite Arethusa's assistance, the two men got down all right. Osbert came second, carefully latching the skylight after him.

"What did you find, darling?" Dittany asked, hugging her beloved to make sure he was intact.

"Deputy Monk has ascertained that Brown has in fact completed what appears to be a first-class job of leakproofing the skylight," Sergeant MacVicar kindly informed them, Osbert's lips being for the moment otherwise employed.

"Stap my garters," Arethusa exclaimed in disgust. "Is that all?"

"It cannot be lightly dismissed, Miss Monk. Since Brown must know the work was done properly, why has the gear not been taken away?"

"Need one ask?" cried Dittany. "Brown works for McNaster. McNaster's been slinking around here trying to worm his way into our good graces so he can pull another of his nasties, and now he's done it. Can't you imagine what Mr. Fairfield's death will do to our membership drive? People will say the museum's a public menace. We won't be able to raise the money to keep it going, and he'll grab it."

"Doucely, doucely," Sergeant MacVicar cautioned. "The gear may have been left simply because Brown has no immediate use for it elsewhere and this is as good a storage place as any. Nevertheless, the fact should not be overlooked, nor should that fragment of gray yarn Deputy Monk found. When I myself performed the melancholy task of examining Mr. Fairfield's lifeless corpse, I observed a snag on the back of the gray cardigan he was wearing. Of course it could have been done some while back."

"No chance," said Dittany. "The sweater was brand-new. He was showing it off to me yesterday morning. He told me his secretary had given it to him as a farewell present because he was coming up here among the icebergs and igloos. We were laughing about it." She suppressed a sniffle and said briskly, "So if the wool matches the cardigan, that proves he was shoved off the roof."

"That would indicate he had been on the roof, Dittany. For what purpose he went there, whether freely or under duress, would still remain to be discovered. However, it would give us sound reason to pursue the investigation. Do you not agree, Deputy Monk?"

"I do."

Osbert's words reminded Dittany of their wedding day. She gazed up at her husband with, as Miss Lydia E. Twinkham had often expressed it, stars in her eyes. Arethusa gave them both a look and went off to brood among the antique carpet beaters and pokerwork mottoes of which fate, by this sinister turn, had again made her acting custodian.

# CHAPTER 5

Sergeant MacVicar, however, remained to strike while the iron was hot. "Dittany lass," he said, "can you remember who was in the museum this afternoon?"

"Well, myself and the Fairfields, of course. And a plumber Andy McNaster sent over. I think he might have been from those Fawcetts in Scottsbeck who run the advertisements about bringing your faucets to Fawcett, which makes no sense whatsoever, because what you have to do is bring the Fawcetts to the faucets."

"A point well taken. Can you describe the plumber?"

"Not too well. He was squatting down with his head under the kitchen sink when I saw him. Sort of middle-aged and fattish with a dark blue jersey on, if that helps any. Oh, and he had a bunion. The side of his left shoe was slit and his sock was hanging out, sort of. White with pink stripes. Rather sissy for a plumber, I thought."

"Ah, yes. That would have been Cedric, sometimes whimsically referred to as Cold-Water Fawcett on account of his habitual pessimism."

"I'll bet Mrs. Cedric is a Hot-Water Fawcett. She keeps him in it, and that's why he's depressed."

"As to that, I could not say." Sergeant MacVicar was always careful about spreading gossip, on account of his official position. "The nickname 'Hot-Water' is generally applied to Harold, second eldest and most choleric of the seven Fawcett brothers."

"The rest of the Fawcetts are just drips, I suppose, if they work for McNaster."

"That is a somewhat unfair assumption, Dittany. All the Fawcetts are well skilled in the craft of the *artifex plumbarius*. You say Andrew McNaster sent Cedric Fawcett to the museum? Voluntarily and of his own free will?"

"Such is my understanding. This Cold-Water Fawcett just waltzed in and said, 'McNaster sent me over. What do you want plumbed?' or words to that effect. Mrs. Fairfield asked him who was supposed to pay and he said it would go on McNaster's tab. So she figured what the heck and got him started in the kitchen."

"This was not the first time Andrew McNaster had volunteered such assistance?" Sergeant MacVicar knew perfectly well it wasn't, needless to say. There were no flies on Sergeant MacVicar.

Dittany shook her head. *"Au contraire.* We've got so used to having some stranger wander in with a bag of tools and say he's from McNaster that we don't even swoon with astonishment any more. We still keep an eagle eye on whoever it is, naturally, because none of us would trust McNaster any farther than we could throw a horse by the tail. Mrs. Fairfield ought to have cleared the plumber with one of the trustees before she told him to go ahead, but that's not her way."

There she went again. Dittany hastened to make amends. "Not that you can blame her for getting a bit restive about wanting to move into her own place. You know how it is when you're somebody's guest, no matter how nice they are. Minerva would never let on for one second that she was sick and tired of having the Fairfields under foot, but a person can read between the lines. Unless they're Arethusa's lines, which you often can't read at all," she added, for she was still miffed at her aunt-in-law. "The Munson boys were painting woodwork in the birthing room."

"The Munson boys, eh? That would be Edward and Albert?"

"No, Eddie and Dave. Bert was offered a part-time job at the paint store in Scottsbeck because the Munsons have been throwing so much business its way this summer. They just finished painting our house, you know. They're doing the museum for half price out of the goodness of their hearts. They'd be home now, I expect, if you want to grill them. This isn't Roger Munson's be-pals-with-your-kids night, is it?"

"No, this is the Male Archers' practice night," sighed Sergeant MacVicar, who'd have been there himself, were it not for the untimely demise of Mr. Fairfield. "Roger will be at the butts with the rest of the men."

The rest of the men included virtually every adult male in Lobelia Falls except Osbert Monk, who was being privately tutored by his wife and showing great promise that he, too, might one day qualify for membership.

"Then Eddie and Dave will be with their father, won't they?"

Dittany suggested kindly, for she could see which way Sergeant MacVicar's heart was yearning.

"No chance. They are still in the intermediate class, which meets tomorrow evening. They may, to be sure, be practicing in their own back yard," the sergeant added in a brighter tone, for hope springeth eternal and a man might still get in a shot or two with a borrowed bow before it became too dark to see the target. His father, who'd served in the Nova Scotia Highlanders, had known a song about that. As they marched down the street in loose formation, Sergeant MacVicar found himself crooning, "I canna see the tarrget. Oh, move the dom thing closerr. It's ower far awa'."

Arethusa, who happened to be nearest, turned her vast and fathomless dark eyes upon him in great amaze. "You're in merry mood, sirrah, for a man with a probable murder on his hands."

"It makes a change, Miss Monk," was the sergeant's succinct reply. "And you will oblige me by keeping that under your mumchance also, eh?"

"Fear not, *mon capitaine.* My lips are sealed. What a wonderful line! I must use it sometime."

Arethusa lapsed into one of those brooding fits that meant some duke or baronet was about to be pinked in the jabot as soon as she could get back to her desk. Sergeant MacVicar, too, had wherewith to brood on. Dittany and Osbert strolled ahead, a slender blue sleeve slipped around a tall beaded-buckskin back and a long tan arm wound protectively around a small blue cardigan.

Each occupied with thoughts of varying natures, they none of them spoke again until they reached the Munsons' back yard. There, sure enough, they found Dave and Eddie industriously plugging away at a plastic-covered target set against piled-up bales of hay. Well-bred youths that they were, the brothers parked their bows against a bale and came over to shake hands.

"Evening, Miss Monk. Evening, Dittany. Evening, Sergeant MacVicar. Howdy, Osbert. We figured you'd be along sooner or later."

"If in fact you were expecting to see me, why did you not come and seek me out?" the sergeant inquired, rather absentmindedly because he was eyeing the target.

"And do you out of the chance to get in a few shots?" That was

Dave, younger and brasher of the two. "You'd better use Ed's bow. It pulls a little stronger than mine."

"M'ph." Struggling not to look too gratified, Sergeant MacVicar picked up the elder brother's bow, fitted an arrow to the string, and sent it, as he knew his small audience expected him to, straight to the center of the bull's-eye. Dave handed him another arrow, which he placed dead left of the first, close enough for the flights to touch but not so close as to ruffle the feathers. The third landed the exact same distance to the right, the fourth directly above, and the fifth precisely below.

"Not bad shooting" was the consensus of the group. Sergeant MacVicar returned a slight nod.

"I have done worse and will again, I doubt not. Now, lads, tell me what I came to hear."

"About what happened at the museum this afternoon, right?" said Eddie.

"Insofar as your memories serve. You were painting woodwork in the birthing room, Dittany tells me."

"Yes, only Mrs. Fairfield doesn't like having it called that any more, I don't know why. It isn't as if she had anything to worry about. I mean," Eddie flushed, for it was one thing to bandy words among his *compères* and quite another to do so in front of Sergeant MacVicar, "I don't suppose she'll be moving into the museum now."

"That is for the trustees to decide," said the sergeant. "Our concern is with Mr. Fairfield's last hours. Can you cast any light on his movements?"

The brothers exchanged shrugs. "Gee, I'm afraid not," Dave answered. "I don't think he so much as stuck his head in the door all day. He didn't seem to be all that interested in how the place was coming along, the way Mrs. Fairfield was. She'd be popping in and out every five minutes to see if we were finished yet and how come the job was taking so long, eh. Mr. Fairfield just sat in the back parlor sticking labels on stuff people brought in and making notes on little cards. Cataloging the exhibits, he called it."

"Why shouldn't he?" Eddie said. "That's what it was. Dave's right, though, Sergeant. We knew Mr. Fairfield was around because we could hear his wife talking to him about one thing and another, but I can't recall laying eyes on him the whole time we were there."

"And how long was that?"

"All day, just about. It must have been close to nine o'clock when we started, because we'd been out to the lake early."

"Indeed? Were they rising well?"

"Not too bad. We got a few smallmouth bass. Dave hooked on to a three-pounder but I guess his tackle was too light."

No doubt Dave had actually struck too soon, as he often did, but esprit de corps ran high among the Munson brothers.

"Anyway," Eddie went on, "we worked till maybe a quarter to twelve, then we went home to dinner and got back at half past, or near enough as makes no difference. We knocked off at half past four. I know that, because we'd promised to go over to Scottsbeck and pick up Bert after he got through at the paint shop. He'd left us the car to go fishing."

The Munsons had been having car problems. Right now, schooled in efficiency by Roger and goaded to frugality by the mounting costs of higher education, the family was making do with one vehicle. Sergeant MacVicar didn't need to have that explained to him, of course.

"Now, during the course of the afternoon, who was in the museum other than yourselves, the Fairfields, and Dittany?"

"Mrs. Boulanger brought over some gingerbread and lemonade, which was darn nice of her. That was maybe twenty past two. A plumber came to work in the kitchen right after she left. The fat one from Scottsbeck who goes around looking as if his dog just died. He was still working when we came away. At least I think he was working. He had the sink pipes out and his tools strewn around."

"And was there anybody else?"

"That other woman, Ed," Dave prompted.

"What other woman?"

"You know, the one who came in the back door."

"I thought that was Mrs. Fairfield."

"Mrs. Fairfield wouldn't have come to the back door, Ed. She was already in the house. This was somebody else."

"If you say so. I wasn't paying any attention."

"What did this woman look like, David?" Sergeant MacVicar prompted. "Did you see her well enough to recognize if you saw her again?"

On that point, Dave was not helpful. He thought he might have caught a glimpse of a blue dress or skirt or something she was wearing, but it might have been green or purple. He hadn't been interested. Dave was off women these days, having had his heart temporarily broken by a redhead from Burketon Station. He didn't mention the redhead, but naturally everybody in town knew about her and thought Dave Munson well rid of a giggling chit who couldn't even hit the black at twenty lousy feet.

"Could you identify her by her voice?" Sergeant MacVicar persisted.

Dave pondered, then shook his head. "I don't think she said anything. Anyway it couldn't have been any of Mum's special pals like Dittany here or Miss Monk or Mrs. Trott or Mrs. Oakes. I'd have recognized them fast enough."

"And so you would. Where did she go from the kitchen, can you tell me that?"

"No, I'm afraid I can't. I'm so used to people wandering in and out of the museum, I don't pay much attention. Maybe the plumber would know."

"Then it behooves us to ask the plumber," said Sergeant Mac-Vicar, nothing daunted. "Good shooting, lads. Come, Deputy Monk. We may as well nip on over to Scottsbeck and draw a bow at a venture."

# CHAPTER 6

It was not to be supposed that Dittany, having been separated from Osbert for two interminable days and, more importantly, nights, would take kindly to the prospect of his tootling off to Scottsbeck without her. When this fact was pointed out to him, Sergeant MacVicar not only understood but kindly volunteered to drive so the newlyweds could sit together in the back seat. Osbert blushed and said he didn't mind driving and why didn't they get Mrs. MacVicar and take her along, too, so she and the sergeant could sit in the back seat instead?

Sergeant MacVicar did not blush, but he did rub his chin and allow his bright blue eyes to twinkle once or twice. In the end, Mrs. MacVicar and Dittany sat in back and discussed archery and garden club affairs, while their spouses sat in front and talked archery and crime detection, for that was how things were done in Lobelia Falls.

Cedric Fawcett, when they finally tracked him down sitting on a bench beside a muddy, sluggish creek, staring lugubriously into an empty Labatt's bottle, was no earthly help at all. There'd been women in and out from time to time, and that was as far as they could get him to go. He hadn't paid any attention to them. Why should he? He'd come to fix the sink trap, the sink trap he had fixed, and what more could they reasonably expect of him?

When had he left the museum?

After he'd fixed the sink trap.

Was that before or after Mrs. Fairfield had been killed?

Cedric Fawcett didn't know. He wouldn't have known unless the body had turned up in the sink trap, which it hadn't, eh.

What had he done after he'd left the museum?

He'd gone home and had a Labatt's, naturally.

What were Mr. Fawcett's plans for the immediate future?

He planned to go and get another Labatt's. He arose from the bench to signify the interview was over and wandered, presumably beerward, through the gathering gloom. Mrs. MacVicar picked up her handbag and asked, "What shall we do next?"

"We might go get a Labatt's," Osbert ventured.

That struck them all as a reasonable suggestion. They went. Nobody would admit to being hungry but they ordered a Welsh rabbit anyway and found it good. As they were taking a poll on whether anyone wanted a final Labatt's, who should stroll over to their table but Andrew McNaster?

"Well, well, look who's here" was his predictable greeting. "I thought you folks would be back in Lobelia Falls picking up the pieces. Say, how about me buying you all a beer?"

"We would not impose on your generosity to that extent, Mr. McNaster," the sergeant's wife replied with stately dignity. "You have already put us in your debt with the assistance your staff has rendered to the museum. We have in fact just been talking to one of your men who was working there this afternoon when the tragedy occurred."

"You mean Ceddie? I thought he'd left before it happened."

"That point is still moot," Mrs. MacVicar told him. "My husband has not yet been able to reach a firm conclusion as to the exact time Mr. Fairfield met his death. Moreover, your Mr. Fawcett was unable or perhaps merely unwilling to tell us precisely when he left. Perhaps you could do so?"

"Who, me? Listen, what's the idea here?" McNaster was a tall, portly man with shiny black hair and shiny red cheeks that gave the impression he was sucking jawbreakers. His lips were red and shiny, too, but right now there was no suggestion of sweetness about them. "I try to do you a favor, and this is the thanks I get. Give a dog a bad name and hang him, eh? Just because I may possibly have made one or two little errors in judgment a while back—"

"We are none of us perfect, Mr. McNaster," said the sergeant, although nobody thought he really meant it. "Therefore it behooves us to vouchsafe unto others that mercy which we are so desirous to receive ourselves, does it not? As my wife has indicated, we four came over to Scottsbeck endeavoring to extract some information that might help us make sense of the sad occurrence to which you have alluded. Thus far our expedition has not met with success. My wife's words to you were spoken not in censure but in hope."

"Then how come she wouldn't let me buy her a beer, eh?"

"Because she's already had two and she doesn't want any more," Osbert Monk put in. "She won't let me buy her one either, if it makes you feel any better. We'd have asked you to sit down with us, but we were getting ready to leave."

"My husband's been away on a business trip and he's tired," Dittany added for what that was worth.

She'd never thought to see the day she'd be deliberately trying to placate Andy McNasty, as he was more commonly known around town, but as a dutiful wife she felt bound to follow where Osbert led. Besides, she knew Osbert was trying to find out how Andy McNasty knew Mr. Fairfield had fallen off the roof instead of out the window as was commonly supposed.

It was sad to see all this diplomacy trickling down the drain. McNaster's reply was as unsatisfactory as Cedric Fawcett's, though less phlegmatically given. The gist of it was that he'd stopped at the inn for supper as usual, seen the commotion over at the museum, and gone to see what was up. He'd known Fred Brown was doing a job on the museum roof. He'd assumed Mr. Fairfield had gone up to inspect Brown's progress, or lack of it, because that was what he himself would have done, though he wouldn't have fallen off the edge because he wasn't an absentminded intellectual like Mr. Fairfield. Now they mentioned it, he'd heard somebody say something about the attic window but those windows hadn't looked to him like the sort a person would be apt to fall out of. So he figured it must have been the roof, wasn't it?

"At this juncture we are not sure of anything, Mr. McNaster," said Sergeant MacVicar. On that equivocal note, they parted.

"My stars and garters!" was Dittany's comment once they'd got back into the car and headed for Lobelia Falls. "What do you make of that?"

"Of all possible encounters," Sergeant MacVicar agreed, "that was the one I should least have expected.

"You were marvelous, Mrs. MacVicar," said Dittany. "How in the world did you ever think what to say?"

"Mrs. MacVicar is never at a loss for a word," said the sergeant, keeping his eyes on the road. "Were praise to the face not open disgrace, I should be inclined to agree that she was indeed marvelous."

Mrs. MacVicar said not to be silly and didn't Dittany think the restaurant cook had gone a little too heavy on the mustard in the Welsh rabbit?

Dittany said Osbert liked plenty of mustard and did Mrs. Mac-Vicar think McNaster had been telling the truth or putting it on?

"He is a man of devious ways," Mrs. MacVicar conceded.

"I wouldn't trust that ornery coyote one inch, myself," said Osbert. "Furthermore, I'd a good mind to get up and paste him one, the way he kept ogling my wife. Not that she isn't oglesome, if that's the right word."

"Please, darling. Praise to the face is open disgrace. What got me, aside from the ogling," Dittany inserted parenthetically, though in truth she hadn't noticed it, having had eyes only for Osbert, who was no mean ogler, either, "was his saying Mr. Fairfield was dumped off the roof. How does he know those attic windows are too small to push anybody out of, unless he's been up there poking around, eh?"

"Strictly speaking," said Sergeant MacVicar, "the attic windows are not too small. A form of so slight a build as Mr. Fairfield's could have been projected from yon orifice if you lined him up straight and gave him a hefty shove. The difficulty would lie in obtaining his cooperation for such a maneuver."

"But what about the fuzz on the railing?"

"We must e'en ask ourselves whether that fuzz could have been put there by conspiratorial hands to make us think the victim was not in fact dumped out the attic window when in fact he was, although I cannot for the life of me think why. As to how McNaster happened to take so keen an observation of the attic windows, we must remember he is by profession a builder. I doubt not it would be second nature for him to notice windows in the same way a milliner, for example, would notice hats."

"A milliner would find few hats to notice these days, more's the pity," said Mrs. MacVicar. "I would remind you, Donald, that while McNaster chooses to call himself a builder, he is by avocation a schemer and conniver. One would wish to believe he has learned his painful lesson and abandoned his perfidious ways, but one would have to be either a saint or the possessor of a very short memory to do so. The circumstances under which we acquired the Aralia Polyphema Architrave Museum preclude our being over-credulous about this sudden outpouring of the milk of human kindness. On reflection, Dittany, and with reference to your earlier question, I think Andrew McNaster was more than likely having us on. If I mistake his motives, you can put it down to human frailty or the mustard in the Welsh rabbit."

"Mustard," said Dittany. "That reminds me, I wonder if Mrs. Fairfield is still awake."

"I don't get the connection, darling," said Osbert.

"That," said Mrs. MacVicar, "is because you don't know Mrs. Fairfield as we do. Donald, you needn't bother pulling that Deacon Jeremiah face at me. With all compassion for her sudden bereavement, we've found her to be only superficially endowed with those qualities of sweetness and light you profess to find so attractive in womankind, despite or perhaps because of the years you've lived with me."

"Deputy Monk, as an old married man to a young married man, I advise you never to try answering a remark like that. Dittany, I misdoubt Dr. Somervell's potion will have assured Mrs. Fairfield a solid night's sleep. Any attempt to grill that most material witness must be postponed until we can be sure of getting rational answers and not incurring the wrath of Minerva Oakes, who has already been sorely tried this night and is herself perhaps asleep by now. The morn, or e'en the morn's morn, will be time enough."

Dittany thought the morn's morn would be stretching patience beyond the breaking point, but she knew Sergeant MacVicar worked in mysterious ways his wonders to perform and there was no earthly use trying to hurry a Highland Scot who didn't want to be hurried. And if everybody else was knocking off for the night and trotting off to bed, who were she and Osbert to buck the trend?

But she did wish to heck they'd been able to find out who that woman in the blue or green or purple dress was, and what she'd been doing in the museum's kitchen. Because the kitchen was next to the back stairs, and the back stairs led to the attic, and going up attic had been her idea in the first place. She had a nasty feeling that if she hadn't obeyed that impulse, Mr. Fairfield might still be alive.

# CHAPTER 7

It might have been vestigial guilt that sent Dittany to the museum as soon as she'd given Osbert his breakfast and seen him happily cuddled up to his typewriter. She hadn't expected to find anybody around the place this morning, not even the odd loiterer on the sidewalk. Lobelia Falls folk had better things to do than lollygag around gawking when there was nothing to see. Therefore, she was utterly flabbergasted to get inside and find Mrs. Fairfield seated at her late husband's desk, writing busily in one of his notebooks.

As she hesitated in the doorway, the widow looked up. "Good morning, Mrs. Monk. You're an early bird today."

"You could have knocked me over with a feather," Dittany told Hazel Munson later. "I just stood there with my mouth open."

In fact, she didn't. She gulped once or twice, then got her vocal cords straightened out. "Mrs. Fairfield, whatever you're doing, you don't have to. Wouldn't you rather go home and bathe your temples in cologne or something?"

"Mrs. Monk, I have no home."

"But Minerva would—"

"Mrs. Oakes has been kindness itself. But one can hardly expect her to wait on a lorn widow hand and foot, can one?"

"I don't see why not. Minerva's a natural-born mother duck, I expect she's over at Zilla Trott's right now, borrowing some camomile tea to soothe your fractured nerves. She'll be sick as a cat when she finds you're not around to drink it. Besides, shouldn't you be doing things about the—about Mr. Fairfield?"

"Oh, that's all done." With a sad little sigh, Mrs. Fairfield turned another page, awkwardly because of her cast, and made another note. "That undertaker from Scottsbeck seems efficient enough. I'm meeting with Reverend Pennyfeather in a while at the parsonage to plan the funeral service, and I've telephoned Mr. Fairfield's nephew in Duluth. There are so few relatives. My husband was the last of his generation, and I'm an only child, sad to say. You are more fortunate than I in that regard, I'm sure."

"Nope," said Dittany. "I'm an only child, too."

Panic seized her, though, as she realized she herself might some day, God forbid, become a widow. She thought of Osbert back home now, with another herd of rustled cattle thundering through his inspired brain, no doubt, and that cowlick behind his left ear swirling so adorably she'd had a hard time tearing herself away from it just now. Maybe she ought to run back this instant and take another good, long look, just in case.

No, this was no moment to be dithering over Osbert's cowlick. She ought to be saying something consolatory to Mrs. Fairfield. Her problem was that Mrs. Fairfield wasn't actually looking overwhelmingly bereft. On the contrary, to Dittany's discerning eye she appeared a weentsy bit smug, sitting there in the curator's chair—albeit the chair was an ugly old wooden thing painted to look like mahogany, with wobbly legs on tiny metal casters that resembled babies' roller skates—plying the gold-plated fountain pen that had been another farewell gift from her late husband's erstwhile colleagues.

"What about the people where he used to work?" she asked.

"I called my husband's former secretary as soon as I got here. I didn't like to keep putting long-distance phone calls on Mrs. Oakes's bill. I don't suppose any of them will come to the funeral, but I daresay they'll send a nice floral tribute."

She tapped the end of the gold pen against her front teeth, scanning her notes. "Now, Mrs. Monk, if you're looking for something to do, you might try making those dining room chairs presentable. I want that room set up as soon as possible so I can start thinking about the upstairs. Wash them down with mild soap and water, being careful not to soak the wood. You'd better do it outdoors. They must be thoroughly dry before you start rubbing in the lemon oil. By the way, the kitchen sink still isn't draining properly. Kindly give that plumber a ring right now."

Bereavement or no bereavement, this was a bit much. "Can't," said Dittany. "You accepted that plumber as a donation from Andrew McNaster, remember? Since we didn't hire him, I don't see where we have any authority to call him in."

"Then how am I to get my sink fixed?"

"Let's wait and see. He may be planning to come back later today."

Dittany could have thought of other things to say, but she refrained. Young as she was, she'd seen enough of death to know it could affect those left behind in strange ways. Maybe all this bustle and bossiness was just Mrs. Fairfield's way of handling her grief. Little did she know there was worse news to come about her husband's precipitous demise.

Dittany wasn't about to be the one to tell. She went and washed the dining room chairs.

As she was setting them out to dry, on the side porch which was screened by a high hedge, because everybody in town would naturally be assuming the museum was closed today out of respect for its late curator and would be shocked to the marrow did they but know not only a trustee but Mr. Fairfield's very widow were here working, a van pulled into the driveway and a man got out. He wasn't the plumber; he was the long-lost roofer.

"Morning, ma'am. Here for my stuff."

"You mean those ropes and buckets you left in the stairwell?" Dittany replied. "I'm afraid you can't have them."

"Huh? Who says so?"

"Firstly, the board of trustees, of whom I'm one. We don't intend to settle your bill until we've made positively sure that skylight isn't going to leak again. Unless you can give us a positive ironclad guarantee, you might as well leave that stuff right where it is till after the next rain."

"Look, lady, when I fix a skylight, it's fixed. I want my gear."

"That brings us to objection number two," said Dittany, "namely and to wit, Sergeant MacVicar. In case you hadn't heard, we had a sudden death here yesterday."

"What'd that to do with me?"

"That remains to be seen," Dittany replied darkly. "Anyway, Sergeant MacVicar's in charge of the investigation, so you'd better trot yourself down to the station and get his permission before you start tampering with the evidence."

"What's all this?" That was Mrs. Fairfield, right on the job. "Is that the plumber you're talking to, Mrs. Monk? Did you tell him about the—why, Frederick Churtle! After all these years. If you've come to borrow more money from Peregrine, I'm afraid you've left it a bit late."

"Haven't changed a bit, have you, Evangeline?" The roofer squinted up at her with what could be dimly discerned through his three-days' growth of whiskers as an expression of deepest distaste. "Hey, you don't mean that was Perry who got killed yesterday?"

"It was, since you're so kind as to inquire."

"I'll be damned." He took a moment to digest the news, then shook his head. "Poor old Perry. How'd it happen?"

"He went up to shut the attic windows Mrs. Monk here left open, and fell out."

The roofer shifted his gaze yet farther upward and shook his head again. "You trying to kid me?"

Mrs. Fairfield's not inconsiderable jaw dropped. "Frederick, whatever do you mean?"

"Cripes, Evangeline, I always knew you weren't anyways near so smart as you took credit for, but I'd never have believed you could be that dumb. Take a look at 'em."

Instead of following his suggestion, Mrs. Fairfield turned to Dittany. "Mrs. Monk, if you have any idea what Frederick Churtle is driving at, would you be kind enough to enlighten me?"

She did look thunderstruck, as well she might. Dittany tried to think of a tactful way to explain. "Well, you remember yesterday when we were up attic?"

"How could I forget? If you hadn't chosen that particular time to go—"

Dittany's tact began to wear thin. She fought the urge to remind Mrs. Fairfield that she had gone alone and would have been better content to remain so, and furthermore that she wasn't the one who'd said to leave the windows open.

"Yes, well, we can't change that now, can we? What I started to say was, don't you recall how tiny those windows are?"

"Why no, I can't say I do. When you say tiny—"

"I mean they're hardly more than portholes. Come out on the lawn and see for yourself."

Mrs. Fairfield heaved a mighty sigh, stepped down to the ground, and did as she was bidden. "Oh, dear. I do see what you mean. All right, Frederick, for once in your life, you were right and I was wrong. But if Peregrine didn't fall out the window, then—"

The roofer snorted. "Then I guess we know now why this young woman says Sergeant MacVicar doesn't want me to take my rigging down, eh?"

"Are you trying to say he fell off the roof? That's absurd, and you should know it better than I. You know how Peregrine always was about heights, Frederick."

"I know. Wouldn't even climb up on a chair to change a light bulb. Puts you on kind of a sticky wicket, eh, Vangie?"

Mrs. Fairfield didn't say anything for what seemed a long time. Then she sighed again, more heavily than before. "Yes, Frederick, it does. If Sergeant MacVicar is—but I mustn't even think of that, must I? After all, you were Peregrine's friend once."

"Evangeline, what the bloody hell do you think you're talking about?"

"Oh, Frederick, how can I tell? Such a dreadful, dreadful—Mrs. Monk, do you think you could possibly find me a cup of tea?"

"I'll put the kettle on," said Dittany. "You go on into the parlor and stretch out on the chesterfield."

"No, no. I mustn't give in. Peregrine wouldn't have wanted that. I'll just go into my office and get back to work. Frederick, if you happen to run across that plumber, I'd thank you to tell him I want him here at his earliest convenience."

"How come his convenience instead of yours? Gettin' soft in your old age, Evangeline?"

"Frederick, this is hardly the time or the place for one of your singularly tasteless jokes. Surely you can't object to delivering a simple message. You owe me a few favors, in case you'd forgotten. Among other things."

Before the roofer could reply, Mrs. Fairfield turned and stalked back inside. Dittany waited to ask the man, "If your name's Churtle, why do you call yourself Brown?"

"I'm a remittance man. I don't want to embarrass me dear old daddy the dook."

"Thank you. And how come you picked today to come after your tackle, when you allegedly finished patching the skylight two weeks ago and we haven't seen hide nor hair of you since?"

"I been busy writing my memoirs. Ta-ta, miss."

He got into his van and chugged off. Dittany went to make Mrs. Fairfield's tea. As she was scalding the pot, she thought of phoning Sergeant MacVicar about this interesting new development. Then she reflected that the phone was on the desk where Mrs. Fairfield would be sitting, that she didn't quite know what to tell, and that Sergeant MacVicar must already know the roofer had been here.

News of any sort wasn't apt to lie around gathering dust in Lobelia Falls, and the MacVicars' own grapevine was almost preternaturally efficient. She rinsed out a pink teacup with For a Loving Grandma printed on it in gold, clearly one Therese hadn't yet got around to putting into the flea market, made the tea, and carried the tray to Mrs. Fairfield.

The widow was at the ledgers again. She took off the plastic-rimmed granny glasses that had been perched halfway down her nose and let them dangle from the black cord around her neck.

"Thank you, Mrs. Monk. This will perk me up. I'm sure I don't have to tell you what a ghastly shock it was having Frederick Churtle pop up like that. It's been thirty years or more since I hoped I'd seen the last of him. You don't really believe what he was trying to make out, do you?"

"It's not a question of what I believe." Dittany was through trying to be tactful. "It's what Sergeant MacVicar believes that matters. He'll be hotfooting it over here, I expect, once he learns you're up and about."

Normally he wouldn't have come badgering a widow quite so soon, but this one was asking for bother. Mrs. Fairfield might be wondering whether she'd have done better to stick with the cologne and the darkened bedroom. She fussed around with the milk and sugar and took a fortifying sip of her tea.

"I'm sure you're wondering, Mrs. Monk, how my husband and I ever came to know a man like Frederick Churtle. The thing of it is, Frederick and Peregrine were boyhood chums back in their hometown and kept up their acquaintance as they grew up, even though their lives were taking very different paths."

She had recourse to the pink teacup again, then shook her head. "No, that won't do. You may as well know the plain truth. My husband, who you must realize was the best-hearted man alive, allowed Frederick to impose on his good nature long after he'd outgrown the acquaintance. Not to put too fine a point on it, Frederick borrowed large sums of money from Peregrine and never paid them back."

"Oh," said Dittany.

"Yes, that's how it was. I daresay we could all tell stories of false friends. Forgive me for airing my personal problems this way, Mrs. Monk. I expect I'm distraught and simply need to talk. It absolutely knocked the stuffing out of me, having that wretched sponger poke his face around here after all these years, running me down and trying to make out Peregrine's death was," she swallowed more tea, "something other than what we know it was. That's what Frederick was getting at, wasn't it?"

"Well," Dittany answered cautiously, "you have to admit he was right about those attic windows. If you'd care to go up and take another look—"

"I couldn't! Not now. I suppose I shan't mind after a while, when duty drives me to it, but not today, please. I simply couldn't face it."

"That's only natural. I should have known better."

"I'm sure you meant well, Mrs. Monk. Do you think those dining room chairs are dry yet? We shouldn't leave them out too long."

There were some people it simply didn't pay to be nice to. Dittany bit her lip, picked up the tea tray, and stalked out of the office.

# CHAPTER 8

She was out on the porch sloshing lemon oil on the chairs to relieve her feelings when Sergeant MacVicar appeared.

"Ah, lass, there you are. Far be it from me, eh, to pass judgment on a woman's housekeeping methods, but it strikes me you are being a trifle o'er generous with yon lemon oil. Indeed, I am somewhat astonished to find you working here at all on such a day."

"I have my orders." Dittany sloshed on another dollop of lemon oil to show what she thought of them. "If you're looking for Mrs. Fairfield, she's in the back parlor impersonating Margaret Thatcher. Did you see Frederick Churtle?"

"Who?"

"The roofer from Scottsbeck who calls himself Brown. He was a boyhood chum of Mr. Fairfield, whose first name was Peregrine."

"I was cognizant of the latter fact. So must you have been at the time your board of trustees hired him."

"And woe to the day we did. I guess I know, but I must have got him mixed up with one of Arethusa's minor characters. Mrs. Fairfield's is Evangeline."

"Now, that," said Sergeant MacVicar, "I had not known. It minds me of Henry Wadsworth Longfellow's immortal line, 'She bore to the reapers at noontide flagons of home-brewed ale.' "

"In a pig's eye she did," snorted Dittany, applying such wrathful friction to her polishing cloth one might have thought her a girl guide trying to start a campfire without matches. "Evangelines don't bear flagons. They sit on their duffs and yell for somebody else to fetch 'em."

"Do I detect a note of acrimony, lass? We must make allowances for circumstances."

"I have. That's why I'm polishing chairs instead of flouncing off in a huff. Getting back to Churtle, did you see him?"

"Ah yes, Churtle. I did not. What about him?"

"He came by a while ago for that mess of hemp spaghetti he left strung up through the stairwell. I told him he couldn't take it away till you said he could, and he left. I supposed he was going to see you."

"If he was, he missed me. Did you tell him why my permission was necessary?"

"I started to. Then Mrs. Fairfield came out and the two of them got into a hairtangle. It turns out he and Peregrine were kids together."

"Indeed? And how did yon Churtle react to the news of Mr. Fairfield's death?"

"He told Evangeline she was bonkers to think her husband fell out the attic window."

"Why did he mention the attic window?"

"Because that was what Mrs. Fairfield told him. She explained how I'd left them open and Mr. Fairfield had to go up and shut them."

Sergeant MacVicar rubbed his chin, his fjord-blue eyes resting thoughtfully on the almost-empty lemon oil bottle. "This was before or after the alleged Brown had been identified as Churtle?"

"Oh, after. Mrs. Fairfield spotted him right away. The first thing she said was, 'Why, Frederick Churtle.' Then it all came out about the old pals stuff and his hitting Peregrine up for money."

"Um ah. How much money?"

"Surely you don't think Mrs. Fairfield would have been vulgar enough to tell me? She apologized afterward for having mentioned money at all."

"Indeed? Noo, lass, could we go back over this entire conversation. Who said what to whom, and in what order?"

Since the conversation had been so short and so fraught with unexpected revelations, Dittany succeeded in repeating the whole thing. Sergeant MacVicar nodded once or twice but did not interrupt. When she'd finished, he asked, "And that was all? Nothing after Churtle told you he was writing his memoirs?"

"I think he said, 'Ta-ta, miss.' Then it was boots, saddle, to horse, and away. I'm surprised he didn't go straight to the station if he was so hot after his blocks and tackles."

"Aye, and why did he choose this particular morn to pick it up, syne he'd been content to leave it here so long?"

"Because he figured we'd all be off baking custards for the widow, and he'd have the place to himself."

"Pairhaps. There's food for thought here, lass. According to your account, Churtle did not deny knowledge of a death here yesterday, albeit he either did not know or feigned not to know the demised was the friend of his youth. Furthermore, and this is the part that puzzles me, when he did find out, he failed to ask when the funeral is to be held. I believe I will pay my respects to Mrs. Fairfield. She is in the back parlor, you say?"

"Yes, only she's calling it her office now. Come on, I'll show you."

Dittany knew perfectly well Sergeant MacVicar didn't have to be shown. He knew she knew. Being a perspicacious man, however, he also knew Mrs. Fairfield had been giving Dittany a rough morning, that Dittany in any event would have no intention of being left out of whatever was going on, that he'd waste his time trying to keep her back because she'd been aye the same since she was a wee bairn, and that considering the lemon oil, he didn't blame her. Therefore, he contented himself with making her presence official.

"Dittany, Mrs. MacVicar always maintains a woman needs another's supportive presence in time of grief and stress. Therefore, you will be good enough to remain whilst I ask Mrs. Fairfield a few questions. I will endeavor not to tax your sensibilities unduly, Mrs. Fairfield."

"Oh, please don't fret yourself about my sensibilities, Sergeant." Mrs. Fairfield touched a folded handkerchief to the corner of her right eye and brought it away, Dittany noticed, perfectly dry. "I'm trying to be a good soldier. I know what a bore it must be for you all, having something like this occur to a stranger within your gates. I shall be so relieved when this apartment finally gets finished and I at least have a place to call my own. Not that Mrs. Oakes hasn't been the soul of kindness, but you know how it is. Or perhaps you don't, never having been in a similar position. I must say, when I broke up my own lovely home to come here, I never dreamed anything like this would happen."

She plied the handkerchief again. "Ah well, you don't want to hear about my troubles. Ask your questions, Sergeant, and I'll do my best to give you sensible answers. If I can just keep my poor wits about me, that is."

"Then suppose we start with something easy. Tell me about Mr.

Churtle. Dittany tells me he is an old acquaintance whom you had not seen for many years."

"That's correct. At least thirty, possibly more. Frederick Churtle was my husband's acquaintance, not mine. They'd been boys together. He was never, I must say, one of my favorite people."

"And why was that, Mrs. Fairfield?"

"As I've already told Mrs. Monk, I resented the way Frederick took advantage of my husband's good nature. I despised him as a person of low habits and no principles. To put it in a nutshell, he drank, gambled, and consorted with loose women. He rioted away his own paycheck every week, then came and mooched off my husband."

"Indeed? A most pernicious state of affairs."

"You don't know the half of it. I couldn't begin to tell you how much money he borrowed from us over the years and never paid back. My husband used to slip it to him without telling me. That was after we'd had a few dustups over Frederick's constant sponging, I must admit. Then at last things came to a head."

"Aye, 'tis ever thus. What happened, Mrs. Fairfield?"

"I'm not quite sure, but I do know Frederick got into some dreadful scrape. I believe he was caught stealing from his employer and had to make good or go to jail. Anyway, he desperately needed five thousand dollars, and Peregrine absolutely insisted on lending it to him out of our savings. I shan't pretend I yielded with any good grace. I made Frederick sign a note for the money, promising to pay within six months. I hoped that would force him to face up to responsibility."

"A vain hope, I mistrust."

"It certainly was. Instead of paying, Frederick skipped town and apparently changed his name so we couldn't catch him. You could have knocked me over with a feather when he breezed in here this morning, brash and brazen as ever."

"You had not the slightest inkling yon Churtle was in this area?"

"Heavens no. How could I? I told you we hadn't seen hide nor hair of him for thirty years. Not that we'd have stayed away on his account, I can assure you. My husband's eyes were opened long ago about his dear old boyhood chum. In any event, the stipend here is hardly conducive to large-scale philanthropy. Not that I'm complaining you understand. I quite realize the trustees would pay more if they could afford to. I will say that if I'd known who this so-called Brown was, I'd certainly have recommended they find another roofer."

"But you never saw the soi-disant Brown working here?"

"No. I believe he'd finished whatever he was supposed to do before my husband and I arrived. Those ropes were already hanging down the stairwell. I did ask to have them taken away because they're such a nuisance, but Mrs. Monk's aunt told me the trustees wanted them left in place until they'd made sure the skylight wouldn't leak again. That made sense, of course, although I can't see how I'm expected to get that stairwell papered with them in the way. I rather wish you'd let Frederick take them away, Mrs. Monk. Now every time I see them, I'll think of him and that outrageous suggestion he made about Peregrine this morning."

"I have been wondering how I might broach that subject," said Sergeant MacVicar.

"Why? Surely you don't think there's any truth in it?"

"Yon attic windows are extremely small, Mrs. Fairfield."

"Well, Peregrine was no giant," the widow retorted sharply, then remembered she was bowed down by weight of woe. "Mrs. Monk did say something about the windows just now. It was she who opened them in the first place, you know."

That was too much for Dittany. "Yes, and I'd have closed them when we left, only you said not to."

The handkerchief came into play again. "Did I? I suppose I meant to send up the Munson boys or somebody. There are always so many people in and out of here, you know. It never occurred to me Peregrine might wind up having to shut them himself."

"We are not sure he did," Sergeant MacVicar remarked.

"What do you mean? Were the windows still open after we found him?"

"Two were shut, two were open, one of which latter was the window under which Minerva Oakes found him."

"Well, of course it was. You'd hardly expect him to turn around in midair and shut it after him, would you?"

"Nay," Sergeant MacVicar agreed, "a man plummeting to his doom might well be excused for overlooking such a trifle. But you see, that raises another question. Not only were the windows unusually small, they were in grievous disrepair. They required to be propped open, which Mrs. Monk had in fact done with bits and pieces she found lying about. Given the meager space he'd have had to squirm through, how would Mr. Fairfield have managed to do so without knocking out the prop and thus being pinned between sash and sill?"

"Peregrine was a very small man." Mrs. Fairfield was looking pretty green around the gills by now, Dittany noticed.

"I grant you that. However, there is the further complication of the window sills."

"The window sills? Attic windows don't have them, surely?"

"I stand corrected. The proper term would have been ledges. On account of the sloping mansard roof, you see, and the windows being set in plumb to the attic floor, there is thus created a flat shelf approximately a foot deep in front of each one."

"If you say so. But what—"

Sergeant MacVicar waved a magisterial hand for silence. "Now, since you have seen ample evidence of the state John Architrave's ancestral home was in at the time it fell into possession of the Grub-and-Stake Gardening and Roving Club, you can well believe, eh, that yon ledges had not been cleaned off for decades. Therefore, had your husband gone out one of the aforementioned windows either by accident or by design, he must inevitably have left a trail among the accumulated dirt and debris, as well as transferring some of this material to his clothing. We found no evidence that he did so, therefore we are forced to conclude that he did not make his final exit by that route."

"Then it must have been one of the second floor windows he fell from."

"Aye, but here again we run up against an enigma. In the first place, Dr. Somervell questions whether the relatively shorter drop could have resulted in such extensive injuries as Mr. Fairfield was found to have sustained. There is the added difficulty that above the spot where his body was discovered, there is only one other window that might conceivably have answered the purpose. This is that odd little porthole affair high up in the stairwell, which is accessible only by a most precariously perched ladder. Why it was ever put there, the Lord in His infinite wisdom doubtless knows."

"But what about those ropes of Frederick Churtle's?"

"A most ingenious suggestion, Mrs. Fairfield. But e'en supposing a man of your husband's years, dignity, and known aversion to heights presumed to make a monkey of himself by means of the rigging, it would have availed him nowt. That window was painted shut sometime around eighteen hundred and seventy-two, from the look of it, and has obviously never been opened since."

"Sergeant MacVicar, what are you trying to tell me?"

"I am trying to point out to you that having ruled out possible alternatives and having found certain evidence to support our thesis, we are led to assume your husband fell off the roof."

"The roof? Oh, but that's impossible. Peregrine would never in the world have gone on the roof. He was scared to death of heights from the time he was a little boy. I can remember that odious Frederick Churtle teasing him about it. Frederick himself doesn't mind heights a bit. He was an elevator repair man when I first knew him. He'd tell dreadful stories about walking across an elevator shaft forty stories high on a narrow plank, and poor Peregrine would get sick to his stomach just hearing about it. Surely you must be mistaken, Sergeant MacVicar. Isn't it more likely Peregrine lived long enough to have crawled away from the spot where he fell, or that he—he bounced when he hit?"

She clapped the by now somewhat less pristine handkerchief to her mouth. Sergeant MacVicar shook his head.

"I fear not, Mrs. Fairfield. He landed in a bed of bee balm, you know. The plants were badly crushed by the impact of his body. There is no such crushing anywhere but underneath where he lay when we found him. Dr. Somervell gives it as his considered opinion that the dent in Mr. Fairfield's head was such as to have effected his instant demise. Also, we have discovered yarn from that gray shetland cardigan he was wearing at the time caught on one of the ornamental spikes that surround yon skylight. Can you explain how it got there?"

Mrs. Fairfield shook her head. "Then—then what you're saying, Sergeant MacVicar, is that my husband killed himself."

# CHAPTER 9

Sergeant MacVicar's blue eyes remained unswervingly focused on her face. "Can you think of a reason why he might have done so, Mrs. Fairfield?"

"I never saw anybody look so much like a largemouth bass in my life," Dittany told Hazel Munson later, not derisively but merely in the interest of accurate reportage.

Nor was she exaggerating. It was some time before Mrs. Fairfield managed to get her lower jaw back under control. Even then she had to wet her lips and swallow a couple of times before her voice came back.

"No. Not really. I suppose one never knows what may be going on inside another person's mind, but I'd have thought Peregrine was the last person in the world to commit suicide. He hadn't been happy about retiring, but then the appointment to the Architrave came along and that cheered him up. Of course when we got here we found it was—well—something less than we'd been given to expect, but that just made the challenge all the greater. Peregrine was quite cheerful about it, really. He said it was like starting a new career."

"And what about his health, Mrs. Fairfield?"

"Not bad, for a man his age. He took blood pressure pills, but that's nothing unusual."

"Any pressing financial worries?"

"Not after I managed to get Frederick Churtle's hand out of his pocket. One doesn't exactly get rich in our line of work, you know, but we'd managed to build up a little reserve, and Peregrine had his pension. The salary here isn't much, of course, but we felt that getting our living quarters provided by the Architrave made it a reasonable enough situation. No, Sergeant MacVicar, unless there was some secret in Peregrine's life I don't know about or unless Peregrine had a sudden attack of brain fever, I simply can't picture him climbing up on the roof and jumping off."

"Then that brings us to the final alternative, does it not?"

"The final—I'm not sure what you mean."

"A mere matter of logic, Mrs. Fairfield. Since we have ruled out the likelihood that Mr. Fairfield effected his own sorry demise either by accident or by design, then it must follow as the night the day that somebody murdered him."

The widow took his words better than Sergeant MacVicar appeared to have been expecting. Dittany wasn't a bit surprised, though. Tough as a boiled owl was her own ungenerous private appraisal, not that she'd ever boiled an owl or would have dreamed of trying to. Anyway, Mrs. Fairfield must have seen it coming. She bowed her head, employed her handkerchief, then replied quietly enough, "I suppose there's nothing else left to believe, is there? But who on earth would want to kill Peregrine?"

"That is what we must find out, Mrs. Fairfield. Have you any ideas as to a possible suspect?"

Mrs. Fairfield began pleating her already overstrained handkerchief. "That's a terrible thing to ask, Sergeant. I'd have to think long and hard before I ventured any kind of suggestion."

"Then I will await the result of your cogitations with what patience I can muster. In the meantime, it might facilitate our investigation if you could give me an account of whatever may have occurred before you left the museum yesterday afternoon."

"What occurred? Why, nothing in particular that I can recall. By the time Mrs. Monk and I came down from the attic, the afternoon was fairly well over. We were both covered with dust by then, my arm was bothering me terribly, and I was about ready to drop from the heat. I'm afraid I wasn't thinking much about anything except getting back to Mrs. Oakes's for a shower and some clean clothes."

"Did you speak to your husband before you left?"

"Oh yes. For the last time. Though of course I didn't know it then. I told him about the windows, as a matter of fact, and showed him a few things we'd turned up in our prowling. Mrs. Monk had taken the only real find away with her, so he never did get to see that, but I don't suppose it matters now."

"And he seemed in good spirits then?"

"Normal spirits, I should say. He was in the dining room, sorting through some odds and ends of china to see if we had anything that would make a decent showing in that bowfront cabinet. It had taken me a few minutes to track him down, I remember. I'd thought he'd be either here in the office or else in the kitchen where the plumber was working. Or alleged to be."

"That would have been Cedric Fawcett from Scottsbeck?"

"I suppose so. It was the same one who'd been here before. I didn't ask his name."

"But you did speak to him?"

Mrs. Fairfield couldn't repress a grim smile. "Oh, I spoke to him, all right."

"And he was still here when you left?"

"I believe he must have been. I left almost immediately afterward. In fact, I have a dim recollection of seeing his truck drive out of the yard as Mrs. Oakes and I were walking toward here later. Though come to think of it, I'd thought the plumber's truck was blue."

"And what color was the truck you saw leaving?"

"It seems to me it was brown. Perhaps Mrs. Oakes will remember."

"Mrs. Fairfield, this is extremely important." Sergeant MacVicar was forgetting to be benign. "Are you positive this truck was coming from the museum? You must realize that would mean its driver may actually have been there at the moment of your husband's death."

"Certainly I realize that, I wish I could swear to it as a fact, but I can't. I believe I saw it pulling out of the driveway and I have an impression it was brown. That's the best I can do. At the time I was worried about my husband, you know."

"But it was not so very late, after all."

"Yes, but I was afraid he might have had one of his dizzy spells. He did have high blood pressure, as I mentioned. Sometimes he forgot to take his medicine if I didn't remind him. One does hate to be nagging all the time. So he'd have had reason to be apprehensive about heights even if it weren't for his phobia. That was Frederick Churtle's fault, too, by the way."

"How so?"

"Back when they were little boys, they were playing on top of a henhouse, which of course they shouldn't have been doing, and Frederick shoved Peregrine off the roof. He landed among a flock of guinea hens and they all started gobbling and screaming at him. You know what an unspeakable racket they make. He was terrified, naturally. And Frederick just stood up on the roof laughing at him. Did you ever hear of anything so heartless?"

She rubbed her hand across her forehead. "How did I ever get started on guinea hens? Please forgive me. You were asking about the truck. Surely if I wasn't imagining it, somebody other than myself must have noticed. I find very little seems to escape the neighbors around here."

"But it was suppertime," Dittany pointed out. "They'd have been eating."

"Not all of them, surely?"

"Certainly all of them. It was Male Archers' practice night. The men would want their suppers right on the dot so they could get out to the butts."

"Aye," sighed Sergeant MacVicar, doubtless still brooding on the shots he himself had missed making when duty so inopportunely called. "Nevertheless, we shall make inquiries on the off-chance somebody can confirm or refute Mrs. Fairfield's supposition. Nor is it without the bounds of probability that Minerva Oakes will be able to cast light on the matter. Now, Mrs. Fairfield, let us get on with this already fruitful reminiscence. Can you state for a positive fact that you and Mr. Fairfield were alone here, save for the plumber in the kitchen, before you left him and went to change your dress?"

"Why, no, I couldn't swear to it. I didn't go searching through the rooms or anything. People do drift in and out, you know. There was that woman in the purple dress, for instance."

"Ah, yes. The Munson boys mentioned her. Were you able to ascertain her identity?"

"No. I only caught a glimpse of her. She was going out toward the back as I was coming downstairs. All I can say is, she was wearing a dress of some silky material in an unusual shade of purple printed with a smallish green and turquoise design of some sort. Rather attractive, really. I remember wishing I could get a look at the front to see how it was made."

"You didn't call out to the woman or attempt to pursue her for this purpose?"

"Hardly. I was filthy dirty, you know. On the contrary, I ducked back hoping she wouldn't take a notion to turn around and see me looking such a sight."

"Dittany, lass, you have made no mention of this woman in the purple dress," Sergeant MacVicar said. "How is it you did not see her yourself, if you and Mrs. Fairfield came down from the attic together?"

"Because we didn't, I suppose. I mean we did, but we split up on the second floor. I was walking ahead and decided to use the front stairs instead of the back because I was in a hurry to get home before Osbert."

In fact, she'd been high-hatting Mrs. Fairfield over that box of quilt pieces. Dittany didn't particularly care to remember that now, despite the lemon oil that had flowed over the dam since then.

"So it's possible this woman was still in the museum when I left," said Mrs. Fairfield. "I remember wondering, now that I think of it, if she was going down cellar with something for the flea market."

"In a silky purple dress with green and blue doodads on it?" Dittany shook her head. "Sounds rather fancy to be prowling around that dirty old cellar in. I wonder if she could have been someone from the inn."

"I am surprised you are not wondering which lady of your acquaintance owns such a frock," Sergeant MacVicar admonished.

"Because I already have and I can't think of anybody. Mrs. MacVicar might know." Mrs. MacVicar usually did. "If not, I could ask around."

"Aye, Dittany, do that. I will make inquiries at the inn."

"With all respect, Sergeant MacVicar, that's pretty finky of you. Can't you let Bob and Ray do it instead? Petsy Poppy's waitressing over there now, you know."

Sergeant MacVicar was not to be baited. "Aye, I misdoubt my deputies would be pleased to renew their acquaintance with Miss Poppy, who was so helpful to the police in the affair of the Hunneker Land Grant."

And a few other affairs, maybe. Dittany wouldn't be surprised if Bob and Ray hadn't already renewed their acquaintance. Petsy was a young woman of awesome physical endowment. She held the further distinction of being the first and so far only female Osbert Monk had ever picked up in a bar.

Far from being jealous, Dittany held a warm spot for Petsy in her own regard. First, Osbert had made his advances in line of duty during his earlier deputization by Sergeant MacVicar and under the tutelage of Bob and Ray. Second, his success with Petsy had caused him to overcome his shyness and emboldened him to propose to the then Miss Henbit after less than a week's acquaintance. Even so, Dittany didn't want the job of interrogating Petsy left to Osbert again.

"I could ask her myself if you like," she offered. "Petsy's a niece of the Mrs. Poppy who's my cleaning woman, you know."

"Oh," said Mrs. Fairfield most inadvisedly, "do you have one?"

Since Dittany had invited the Fairfields to tea one day the previous week, and since she'd been at considerable pains to have the house looking decent for the occasion, she pointedly left the widow's question unanswered. Mrs. Fairfield was actually starting to look somewhat abashed when Arethusa blew in and gave her an excuse to pretend no awkwardness had occurred.

"Egad and a rousing gadzooks" was Arethusa's tactful greeting, "whatever are you doing here, Mrs. Fairfield? Shouldn't you be prostrate in a darkened room? With a wreath of lilies around your brow," she added after a pause for reflection.

"No, no." Mrs. Fairfield had got the long-suffering cadence down pat by now. "My husband would have expected me to carry on. Having put one's hand to the plough, you know. What a handsome Brussels lace tablecloth you're carrying. Is that for us?"

"Yes, but it's Battenburg." Arethusa spread the cloth out to give them a better look. "Miles of little tapes, you see, stitched all together by hand, with crocheted thingamajigs intercalated among the interstices. Hideous waste of time, but rather a pleasant effect. 1897."

"I should say at least forty years earlier."

"Then you wot not whereof you speak. My great-grandmother wrote in her diary on April 14 of that year, and I quote, 'Today I completed the Battenburg lace tablecloth on which I have been working all winter to the detriment of my eyesight and the annoyance of my husband who deems my nightly preoccupation with needlework prejudicial to his enjoyment of what he pleases to consider his conjugal rights.' We'll use it on the dining room table, with that silver gilt epergne Samantha Burberry's mother-in-law gave us full of wax fruit and artificial flowers in the tastelessly flamboyant, though admittedly eye-catching, mid-Victorian manner."

"Oh?" It was a remarkably chilly "Oh?" for one whose mind might at that time have been expected to be dwelling on the eternal verities. "Do you find the tastelessly flamboyant mid-Victorian manner altogether appropriate for a genuine Queen Anne table?"

"Not at all," said Arethusa. "I mention it only because what we have is a tastelessly flamboyant mid-Victorian imitation of a Queen Anne table."

Mrs. Fairfield looked as if she were going to say something else but had recourse to her handkerchief instead. Then she said bravely, "Sergeant MacVicar, if you have no further use for me here, I ought to be getting along. Reverend Pennyfeather will be expecting me about the funeral. Just leave the tablecloth in the dining room, please, Miss Monk. I'll attend to it when I get back in an hour or so."

Arethusa shook her luxuriant raven tresses, which she was wearing today *à l'espagnole,* complete with a spit curl on either cheek. "You will do no such thing, Mrs. Fairfield. Mrs. Pennyfeather is giving you lunch with the deacons at the parsonage. After that, Mrs. Oakes expects you back at her house for a nice little lie-down before she and Mrs. Trott escort you to the funeral parlor, where various members of the community will be waiting to pay their respects. You then return to Mrs. Oakes's for tea with the museum trustees. That includes you, Dittany. I dropped in at the house but that idiot nephew of mine said you were over here, which is why I came, come to think of it. Where was I?"

"I think you were about to ship Mrs. Fairfield back to the funeral parlor after we'd finished tea." Dittany told her.

"So I was. Well, that's our program and we'd better get cracking. Mrs. Pennyfeather's making *croustades aux crevettes à la nantua* out of respect for Mr. Fairfield's memory, and they've got to be eaten hot."

"But I'm not dressed for anything so grand," Mrs. Fairfield protested.

"True, i' faith," said Arethusa, viewing without favor Mrs. Fairfield's stockingless legs, denim skirt, and short-sleeved plaid cotton blouse. "You should have worn black, or at least something dark and dignified. People expect it. Sergeant MacVicar will run you back to Minerva's to change. *Tout de suite.*"

"But the museum?"

Mrs. Fairfield wasn't liking this high-handedness a bit, Dittany could see. She'd have hated it herself. But then, were she, perish the thought, a new-made widow, she wouldn't be here dithering about dining room tables. She'd be out in her own back yard, erecting a funeral pyre to commit suttee on. Perhaps she'd better not mention that, though. It was just the sort of thing Arethusa might want added to the agenda.

# CHAPTER 10

"Arethusa," said Dittany a little later, back on Applewood Avenue, "weren't you laying it on a bit thick back there?"

"How should I know, forsooth? We've never buried a curator before."

The chairman of the board hauled a chair up to the kitchen table and sat scowling in the direction of the den, whence her nephew's typewriter could be heard galloping like the hoofbeats of a wild stallion on his way to visit some likely-looking mare; not that any stallion of Osbert's invention would be caused to make its intentions known on paper. Readers of Westerns are a pure-minded lot, and Osbert wouldn't have wanted to offend their sensibilities.

Arethusa was not thinking of Osbert's readers' sensibilities. She was moodily selecting the fattest little onion from the dish of mustard pickles Dittany had just set out. "In my personal opinion, we're planting the wrong half of that connubium, though I suppose I shouldn't say so."

"No, you shouldn't," Dittany replied in a rather offish tone, for she had been planning to eat that onion herself. "At least not until after the funeral," she modified. "I foresee we're going to have to straighten that lady out one day soon."

"And I foresee who's going to be the straightener." Arethusa snapped viciously at a piece of pickled cauliflower, getting mustard on her chin. "You do realize, ecod, that la Fairfield expects us to keep her on as curator in her husband's place?"

"I also realize she'll try to make us look like a pack of rats when we start trying to give a poor, lorn widow the heave-ho." Dittany slapped a platter of salad on the table and went to call Osbert.

"Dinner's ready, darling."

"So soon?" The typewriter slowed to a trot, then a walk, then Osbert tied it to the corral fence and came into the kitchen. "You here again, Aunt Arethusa?"

"An affectionate nephewly greeting, i' faith! Can you never say anything pleasant?"

"If I must. That color looks good on you."

"My Peruvian blouse?"

"No, your Coleman's Mustard."

"Schoolboy humor. Pah!"

"Yes, Aunt Arethusa. I suppose you've scoffed all the pickled onions as usual."

"Dittany, how can you tolerate this graceless lout?"

"With the greatest of ease." Dittany dropped a kiss on Osbert's cowlick and helped him to the biggest piece of chicken before his aunt could grab it. "Did you have a productive morning, darling?"

"Great! I rustled a whole herd of yaks."

"A parlous geste," sneered his aunt, "since there are no yaks nearer than Tibet. I'm not even sure there's a Tibet any more, the way they shove boundaries around these days."

"If they move boundaries, why can't they move yaks?" Dittany asked reasonably. "Lettuce, darling?"

"Don't ask him that," cried Arethusa. "He'll take it as an invitation to further displays of lewdness and lechery."

"Really, Arethusa, you do have a prurient streak in you. Have some lettuce yourself. It cools the blood."

"It doesn't cool mine," said Osbert recklessly. "Now that Aunt Arethusa's brought up the subject, darling—"

"I have not. *Unberufen!*"

"What's that supposed to mean? You can't go around unsaying things at a whim. And you needn't try to make us think you can speak German just because you once ate a bratwurst, either."

"Shall we talk about something uncontroversial?" said Dittany.

Arethusa shrugged, racked her brain for a moment, then obliged. "What's happened to that creature you optimistically refer to as a dog? I haven't seen it around lately."

"Poor Ethel's suffering the pangs of unrequited love," Dittany told her. "She's fallen for a woodchuck who lives over on the Enchanted Mountain; one of those strong, silent types. I've told her it can never be, but you know how girls are. She just won't listen. She comes dragging home every so often for something to eat, then goes back and flops down beside the woodchuck's burrow. When it comes out, she starts making mournful noises, then it bounces off, playing hard-to-get. I'm hoping passion runs its course before cold weather sets in and the woodchuck decides to hibernate. We may have to go out and build an igloo around her. Speaking of building, I wonder why that roofer goes around whomping on shingles under an alias."

"Possibly because his aunt bullied his parents into naming him Osbert," said her husband. "What roofer?"

"The one who either has or hasn't fixed that leak in the skylight at the museum. He turned up this morning wanting his gear."

Osbert paused in the act of buttering a slice of brown bread to regard his mate with thoughtful eyes. "He did, eh? Under an alias, you say? What alias?"

"Actually I'm not sure about the alias," Dittany admitted. "I'd assumed his name was Brown because he drives a brown truck with Brown the Roofer painted on it, but maybe he bought out Brown's business and hasn't got around to repainting the truck or something. Anyway, he's an old buddy of Mr. Fairfield who used to borrow money and not pay it back under the name of Churtle."

"Thus proving we should neither a borrower nor a lender be," said Arethusa with her mouth full of lettuce. "I wonder if Churtle is a derivation of 'churl'?"

Osbert did the only sensible thing and pretended he hadn't heard. "How did you find out Brown was Churtle, darling?"

"I was out on the porch over there, cleaning up some walnut side chairs Grandsir Coskoff's first wife's mother brought with her when she immigrated from Grand Rapids. At the behest of the Empress Evangeline, I may add."

"Of who?"

"He means whom," said Arethusa, finding the last pickled onion and chomping it triumphantly.

"I was referring to Mrs. Fairfield, our self-appointed head honcho. Anyway, this roofer hauled up and told me he'd come for his ropes and buckets. So naturally I told him he couldn't have them till Sergeant MacVicar said he could. That led to a discussion of our recent fatality, which in turn led to Mrs. Fairfield's charging out to stick her oar in. She reared like a spooked mustang when she saw the roofer and called him Frederick Churtle, among other things."

"How did she know he was Frederick Churtle?"

"Because Frederick and Peregrine—"

"Who? And don't go yammering 'whom,' Aunt Arethusa. I refuse to get involved with the accusative case."

"Mrs. Fairfield got involved like anything," said Dittany. "As to Peregrine, that was her husband's first name. Doesn't it make you feel a little better about Osbert?"

"Nope. I rather like Peregrine, as a matter of fact. It makes me think of buzzards soaring above the buttes."

"It would," snarled Arethusa. "What about Peregrine, Dittany?"

"He and Frederick Churtle were pals from their cradle days and remained so for some time after the Fairfields were married, despite Evangeline's conviction that Churtle was a drunk, a waster, and a rioter away of his substance. Also a rioter away of Peregrine's substance, as she learned to her expressed chagrin. Fred kept hitting Perry up for loans and never paying them back."

"But perhaps he had debts of honor?" Arethusa suggested.

Osbert snorted. "I never could figure out why it was so dad-blanged nobler in the mind to pay your gambling losses by cheating the baker out of his bread money. And don't bother trying to explain. I want to hear the rest about Perry and Fred."

"Well," Dittany went on, "the mooching continued for some unspecified length of time. Then Mrs. Fairfield, who also makes me think of buzzards over the buttes, vowed she'd put a stop to it. Fred got into a really bad scrape and nicked Perry for five thousand dollars to bail him out. Mrs. Fairfield couldn't stop her husband from forking out, but she did make Fred sign a note for the money. Thereupon, he vanished into the sunset and never resurfaced again until this morning, by which time the statute of limitations for getting her cash back must have run out."

"Maybe that's why she was so miffed with him."

"I suppose so, but it does seem to me that if I happened to bump into an old pal of my husband's on the eve of his funeral, I'd want to bury the hatchet for auld lang syne. I mean, wouldn't you think having Fred Churtle show up would recall those halcyon days when Perry and Vangie were still lovestruck young kids? Not that I can visualize Mrs. Fairfield as a blushing bride, but there it is."

"There what is?" demanded Arethusa, licking mustard off her fingers. "Tea and cookies, perchance?"

Thus reminded of her duties as hostess, Dittany got up to clear away the plates and fetch dessert. Osbert sprang to help her. They happened to meet in the pantry by the cookie crock, so it was some time before they got back to the table where Arethusa sat gathering her brows like gathering storm, nursing her wrath to keep it warm, as Sergeant MacVicar would indubitably have observed, given the opportunity.

"Does Sergeant MacVicar know about Churtle?" Osbert wondered, perhaps catching that same hint from his aunt's by now well-gathered brows.

"Need you ask?" said Dittany. "He came along right after Churtle left and give Mrs. Fairfield the third degree. She'd offended his sense of decorum by going to work instead of staying at Minerva's nursing her tear-tortured eyeballs. She offended mine, too, though I know it's mean to say so. I think she was bending over backward not to be a burden on anybody, for fear we'd get fed up and give her the heave-ho."

"Meseems she was taking a great leap forward to let us know she intended to intimidate us into keeping her," Arethusa retorted less charitably. "That reminds me, I must alert Minerva to invite the rest of the board to tea."

"Arethusa," cried Dittany. "Do you mean you made up all that about Mrs. Pennyfeather and the shrimps on toast and whatnot? How could you?"

"Silly question. I always can. However, there was a modicum of truth to my remarks. I'd seen Mrs. Pennyfeather at the market buying shrimp for old Deacon Hayes. She told me he likes them better than anything else since he cracked his upper plate and doesn't dare chew hard, and she was having him over this noon because it's his birthday. As Mrs. Fairfield was going to be there at eleven, I knew they'd ask her to stop and eat with them. The Pennypackers couldn't turn anybody away from their table if they had only one crumb to divide among them. And if by 'how could you?' you mean, 'why did you?' I should think the answer was obvious."

"Not to me," said Osbert.

"It is to me, now I think of it," said Dittany. "Have another cookie, Arethusa. Osbert, you'll be interested to know Mrs. Fairfield claims she saw that woman in the purple dress Dave Munson mentioned."

"Dave said the dress was blue."

"He also mentioned green and purple, if you recall. Mrs. Fairfield said it was purple with a chartreuse and turquoise design on it."

"Sounds god-awful, eh. Did she say who the woman was?"

"No, she only noticed the dress. I think it must have been a stranger from the inn, unless somebody we know has a new dress nobody's heard about yet, which hardly seems likely. Arethusa, whom do we know who'd buy an outfit that color?"

"Almost anybody, if it was a big enough markdown. Me, for instance. How do you think Sir Percy would look in a rich purple velvet suit and a turquoise satin waistcoat?"

"And a chartreuse periwig? That's a thought. Maybe the woman was really Andy McNasty in drag."

"What for, egad?"

"Casing the joint in the interest of fell designs and evil machinations, one would naturally assume. We'll find out sooner or later, no doubt."

"Zounds! You don't think it was McNaster who heaved Mr. Fairfield off the roof?"

*"Pourquoi pas?* Andy knows about roofs, or ought to. Furthermore, Frederick Churtle does his roofing work."

"Aha! The plot thickens. You baked these cookies a soupçon too long."

"Osbert likes them nice and crunchy."

"But then I still have my own teeth," said Osbert. "What does Sergeant MacVicar intend to do about the woman with the dress?"

"He was about to ask his wife if she knew who owned one like it. If she didn't, which I find hard to believe, he was going to send a posse over to interrogate Petsy Poppy."

"He is? I could—"

"Not on your life you couldn't. You're a married man now, in case the fact had momentarily escaped your memory."

"Darling, you can't possibly imagine I have any fell designs on Petsy just because I once interviewed her in line of duty."

"Duty, forsooth!" His aunt emitted a particularly nasty snicker. Dittany gave her a look.

"Lay off, Arethusa. Darn it, I wish you hadn't roped me in for this tea party at Minerva's. I keep having guilt pangs about not showing Mr. Fairfield those quilt pieces. If I hadn't taken a notion to go up attic in the first place, the poor old coot would probably be alive now."

Osbert wasn't having any of that. "Darling, if somebody was planning to murder Mr. Fairfield, whatever you did or didn't do can't have made a particle of difference one way or the other."

"It makes a difference to me," snapped Arethusa. "Quit nattering and go fetch those pieces. Pronto, as this semiliterate lout would no doubt put it."

Dittany gave her another look and went to get the wooden box. Arethusa, who had due respect for fine handwork even if she had none for her otherwise celebrated nephew, washed her hands free of pickle juice before she started turning over the exquisite scraps of satin and velvet.

"Lovely, lovely. Just look at this golden bumblebee. It reminds me of something, though I can't think what."

"The birds and the flowers?" Osbert suggested.

"Gadzooks, you randy rake, meseems I liked you better with inhibitions."

"Fiddle, Aunt Arethusa. You thought I was a wimp."

"If by wimp you mean milksop, cotquean, or whey-faced molly-coddle, you could be right, though the correct expression might be that I disliked you less. The point is moot, since I'm stuck with you regardless. Getting back to this bee, have you ever seen a more impressive bug?"

"It's got one black antenna and one yellow," said Osbert. "I wonder why."

"Perhaps because whoever did it ran out of black or, as the case may have been, yellow thread and didn't feel like running out to get some more," Dittany suggested. "There's a whole swarm of bees, it looks like. Mrs. Fairfield thought the bride, who evidently never got to be one, may have belonged to a sewing circle called the Busy Bees. Or else her name was Betsy or Beatrice."

"Or Bedelia, Belinda, Bertha, or Bathsheba," Osbert added helpfully.

"Berengaria, more likely," said Arethusa. "Hola, here's a brown baby bee. Or is it a wood louse?"

"Nobody would embroider a wood louse on a bride's quilt," Dittany objected. "Except possibly her younger brother. I think that's meant to be a worker bee. They'd want one to fix the queen's tea, I expect. Speaking of which, hadn't you better phone Minerva and let her know she's giving a party?"

"Gadzooks, yes. Better still, you call her. I have to go home and embroider a gown for Lady Ermintrude." Arethusa scooped the quilt pieces back into the box, stuck it under her arm, and left.

# CHAPTER 11

"She's gone loco," said Osbert. "I knew all that garter-stapping would catch up with her sooner or later."

Dittany kissed the tip of his nose. "Darling, why don't you go rustle another yak while I call Minerva?"

"Yes, darling. That worker bee had one red whisker."

"How nice. I hope Arethusa doesn't put those quilt pieces down some place and forget where. We've got to get started on that quilt while people are still feeling sympathetic. I'd better find out if Minerva wants me to—oh, is that you, Zilla? Where's your buddy? Well, holler out and tell her to leave the weeding for another day. She doesn't know it yet, but she's giving a tea. No, just the trustees. You, me, Hazel, Therese, and Arethusa. And Mrs. Fairfield, of course. Should I whomp up a batch of—oh, they have? Yes, naturally they would."

She turned to Osbert. "Zilla says everybody's been bringing cakes and things. What, Zilla? No, the tea was Arethusa's idea and I must say I think it's a good thing to do. No, of course Mrs. Fairfield isn't prostrated. She was over at the museum throwing her weight around all morning, and now she's at the parsonage eating shrimp wiggle. Look, here's the drill. When she gets back to Minerva's, make her lie down for a while. Then you and Minerva escort her to the funeral parlor. Visiting hours are two to four, then seven to nine. Get her back to the house as soon after four as you can make it. Some of us will be over there early to fix the tea. Right. Over and out."

She hung up. "There, that's settled. Now I'll give Hazel and Therese a buzz."

"Just a second, darling," said Osbert. "I've been thinking. Dave Munson said he saw that woman in the purple dress sometime during the middle of the afternoon, didn't he? Three o'clock or thereabout."

"Yes, I think so."

"And what time was it when you and Mrs. Fairfield came downstairs?"

"Around a quarter to five, I know the Munson boys were gone by then. Darling, I see what you're getting at. If that woman wasn't messing around down cellar all that time in her good dress, what the heck was she doing?"

She and Osbert stared at each other for a moment, then Osbert said, "I think I'll step around to the station."

"Yes, why don't you? See if Mrs. MacVicar's come up with any word on the dress."

Dittany suspected the solution to that particular enigma lay in the end-of-summer markdowns. She herself hadn't been around to the sales. She'd been too busy at the museum, and she had a closetful of gorgeous new clothes anyway, now that Osbert had found something to spend his money on. But it simply wasn't possible none of her friends had seized the chance to pick up a bargain or two. Even the home sewers would have joined in the hunt, because they'd all been too busy running up school clothes for their kids or curtains for the museum to make anything new for themselves. In truth, Dittany would have gone herself, sudden affluence or no, if she'd had the time. There was still the thrill of the chase. She gave a moment's wistful thought to clearances of yesteryear, then got at the dishes.

These done, she began wiping around with a sponge. Next thing Dittany knew, she was housecleaning full tilt. Theoretically, Mrs. Poppy now came every week instead of only twice a month as in the pre-Osbert period. What it boiled down to, however, was that Mrs. Poppy thought up twice as many reasons why she couldn't come at all. So things did tend to pile up. Dittany refused to admit to herself that Mrs. Fairfield's snide crack had been the propellant for this burst of domesticity, but she knew such fits didn't take her often and it was well to make the best of them when they came.

Besides, cleaning was good therapy. By the time she wrung out her mop and hopped into the shower, Dittany found herself positively looking forward to the lemon squares, macaroons, and brandy snaps at Minerva's. She put on a lovely sheer black crepe frock she'd bought in Ottawa on her honeymoon, added a black cartwheel hat and a pair of white shortie gloves circa 1955 that her mother had left behind when she'd embraced Bert and the life of a fashion eyewear salesman, and went downstairs.

Osbert was just back from his visit to Sergeant MacVicar. "Darling," he exclaimed, "you look just like a lady going to a tea party."

"That was the effect I aimed to convey. How did you make out with the sergeant?"

"We nipped over to interview the Munson boys. Dave's willing to swear it was no later than half past three when he saw that woman. He was watching the time because they had to pick up their brother in Scottsbeck."

"I remember. But that means she'd been hanging around a whole hour and more when Mrs. Fairfield saw her. Unless she went out and came in again. Did you see Petsy?"

"Ray did. She told him a woman in a purple dress had stopped there for dinner about half past one and dawdled quite a while over her meal. It looks as if the woman must have wandered over to the museum afterward to kill time and just stayed."

"But whatever for? There's not that much to see, and nowhere to sit down if she wanted to rest. And if she went to the inn, she couldn't have been any of our crowd, so she wouldn't even have known there was all that flea market stuff in the cellar."

"I know, darling. So that leaves us with only one other possibility, wouldn't you say?"

"Of course! She must have been talking with Mr. Fairfield."

"That's what Sergeant MacVicar and I think. Not that it means anything, necessarily, provided she left the museum before Mrs. Fairfield did. Since she was seen at the rear of the house both times, that probably means she'd left her car in the parking lot at the inn and cut through the hedge to the back door instead of going around by the sidewalk. Lots of people do."

"You don't have to tell me," Dittany snarled. "We've put in three new privet bushes so far, and every one of them's been trampled down before we could put the shovel away. Next time we're going to plant poison ivy. But, darling, if this woman went into the dining room at half past one and wasn't seen presumably entering the museum till half past three, that must have been one heck of a big dinner she ate. What time did she leave the inn, did they tell you?"

"They couldn't say. The noontime help were going off and the suppertime crew coming on. This time of year they're all part-time workers and don't know what they're doing anyway, as far as I can make out. As to the parking lot, cars are always coming and going. Nobody knows which is a worker's and which is a guest's. Sergeant MacVicar's questioning everybody he can get hold of, but so far he hasn't had any luck finding out what kind of car the woman was driving, assuming she came in a car at all."

"But surely he was able to get some kind of description of the woman herself."

"Oh yes. She was middle-aged, whatever that's supposed to mean these days, medium height, medium build, had a scarf over her head so you couldn't tell what color her hair was, and kept her sunglasses on so you couldn't tell what color her eyes were. She seemed pleasant enough but didn't say much except to give her order. She had steak Diane, whatever the heck that is, cooked medium rare. She didn't mind waiting for it because she had a book to read. It was a real book with a cover on it, not a paperback, and looked dull."

"Why?"

"I don't know why, darling. I'm only quoting. To continue my report, she ordered half a bottle of an unassuming Bordeaux, drank some of it while she was waiting and the rest with her dinner. She skipped the string beans but ate the potato, had Roquefort dressing on her salad, coffee instead of tea, and trifle with extra cream. She left the exact amount of her bill plus a two-dollar tip which is a darn sight more than most of them leave, according to Petsy."

"Aha, so you did get to talk with Petsy."

"Sweetie pie, I couldn't help it. She galloped over and hailed me like a long-lost cousin. Anyway, Sergeant MacVicar was right there. Can you picture me attempting any moral turpitude with him looking on? Not that I would anyway. Look, darling, shouldn't you be getting on to your tea?"

"Trying to get rid of me, eh? What are you planning to do while I'm gone?"

"I have to round up those yaks. It'll take me a while. They've escaped the rustlers and fled into the mountains, where they're mingling with the bighorn sheep to throw their perfidious pursuers off the scent. Yaks are crafty critters, you know."

"I didn't, actually. Okay, you crafty critter, I'll leave you to the yaks."

Dittany set off, keeping a firm grip on her hat brim. It wasn't far to Minerva's because nowhere was far from anywhere in Lobelia

Falls. She was rather sorry about that, since she was not averse to flaunting her new outfit before those of her neighbors who might be whiling away a lazy August afternoon by sitting quietly in their own living rooms with their eyes glued to the slits in their drawn lace curtains. No doubt some of the elder ones would recognize the hat, but Dittany didn't care. It would show she still clung to her roots.

When she got to Minerva's, she found the rest of the party already assembled. Minerva had set her tea table out under the big oak in the back yard. Mrs. Fairfield was occupying a Victorian spring rocker that had obviously been dragged outdoors for the express purpose of letting Mrs. Fairfield sit in it. She'd put on one of those dark nylon jersey wash-and-wear dresses with matching jacket that are touted as being right for any occasion and changed her sneakers for sensible low-heeled pumps. Her usually bare legs were for once encased in darkish nylons—she'd had to get Mrs. Oakes to help her put them on, she told the company, because stockings were the hardest thing to manage with her cast. Peregrine had been wont to help her before—she made genteel play with a fresh white handkerchief.

Altogether, Mrs. Fairfield looked exactly the way the grieving widow of a museum curator ought to look and was conducting herself with exactly the proper degree of mournful decorum. Arethusa was keeping a stern eye on her though, Dittany noticed, just in case.

Dittany herself found Mrs. Fairfield a more touching sight than she'd expected to. After having greeted Minerva with a courteous, "I'm sorry to be the last one. Osbert was having trouble with some yaks," she went over to the guest of honor and made her manners just as though there had been no earlier stiffness between them.

"Good afternoon, Mrs. Fairfield. I'm so glad you felt up to joining us. Did you get some rest after your luncheon?"

"Yes I did, thank you. Everyone is being very kind."

Mrs. Fairfield gave her a resigned little smile and took the merest possible nibble from the edge of a macaroon. Dittany herself had worked up quite an appetite with all the mopping and swabbing. She collected her own tea and a representative assortment of goodies, and found herself a seat beside Hazel Munson.

"How's it going?" Hazel asked sotto voce. "Have they found out anything yet?"

"It looks as if Mr. Fairfield may have had a lady caller shortly before he died," Dittany murmured back.

"Who was she?"

"Nobody knows. She had dinner at the inn, then came in the back way, or so we assume. Your Dave caught a glimpse of her about half past three, and Mrs. Fairfield saw her when we came down from the attic a little after four-thirty. Neither of them saw her face though, just the back of her dress. Purple with turquoise and chartreuse doodads. The only reason we can think of for her having stayed all that time is that she must have been talking to Mr. Fairfield, and we don't know whether or not she actually left the museum before he died."

Hazel finished her scone and began work on a ladyfinger. "You'll never get me to believe that weedy little runt was involved in a *crime passionnel.*"

"Shh!" Dittany hissed from under cover of her hat brim. "Don't make me laugh. Minerva's feelings would be hurt. I'll talk to you later."

They straightened their faces and joined in the general effort to keep the conversation genteel and noncontroversial. That was no small job. Even the weather was a touchy subject in a group devoted on the one hand to gardening and on the other to archery. Fine for the butts meant dry for the dahlias, and as soon as one remarked on the former, somebody else was sure to riposte with the latter. However, the situation didn't get out of hand until Zilla Trott remarked, "That roofer sure picked a fine time to come after his gear, eh."

"Oh?" said Therese Boulanger in what she meant to be a tone of gentle admonition.

It took more than a little gentility to stop Zilla. "Yep. Caroline Pitz told me she saw his truck stop by the museum yesterday just at suppertime. She'd stepped out into the front yard for a handful of lettuce and there he was, bold as Billy.

"I cannot for the life of me imagine why Caroline chooses to grow her lettuce in the front yard," Therese rejoined in a desperate attempt to divert the flow of conversation.

She might as well have tried to stem Niagara with a teaspoon. Even Mrs. Fairfield was exclaiming, "He was?"

Zilla nodded, the afternoon sun picking out burnished highlights on the bridge of her nose. "So Caroline told me. I've never known her to be wrong about anything but wheat germ and politics."

"Where does Mrs. Pitz live?" Mrs. Fairfield was demanding.

"Directly across the street from the museum."

"And this was at what time?" She was forgetting to sound bereft.

"Quarter past six, somewhere around there. She said they were just about to sit down. Men's practice night, you know."

Mrs. Fairfield waved the men's practice night aside with an impatient gesture. "And what was the roofer doing there? You must realize how important this is, Mrs. Trott."

"Why, I—oh, for Pete's sake! I don't know what'd got into me today. Brains addled with the heat, I suppose. I'm sorry, Mrs. Fairfield. I shouldn't have brought it up."

"On the contrary, I'm only sorry you didn't tell me sooner. Sergeant MacVicar must know this, at once."

Zilla looked somewhat taken aback. "I wish there were more to tell. Caroline said she couldn't linger because she had supper on the stove. She'd have liked to make sure he got his stuff out. It's been such a pain in the neck, you know, those big ropes dangling down in everybody's way all this time. They make me think I'm being sent to the gallows. That roofer's name should be Ellis* instead of Brown."

"As a matter of fact," said Mrs. Fairfield, "his name is not Brown. It's Churtle. And he didn't take his ropes last night but came back for them this morning. I know because I went over there myself this morning. To be near Peregrine, I suppose." Remembering her assigned role, she raised the white handkerchief to her eyes again, evoking sympathetic murmurs from Minerva, Zilla, Therese, and Hazel, but not from Arethusa or Dittany.

"Sorry," she said with a pathetic sniffle. "As I was saying, and Mrs. Monk will bear me out because she was there with me, this alleged Brown came back and I recognized him as a person my husband had known years ago, before we were married. Without wanting to blacken anybody's name, I'll only say I personally didn't shed any tears when we lost sight of him. That was thirty-eight years ago, now that I've had a chance to think back and figure it out, so you can imagine what a jolt it gave me to see him

---

* Ellis was the traditional *nom de* noose of Canada's official hangmen. Capital punishment was abolished December 29, 1967.

there today. Mrs. Oakes, do you suppose I could have a spot more tea?"

"Of course." Minerva leaped for her cup, then started passing cakes and cookies and crumpets in a veritable whirlwind of hospitality. "Do try one of these hot milk sponge cakes, Mrs. Fairfield. You've got to keep up your strength."

"I suppose I must." Mrs. Fairfield nerved herself to consume the dainty, then took another in an offhand sort of way as if she didn't want herself to know she was doing it. "It does seem odd Frederick Churtle happened to show up at the museum just when Peregrine —but we mustn't jump to conclusions, must we? I suppose what happened was that Frederick simply found the door locked and went away."

"But the door wasn't locked," Minerva reminded her. "Don't you remember? We turned the knob and went right on in."

Mrs. Fairfield stared at her for a moment, then nodded. "You're right. We did, didn't we? Peregrine would have locked up, of course, when he left. But he—he never left. If you'll all excuse me, I think I'd like to go back upstairs for a while."

This time, even Dittany couldn't begrudge a sympathetic murmur. Arethusa merely helped herself to the last cream cake.

Minerva wiped her eyes on her napkin. "Poor soul, what must it be like for her, here among strangers without even a bed to call her own?"

"Yes, well, that brings us to the next order of business," Arethusa replied with her mouth full. "What are we going to do about her?"

"Do about her?" Therese Boulanger gasped. "Arethusa, how can you bring that up at a time like this?"

"Because, ecod, it's later than you think. Ask Dittany."

"Whatever it is, we can't discuss it now with poor Mr. Fairfield barely settled into his coffin and the upstairs windows wide open," snapped Minerva. "Here, Dittany, try a piece of Hazel's spice cake."

"Thanks. I'll take it to eat on the way.

"With your white gloves on?" snickered Zilla. "What's the all-fired rush?"

"I have to find Sergeant MacVicar and tell him what Caroline Pitz said about Fred Churtle."

"Can't Caroline tell him herself?"

"Come to think of it, I shouldn't wonder if she already has."

Dittany picked up her fork and began to deal with the spice cake in a more seemly manner. "I'd better tell him anyway, though, just in case."

"You're awfully thick with the MacVicars all of a sudden, aren't you? I heard the four of you went over to Scottsbeck last night for a Welsh rabbit."

"The Welsh rabbit was incidental. What we really went for was to grill Cedric Fawcett, the plumber who was fiddling around with the museum sink yesterday. At least Sergeant MacVicar and Osbert tried to, only Fawcett didn't say much except about wanting another beer. Mrs. MacVicar and I just rode along with them for the heck of it. Osbert's deputizing again, you know."

"Deputizing? Whatever for?" Hazel demanded. "We don't have to call out the guard just because somebody had the rotten luck to fall out an attic window, do we?"

"Go take a close look at those attic windows, then ask me again."

"Dittany!" Therese uttered the name in a sort of ladylike yelp. "You're not implying there was some kind of hanky-panky about Mr. Fairfield's accident?"

Dittany pulled her chair closer and lowered her voice. "Keep this under your hats, girls, but—"

# CHAPTER 12

"My stars and garters!" said Minerva Oakes.

It was clear she'd voiced the consensus of the gathering.

"So you see why I have to make sure Sergeant MacVicar knows Fred Churtle was there last night?" Dittany finished when she could get a word in edgewise.

"Well, of course," cried Hazel. "This Churtle probably came by to hit Mr. Fairfield up for another five thousand dollars and tossed him off the roof in a fit of pique when he wouldn't come across."

"A fine way to treat an old pal you haven't seen for thirty-eight years," Zilla snorted.

"Now, let's not go jumping to conclusions," said Therese. "A person's innocent till he's proven guilty, you know."

"Huh! Not if certain people around here whose names I don't have to tell you get wind of the story, which you can darn well bet they will if they haven't already. Churtle's going to be damned regardless, unless Sergeant MacVicar can prove it was somebody else. You go ahead, Dittany, I'll talk to you later."

That was a needless remark of Zilla's. They all would. And so would those members of the club who didn't get invited to Minerva's, and a few more people besides. Dittany put down her fork and picked up her handbag.

"Thanks for the lovely tea, Minerva. I expect I'll see you later on at the funeral parlor."

Little did she know how wrong her expectation would prove to be. Events began taking a new turn as soon as she got to the police station. There, whom should she find but her own beloved Osbert, deputizing for all he was worth.

"Hello, darling," he said. "I'm holding the fort. Ormerod Burleson's still away on holiday, Mrs. MacVicar's at the sales, the sergeant's off trying to trace that woman in the purple dress, and Bob and Ray have been called out to arrest Cedric Fawcett."

"Not our plumber? What did he do?"

"He assaulted Andy McNasty with a snake."

"A rattlesnake?"

"No, one of those squiggly things they poke down drains. He wrapped it around Andy's neck, then he squished a plunger down on top of Andy's head. He was threatening to twist Andy's ears off with a wrench when Andy's secretary laid him out with a bottle of Dr. Brown's Celery Tonic and called the police."

"That beer-swilling slug? Are you sure you've got the right Fawcett?"

"I know, darling, I couldn't believe it, either. But it turns out Cedric has quite a reputation for coming to a slow boil, then wading in with whatever he can lay his hands on. His brothers have had to buy him off a few other times, according to Ray, but this time I guess Andy's determined to press charges. Bob says he didn't mind the snake so much, but he looked upon the plunger as an unpardonable affront."

"One can see why. Not that I have any particular *tendresse* for Andy McNasty, and not that there weren't a few times back there last March when I could cheerfully have whammed him one myself. But, darling, if Cedric Fawcett's such a wild man, don't you think he might possibly—"

"Yes, darling, I do think he might possibly, and so does Sergeant MacVicar, especially since Fawcett and Mr. Fairfield appear to have been alone together in the museum after Mrs. Fairfield left. The hitch is, you can't haul a possibly into court on a murder charge. Unless Fawcett breaks down and confesses, we have nothing whatever to show he had any hand, or plunger, as the case may have been, in Mr. Fairfield's death. We're hoping this woman in the purple dress may be able to cast some light on the matter, assuming she ever turns up. It's not like tracking yaks, you know," Osbert explained earnestly. "All she has to do is change her dress, and she becomes the Invisible Woman. She could be anywhere by now. Well, maybe not anywhere, but someplace we'd never think to look. I mean, what if that was a rented car she was driving, and she simply dumped it at the nearest airport and got on a plane?"

"The only near airport's Charlie Evans's pasture, and all he does is fly around in that little old monoplane dusting crops," Dittany pointed out. "A woman in a nice purple dress with turquoise and chartreuse squiggles would hardly care to squeeze in there with all that bug juice. Not to confuse the issue, darling, but I have a further complication for you. Does Sergeant MacVicar know Frederick Churtle's van, presumably containing Frederick Churtle, was seen leaving the museum yesterday at suppertime?"

"Darling, are you sure?"

"Mrs. Fairfield claimed she saw what she thought was a brown truck pulling out as she and Minerva were walking toward the museum last night on their way to find Mr. Fairfield's body, though of course they didn't realize at the time what they were heading for. Caroline Pitz has now confirmed it was Brown's, which is to say Churtle's. She got a good look at it when she went out to pick lettuce for supper."

"Why didn't she tell Sergeant MacVicar?"

"Why didn't he ask? Remember, darling, most people still think Mr. Fairfield fell out the attic window. Caroline knew the roofer's equipment was still in the hallway and she naturally assumed he'd come to do something about it. You can't blame her for that."

"I could, but I shan't if you don't want me to. Only I do think Sergeant MacVicar should know about this right away."

"That's why I hurried over here instead of staying to help Minerva wash up, darling."

"Oh well," said Osbert, "Aunt Arethusa will have licked the platters clean by now, anyway. Ah, here comes Mrs. MacVicar. I expect that means I'm off the hook. Come on, I'll walk you home. You look right purty in them glad rags, Miss Dittany ma'am."

"Why, thank you kindly, Deputy Monk."

They acquainted Mrs. MacVicar with this new development, got her assurances that she'd let her husband know as soon as she could get hold of him, and headed back for Applewood Avenue. As Osbert was opening the back door, a mass of blackish fur hurtled through the air and two paws the size of dry mops planted themselves in the pit of Dittany's stomach. Her mother's hat went flying and she'd have followed it if Osbert hadn't grabbed her.

"Ethel," he roared. "Unpaw Mummy, you beast. Look what you've done to her dress. Aren't you ashamed of yourself?"

Ethel was not. On the contrary, she made it plain she was in no shape to handle criticism. Hurling herself at their collective feet, for Ethel was a large enough animal to manage this with no strain, she burst into mournful lament.

"Now you've hurt her feelings," said Dittany. "What's the matter, Ethel? Had a falling-out with your woodchuck?"

The whimpers became howls. They apologized, petted, whee-
dled, sympathized. Osbert examined Ethel's paws for possible
thorns, abrasions, or woodchuck bites. Ethel didn't wince, but
neither did she shut up. At last they got her into the kitchen, filled
her bowl with what cates and dainties their larder afforded, and
urged her to eat. She took a despondent nibble or two much in the
manner of Mrs. Fairfield with the macaroon, sighed heavily, cast
dimmed eyes up at them from under the mat of fur that hung
down over her eyes like a sheepdog's, albeit Ethel was not in fact a
sheepdog and might not actually have been a dog at all, and laid
her head against Dittany's knee to the further detriment of the
black crepe dress.

"She's pining away," Dittany moaned. "Osbert, what are we
going to do?"

He knelt on the varnished linoleum beside the doggie dish.
"Ethel, old pard, this isn't the end of the trail. You can't hang up
your saddle and turn your face to the sunset over one lousy woodchuck. Come on, let's see you tie on the old feedbag. A full belly
makes a stiff upper lip, you know. Here, try some roast beef."

Ethel condescended to let a morsel pass her lips and appeared to
find it good. At least she left her mouth conveniently open in case
anybody might be planning to give her another piece.

"See, darling, all she needed was a little tender, loving care.
Attagirl, Eth, eat it up."

"Maybe if I hold the dish to her mouth, she'll lap the gravy,"
Dittany offered.

Ethel considered the matter, then essayed a trial slurp.

"She's getting gravy all over your dress, darling," said Osbert.

"What's a dress compared to the comfort of a dog in distress?"

"Nobly spoken, sweetheart. Here, let me help you hold the
dish."

It was in this touching tableau that Sergeant MacVicar found
them.

"Sergeant," cried Osbert, "we were just on our way to find you."

"The fact leaps to the eye," the sergeant remarked with gentle
irony.

"But Ethel came home in dire straits," Dittany amplified, "and
we couldn't leave her to pine alone and desolate." Her mother had
sung a couple of seasons with the Scottsbeck Savoyards and she'd
learned a good deal of Gilbert and Sullivan as a result. "We think

the woodchuck must have given her the mitten. Did you find the woman in the purple dress?"

"Would that fate had allotted me some easier task, like searching out yon proverbial needle in the haystack. However, the RCMP have put out an all-points bulletin and Mrs. MacVicar has instituted inquiries among her acquaintance, so I am not without hope. Mrs. MacVicar finds it hard to believe that nobody in Lobelia Falls will be able to come up with a description of this mysterious female and the car she was driving."

"Speaking of description," Dittany said eagerly, "Caroline Pitz saw—"

"Frederick Churtle, as we now know him to be, parked in the museum driveway yesterday as she was picking lettuce for supper in her front yard," Sergeant MacVicar finished for her. "Mrs. Mac-Vicar apprised me of that fact some hours ago. I myself have ascertained that Churtle, or Brown as we may call him for purposes of convenience, resides over in Scottsbeck at 42 Glendale Street, which runs off Burnside Road, which in turns runs off Summit Avenue which, as you know, runs past the shopping mall. There is no summit, no glen or dale, and no burn in the vicinity, but that is beside the point."

"Then what precisely is the point?" Dittany asked him, knowing how risky it was to let Sergeant MacVicar get off on a side issue. "Do you want us to ride over to Scottsbeck with you and sit on Churtle's, or Brown's, stomach while you give him the third degree?"

"Noo, lass, we must not make light of serious matters. To be precise, I came hoping to persuade Deputy Monk to interview Churtle, or Brown, single-handed. Myrmidons Bob and Ray are still off getting Cedric Fawcett stowed in the choky, and I must remain available in case word comes through about yon woman in the purple dress."

"Of course, sir, I'll be delighted," said Osbert.

"Me, too," said Dittany.

Sergeant MacVicar looked first perturbed, then resigned. "I will leave you to work out a modus operandi between you. Good e'en to you both. And to you also, Ethel," he added kindly. " 'Tis better to have loved and lost."

"Considerably better, in Ethel's case," Dittany agreed. "We'll see you as soon as we get home from Scottsbeck."

# CHAPTER 13

"Darling," said Osbert, "I still think you and Ethel should have stayed home and rested quietly."

"So you could gallop off flexing your machismo?" Dittany snuggled closer to his shoulder. "You know it's better for her to get her mind off that woodchuck. As for me, I couldn't have borne to sit there wondering whether Churtle was whanging you with his shingle snipper or hitting you up for a loan."

They were riding in Osbert's pickup truck, an elderly vehicle of sober habits he'd bought with the advance from his very first novel, *Red Tails in the Sunset: A Backward Look at the Last Roundup of the Longhorns.*

Before his marriage, he'd been wont to use the pickup for camping expeditions. Dittany herself hadn't camped since her Girl Guide days, but she was amenable to the truck, because Osbert loved it and because they had no other means of transportation. Old Faithful, the 1966 Plymouth Dittany had ridden in since she was knee-high to a hubcap, had finally folded its fenders and been carted away to that Great Recycling Center whence no car returneth. They planned to get a new car sometime, but it wasn't high on their list of priorities. Besides, Ethel liked the truck, too. Having the entire back to herself gave her plenty of room to spread out and let her ears flap in the wind.

"I do believe the change is doing her good," Dittany remarked as she and Osbert got out at 42 Glendale Street. "No, Ethel, stay. You mind the truck while Daddy detects."

She herself was having some qualms about confronting Frederick Churtle on his own turf, but she needn't have worried. The roofer wasn't home.

"He's gone fishing," they were told by a woman who must have been Mrs. Churtle but probably thought she was Mrs. Brown.

"Do you know where?" Osbert asked her.

"Upstream. Where he always goes. He's got a lean-to. Don't ask me where, for I don't know and I don't care. Just so he doesn't bring 'em home for me to clean. Excuse me, my program's on."

She didn't exactly shut the door in their faces, but she left them no room to doubt the interview was over.

"Now what do we do?" Osbert fretted. "Where the heck is upstream?"

"Let's ask the Munson boys," said Dittany. "They'll know."

So back they drove to Lobelia Falls, Ethel looking perkier at every turn of the wheels. The Munson boys weren't home; they'd gone fishing upstream. However, their father was able to tell precisely which stream they'd gone up and where he thought Churtle's lean-to was most apt to be situated. It was a paltry matter of ten miles on a dirt logging road, then a short portage and another five miles or so by boat to Little Pussytoes. They thanked Roger and went home to collect their camping gear and Osbert's canoe.

While Osbert was loading his lightweight craft on the truck, Dittany packed a basket of food, added a box of dog biscuits and one of matches, having no faith in that tale of rubbing two sticks together to start a campfire, threw in a couple of blankets and a bottle of fly dope, and announced she and Ethel were ready to travel.

Roger Munson's directions were, of course, faultless. They found the dirt road with no trouble at all, notwithstanding the fact that it looked like the driveway to an abandoned farm and had a few dead limbs laid across it to add to the thrill of the hunt.

"Churtle must have done that," Osbert mused. "You'd have thought he wanted the road left clear in case he has to make a fast getaway."

"Maybe he's got a wild stallion tethered up at his camp," Dittany suggested, "and is planning to gallop back with pistols blazing and jump over. Make the horse jump, I mean."

"Good thinking, dear. I suppose we might as well put the branches the way he had them. No, Ethel, they aren't to play fetch with. Stay in the truck, like a good girl. Heaven forfend she should go roaming and find another w-o-o-d—"

"Shh!" Dittany warned. "Remember she grew up with the Binkles. You know how literate they are."

Ethel had in fact been adopted from a pound by their neighbors Jane and Henry Binkle, who owned a bookshop. However, a rapport had soon developed between Ethel and Dittany. In due course, she'd packed up her dog license and flea soap and moved next door. For a wedding present, the Binkles had made Dittany and Osbert a formal gift of her doghouse, which had stained-glass windows and wall-to-wall carpeting. Ethel never stayed in it, but it did add class to the dooryard.

As they penetrated farther into the woods, Dittany began to wonder if perhaps she should have packed the doghouse along with the matches and the dog biscuits. Even though they were but two months along from the longest day of the year, it seemed to be getting dark awfully early. Or maybe it was on account of the trees. She hadn't quite realized how many trees there were in Ontario.

Anyway, they were still on the right road, if road it could be called. Every so often, Osbert spied a splotch of crankcase oil that told him some vehicle in no better shape than his own had passed this way not long hence. He kept pointing these out to Dittany and she kept uttering appropriate little cries of delight, though in truth she was too busy trying to keep from bouncing off the seat to notice them much.

After a remarkably long ten miles, they came, as Roger had predicted, to a place where even this abject apology for a road ended in a pindling footpath. Here, Osbert was relieved and Dittany secretly disturbed to see a brown van with Brown the Roofer painted on its side and a CB radio antenna sprouting from its fender.

"Likes to keep in touch, I see," Osbert observed. "Come on, Ethel. Let's just make sure where this path goes."

Roger was right again. It meandered roughly half a mile and wound up as promised on the bank of a wide stream.

"He must keep his boat here. See, Dittany, here's where he pulled it out of the bushes and dragged it down to the water."

"I didn't know you were so up on all this woodcraft stuff, darling," she said dutifully. "Now what do we do?"

"We go back for our gear. You don't have to help with the canoe, darling. I've carried it farther than this lots of times."

"You're not just trying to prove you aren't a whey-faced molly-coddle?"

"My love, can you doubt me?" cried Osbert, much aggrieved.

"All right, then, you take the canoe and I'll carry the rest of the stuff."

"All of it?"

Well might he ask. When they got back to the truck, even Dittany cast a dubious eye over the basket, the blankets, the outsized box of dog biscuit, and the rest of their impedimenta. Osbert picked up the bottle of fly dope. "Here, darling, you take this."

"But what about the rest?"

"We'll let Ethel manage it."

Whipping out the hunting knife he'd hung from his belt, Osbert cut a couple of saplings, lashed them together at one end with a piece of baling twine out of the truck, wrapped their assorted luggage in the blankets to make a neat package, then tied the pack to the saplings with another length of baling twine.

"Come on, Ethel, we're going to make an Indian dog out of you."

"A travois!" cried his wife. "Oh, darling, you are brilliant."

"Not really, darling. I tried it out with a yak this morning. Back her into the shafts, will you, while I fasten the—hold still, old girl. No, darling, not you. Her. Come on, Ethel, raise your paw so I can get this rope under you. Good dog. Now you walk behind her, Dittany, and keep an eye on the travois in case it gets caught on a bush or anything. Here, I'll tie this last hunk of rope to the tip so you'll have something to steer by."

Osbert hoisted the canoe to his shoulders and walked on ahead. Ethel followed, tremendously pleased with herself and managing the travois as if she'd been a working dog all her life. Dittany brought up the rear with her bottle of fly dope and her steering line.

She was not at all scared, she kept telling herself, even when a great horned owl let go with a tune-up whoop in preparation, no doubt, for a busy night among the murmuring pines and the hemlocks standing like druids of eld with beards at rest on their bosoms. She kept her eyes on the travois so that she would be less apt to notice any large green eyes shining out at her. She'd have preferred to keep watching that adorable cowlick behind Osbert's left ear, but this was impractical, his head being inside the canoe. In fact, Dittany could see nothing of him at all except his Levis, his hiking boots, and his flannel-clad elbows balancing the canoe. She was no end relieved when they came to the stream.

Osbert disembarrassed himself of the canoe in an adroit feat of gymnastics and began unwinding Ethel from the travois. "Atta pup. You did fine. Come on, let papa have the blanket."

"Do you honestly think we'll all be able to fit into that thing?" Dittany thought the canoe looked awfully inadequate.

Osbert only grinned. He folded the blankets into a soft pad for Dittany to sit on, stowed their impedimenta at various strategic points, and boosted Ethel aboard with stern orders to lie down and keep still. He then assisted his wife to her cozy seat in the bow, shoved off, and settled himself in the stern to paddle.

"You should have kept that big hat on, darling," he remarked. "You'd look like one of those girls on your grandmother's old sheet music."

"I'll know better next time." Dittany was beginning to enjoy herself. A canoe was a peaceful way to travel. You slipped through the water with hardly a sound, except for the lap-lap of the water and the plop-plop of the drops falling off Osbert's paddle when he raised it for another stroke. One of the old songs had been about paddling your own canoe. She'd have to get him to teach her.

Gramp had liked that song. She wondered if he'd ever paddled a canoe up Little Pussytoes himself, back when he was a young fellow with a Model T and a girl who'd turned out to be Gram, or later on when he and Gram had an Essex Super Six and a son who'd turned out to be Daddy. Her father himself had been a bit old for canoeing, Dittany supposed, by the time he'd married the leading lady of the Traveling Thespians and begat his own little Henbit.

She was thinking in an Among My Souvenirs way about her parents and grandparents when Osbert murmured, "Light up ahead, darling. Maybe I'd better put you and Ethel ashore here and push on by myself."

"Abandon two helpless females to the forest primeval? Not on your life! Churtle's not going to riddle us with bullets, I shouldn't think. I suppose he might pelt us with sinkers and bobbers, or sic his night crawlers on us. Who cares? I'm not afraid of a few lousy angleworms."

"Darling, you put me in mind of Isabella Bird Bishop."

"Who?"

"You know, one of those intrepid Victorian lady travelers. Like Fanny Bullock Workman."

"Oh, of course. I couldn't place her for the moment." Dittany

contrived to speak lightly for the blood of the Traveling Thespians
was in her veins, but her heart was almost, though not quite, in her
mouth as the canoe turned in toward shore.

Now they could see the lean-to of which Mrs. Brown/Churtle
had spoken. A dinghy with a small outboard motor was pulled up
on shore. A cozy campfire burned within a ring of stones. Silhou-
etted against its light was a dark figure that could have been a bear
but proved to be Frederick Churtle. Far from showing hostility, he
acted pleased to have company.

"Ahoy out there!"

"Ahoy yourself," Osbert called back. "Mind if we pull in?"

"Not a bit. Here, let me give you a hand. Name's Brown. Say,
that's some pup you've got there."

"Her name's Ethel. I'm Osbert Monk and this is my wife, Dittany."

"Mr. Brown and I have already met," Dittany said in the tea
party voice she'd been practicing earlier. "What a pleasant camp
you have here," she added politely, since Churtle was gallantly
extending a hand to help her ashore.

Ethel naturally assumed the hand was meant for her and rushed
to find out if there was a dog biscuit in it, giving them all a dunking.
By the time they'd got sorted out and been invited to dry off at
Churtle's fire, the time for formality was past.

"Yep," Churtle was saying, "I come out here a lot. Roofing's a
nerve-wracking profession, you know. Or maybe you didn't. But
let me tell you, there's an awful lot of psychological stress in a
bucketful of hot tar. So I throw the old fly rod in the old buggy and
come out here to unwind. Pity you folks didn't happen along
earlier. I caught me a nice mess of trout for supper. Right out of
the stream and into the frying pan, that's the only way to eat 'em.
Say, what brings you out this time of night, if you don't mind me
asking? Unless you got a camp along here someplace?"

"No, we haven't," Osbert told him. "Actually, what brought us
was you."

"Huh? Cripes, don't tell me you're Renfrew of the Mounted in
disguise."

"Oh no, nothing like that. Just Acting Deputy Monk of the
Lobelia Falls Police Department."

"That so? Aha! Now I get it." Churtle turned to Dittany. "You're that young woman from the museum who's been giving me such a hard time about my bill. Look, if it's about those ropes of mine—"

"It's not," said Dittany. "Not exactly, anyway. You talk to him, Osbert. It will be more official."

Osbert happened to be taking off his wet socks at the moment, but he straightened up and looked as official as he could manage in his bare feet. "The thing of it is, your van was seen leaving the museum last night just about suppertime, which was when Peregrine Fairfield is presumed to have fallen to his death."

"Not from those attic windows he didn't," said Churtle. "I told Evangeline so this morning in front of your wife, and I'm telling you now."

"You don't have to convince us, Mr. Churtle. We don't believe it, either. We think Mr. Fairfield fell off the roof."

"Well, then, that's a different kettle of fish. And roofs being my field of expertise, eh, you've come for a consultation." Mr. Churtle pursed his lips and put his fingertips together. "Now, I'll grant you it could have happened, generally speaking. I could fall off that roof myself if I put my mind to it, which would be an unusual thing for a man in my profession, especially one naturally endowed with the surefootedness of a cat and the nerves of a lion tamer."

"I thought you said you were subject to severe mental stress."

"Not about being on roofs I'm not. The stress comes mostly from wondering whether I'm ever going to get paid for my work." He favored Dittany with another reproving glance. "But getting back to old Perry, it just so happens that's another subject on which I can speak with authority. As your wife here can tell you, it having been brought out this morning in the course of what for want of a ruder word I'll refer to as a confrontation with Perry's widow, I knew Perry Fairfield since him and me was toddling tots together. And I can tell you straight from the shoulder there's no way Perry Fairfield could of fell off that roof because there's no way on God's green earth anybody could of got him to go up on it."

# CHAPTER 14

Churtle put another stick on the campfire and warmed to his thesis. "See, Perry had what you might call a fixation, or maybe a neurosis or even a phobia. I don't think phobia would be too strong a term, though in most respects Perry was sound as a bell. The only other sign of mental aberration he ever showed was when he let himself get hooked and netted by Evangeline Sawn."

"That's the present Mrs. Fairfield," Dittany explained to Osbert. "I don't know if I happened to mention her first name's Evangeline. You know, the one who bore to the reapers at noontide flagons of home-brewed ale."

"*L'enfer* she did, if you'll pardon my French," said Churtle. "Evangeline never bore anybody anything except a grudge, only when she bore down on poor old Perry. Which she did, day and night, night and day from the minute he said 'I do' when he ought to of said 'I don't.' The poor cuss couldn't call his soul his own without her saying it wasn't."

"Yes," said Dittany rather nastily because she'd just got bitten by a mosquito the size of a hummingbird, "she told me how she used to get at him about lending you any more money."

"I figured she would," said Churtle, quite unperturbed. "No skin off my nose. I was glad enough to do it for my old comrade. Yep, wasn't much I wouldn't of done for Perry Fairfield."

"You considered it a favor to relieve him of all his spare cash?"

"Well, see, that's not quite how it was. Look, would you folks care for a mug of tea?"

"Why not?" said Dittany, feeling she might have been a bit hasty on account of the mosquito. "I've got some cookies in the lunch basket."

"I'll get them," said Osbert, heading for the canoe.

"Bring Ethel's dog biscuit, too, eh?"

"I'll go with you and fill the kettle, Deputy," said Churtle, "if you two ladies don't mind staying here alone."

"Oh, we might as well join the party." Dittany wasn't about to let Frederick Churtle sneak up behind Osbert and conk him with a paddle unbeknownst, though she didn't care to say so for fear of spoiling this new atmosphere of bonhomie, spurious though it might be.

However, it appeared Frederick Churtle had nothing more sinister on his mind than boiling up a soot-encrusted kettle, and the distance from the campfire to the canoe wasn't more than twenty feet anyway. They completed their mission without incident, got the kettle balanced on an iron grid rigged across the stones, and resettled themselves.

Churtle resumed his tale, or at least started to. "No, that's not how it was at all. Poor old Perry."

He fell silent. Osbert waited a decent length of time for him to gaze into the campfire and heave a few nostalgic sighs, then said, "Were you intending to tell us how it really was?"

"Why not? It can't hurt him now, poor cuss. See, I did it for Perry."

"So you mentioned. We're still trying to figure out why."

"Why? I'll tell you why. Because Perry asked me to, that's why. And if you want to know why Perry asked me, I'll tell you that too. It was on account of Perry needed the money."

The kettle was boiling. Churtle got up and made the tea. Anybody with half an eye could have seen he was brooding darkly on this mysterious paradox. Or perhaps he was wondering how a tale so intriguingly begun might plausibly be wound up. Anyway, he waited until he'd filled and distributed three tin mugs and Dittany had passed the cookies. Then he took a sip and a bite, said, "Very good, Mrs. Monk," and got on with his story.

"Like I said, Evangeline was trouble from the word go. Now, mind you, I'm not saying she was the worst wife in the world for Perry. Between you and me and the bedpost, Perry was so darned woolly-minded he'd forget which end his head was hitched on to if he didn't have somebody around to remind him. He was always living in some other century than the one he was in, if you get what I mean. That's how come he wound up in the museum business, I suppose. As far as his work was concerned, he managed fine, long as Evangeline was around to keep him up to snuff. It's just that when it came to what you might call practical matters, Perry plain downright couldn't cope."

"What sort of practical matters?" Dittany wanted to know.

"Any sort. Take a for instance. When Perry got married, he still had a little life in him Evangeline hadn't squoze out yet. He might decide to stop in and hoist one with the boys on his way home from the museum even as you and I, like the poet says. Only with Perry, the first thing you knew, he'd be setting 'em up for the house and bang would go his paycheck. So then Evangeline got to collaring his week's pay and just giving him enough to get by on, but Perry'd forget he didn't have the money and set 'em up anyway. So he'd wind up with a bad case of the shorts."

"I can imagine," said Osbert.

"Yeah. So what Perry did, he started stealing from himself, as you might say. He'd tell Evangeline I was in a jam and he had to lend me ten or twenty, however much it was he needed himself. What the heck, my shoulders were broad. I didn't mind. So this went on for a while and naturally these so-called loans never got paid back. I wasn't about to fork over what I'd never got in the first place, not to Evangeline I wasn't. I was just about getting by, myself, in those days."

Dittany passed him another cookie in silent compassion for those lean times of yesteryear. It was easy to feel mellow out here under the stars with the stream gurgling gently by and the pine knots hissing in the campfire and Ethel snuffling peacefully at one's feet instead of howling her plaintive love notes at an unresponsive mammal.

Osbert must have been less affected by the romantic atmosphere or more conscious of his duty as Sergeant MacVicar's deputy. He inquired coldly, "What about the five thousand dollars?"

"Huh? Oh, that. Poor old Perry."

Churtle poked up the fire, then reached over to rub Ethel's ears. "I guess you might call that Fairfield's Folly."

"How so?"

"Soo, what happened was this nice-looking old geezer wearing gray spats and a little white goatee came into Perry's office at the museum one day with a couple of artifacts. Had 'em in an old tapestry valise, Perry said. Don't ask me what an artifact is, but I guess it's something museums like to get their hands on because Perry was all het up about these two. Anyway, Perry authenticated 'em six ways from Sunday, then he asked the old geezer wouldn't he like to donate 'em to the museum?

"Well, the old geezer showed Perry a darn in his spats and said he couldn't afford to, and he didn't have time to hang around trying to strike a deal with any museum committee because he was just passing through town on his way to visit his dear little golden-haired granddaughter. But he'd sell 'em cheap to a private party who'd give 'em a good home. But he'd only take cash because somebody'd given him a bum check once and he'd vowed a solemn vow he'd never take another, being too honest and innocent himself to spot a crook when he run into one. So what did Perry do but trot himself over to the bank and draw five thousand bucks out of the bank without telling Evangeline.

"Perry's idea was, he'd buy the artifacts himself and turn 'em over to the museum. That way he'd get back his five thousand bucks and make himself a little something on the side. What they called a finder's fee. It was strictly on the up-and-up. Perry was so honest himself it was pitiful."

"Except when he lied to Evangeline," Dittany pointed out.

"Ah, but that was in self-defense. So anyway, he went up to the old geezer's hotel room and they had a sociable drink or two and sat around authenticating for a while. Then the old geezer took the artifacts and wrapped 'em up in a couple of racing tip sheets he had lying around the room and put 'em back in the valise and handed it over to Perry. So Perry forked over the five thousand and took the valise and scooted back to the museum with it before the old geezer could get to feeling sentimental and change his mind. But when he opened the valise and unwrapped the artifacts, all he had was a couple of busted sidewalk bricks with mortar on 'em."

Churtle shook his head at the folly of those who put their faith in nice old geezers wearing gray spats. "So he hightailed it back to the hotel figuring the guy'd made a mistake, but as anybody but Perry might have expected, the guy'd already checked out and vamoosed. So there's Perry up a gum tree and stuck there. And here comes Evangeline with blood in her eye because she's gone through his pants pockets and found the bank book with five thousand dollars taken out, which he forgot to hide. So what's he going to do? So naturally he thinks of his pal Fred Churtle and spins her a yarn about me being in a real bad jam and needing to be bailed out. So what could I do? Cripes, the poor bugger was bawling his eyes out when he snuck over to the shop and told me what he'd done."

The roofer shrugged. "Evangeline swallowed his yarn hook, line, and sinker, which was fine for him but not so hot for me. She went yapping all over town about me being a crook and a drunkard and a no-good bum and a few other things I better not mention in front of a lady. So naturally the stories got back to my boss, and he fired me for giving his business a bad name."

"But couldn't you have simply told the truth?" Dittany protested.

"Sure, and who'd believe me? Here's Perry in a nice blue suit and a clean white shirt, sitting there in his office among the high muckymucks, and here's me in my overalls with my bucket of tar. Besides, even if I did manage to convince anybody, the damage was done. All I'd accomplish would be to get Perry fired as well as myself, and what was the sense of that? So I just said what the heck, kissed my landlady good-bye, came as far west as my old flivver would carry me, changed my name, and set up in business on my own. This way, I figured nobody could fire me but myself."

"You never tried to keep up with your old chum?" Osbert asked him.

"Heck, no. Couldn't afford to. With a friend like Perry Fairfield, I'd never need an enemy, would I? Not that I held anything against Perry, mind you. I knew it was all Evangeline's fault, in a manner of speaking. Perry and I were just pawns of fate, but I was tired of being a pawn by then. Besides, what the heck, if I'd written to Perry, she'd have burned the letter. If I'd called him up, she'd have ripped the phone off the wall and sent it out to be fumigated. No sense beating a dead dog, is how I looked at it. Sorry, Ethel. More tea, anybody?"

"Not for me, thanks," said Osbert. "There's still one thing you haven't explained, Mr. Churtle. If you never saw your friend Perry again, what was your van doing in the driveway of the museum yesterday at the time he died?"

"I was wondering when you were going to get back to that," said Churtle. "Now, I'm not going to try to make you believe I didn't know Perry'd been hired by the museum, because I saw it in the papers. And I'm not going to try to make you believe I wouldn't have liked to get together with my old buddy and chew the fat a while, because I would, in spite of everything. But I was darned if I was going to tangle with Evangeline again."

He spat reflectively into the fire. "I've got a nice business built up here in Scottsbeck, and I've got a family to think of which I didn't in the old days. I'm not about to have her stirring up trouble for me again with that viper's tongue of hers. But there I was with my gear still in the museum and it put me kind of between a rock and a hard place, if you get what I mean. So yesterday late afternoon I happened to be over to Lobelia Falls trying to get a check out of Andy McNaster, if you want the truth, so I figured seeing it was getting late and Perry would most likely have knocked off for the day, I'd just swing by and take a chance on collaring my gear when nobody was around.

"So I went over and parked in the driveway, which there was no reason I shouldn't, me being on legitimate business as Mrs. Monk here can tell you. The place looked empty, but I thought I'd just take a stroll around the outside to make sure. See, knowing Evangeline of old, I knew if she was there, I'd hear her talking because the windows would be open on account of the heat. If she was I'd just pussyfoot the heck out of there. So anyway, I'm walking around the building looking up at the roof, making as if that was what I was there for in case anybody happened to be watching. All of a sudden I'm stumbling over something and be darned if it isn't Perry."

Dittany gasped and Churtle nodded. "Yep, it sure took a hike out of me, I can tell you. There he was, dead as a mackerel. I could tell just looking at him. Cripes, what a jolt!"

"What time was this?" Osbert asked him.

" 'Bout a quarter past six. I'd waited till then, see, because I knew it would be close to suppertime and I figured they'd have left, like I said."

"But the place would have been locked up," Dittany protested.

"Oh, I'd have just pried open a window and crawled in if I had to. Happens all the time in our business. People are always going to leave keys for you, and they never do. But anyway, there I was and there he was and I knew darned well what would happen if Evangeline came along and caught me there, so I just said, 'So long, old buddy,' and hightailed it out of there. And that's my story and you'll just have to take it or leave it 'cause I can't do any better."

# CHAPTER 15

"Do you think he was telling the truth?"

It was morning. Dittany had spent a not uncomfortable night with Osbert in Fred Churtle's lean-to, the roofer himself having gallantly insisted he often preferred to sleep outside in the warm weather anyway, and that he'd enjoy having Ethel for company.

Ethel had enjoyed him, too. She was a new dog today, the sparkle back in her eyes, the thump back in her tail. Now she was sitting up in the canoe, whoofling with pleased interest at each new loon and grebe. Only once, when she spied a small, furry quadruped, did she tilt back her head in a plaintive woo-woo-woo. But it turned out to be an otter, so Ethel quieted down and went on taking her census of the waterfowl.

Dittany, who was in the bow learning to paddle and getting on pretty well now that she'd discovered paddling a canoe requires essentially the same technique as sweeping off a porch, which she'd been doing ever since Gram Henbit bought her a child-size broom at the age of four, ventured to turn her head. "Did you hear me, darling?"

"Eh?" Osbert gave her a somewhat fatuous smile. "Sorry, darling. I was trying to think of a word to describe the way your hair looks this morning. 'Mist-bespangled aureole of shimmering golden light' sounds awfully pallid and puny, don't you think?"

"Darling, I'd hate to think I'm corrupting your crisp, virile prose style. Why don't you settle for wet and stringy? What I said was, do you think Mr. Churtle was spinning us a yarn last night?"

"He made it sound pretty convincing, I thought."

"Like when he told me yesterday he was writing his memoirs?"

"But why shouldn't he? Everybody else does. Watch out for that big stone, darling."

"Oh, gosh, I'm sorry. I thought it was another otter."

Dittany decided she'd better keep her mind on her paddling. Frederick Churtle, or Fred as he'd got to be known during their

long fireside chat, could wait till they got safely back. Osbert had
gently let him know any attempt to lose himself in the wilds would
be taken as a confession of guilt and he wouldn't get far anyway
because Sergeant MacVicar's three sons were all Mounties, so Fred
had promised to show up as soon as the fish quit biting.

In sober truth, Fred hadn't had so much as a nibble up to their
time of departure and the fish breakfast to which he'd made grandiose allusions the night before had turned out to be bacon and
eggs from Dittany's basket, but fishermen's lies don't count. The
Monks were both confident he wouldn't let them down.

Once ashore, they decided to leave the canoe hidden under a
shadbush in case they decided to pay another visit to Fred, who
wasn't a bad old scout provided he didn't turn out to have bumped
off his boyhood chum in revenge for the chickenhearted lie that
turned his life upside down. Ethel hurled herself into the back of
the truck. Osbert and Dittany got in front, and they bumped their
way home. The house looked a tiny bit unfamiliar, as houses always
do when their owners have been away. Ethel was disturbed by
this, and said so.

"What's she howling about now?" was Dittany's first reaction.
Her second was, "Who's been in here?"

Osbert dumped an armload of blankets and looked around the
kitchen. "What do you mean, darling? It looks all right to me."

"That's the problem. Every drawer and cupboard's shut tight as
a drum. I always forget and leave something hanging open, and I
know perfectly well I dropped that cup towel on the floor and
forgot to pick it up after I used it to dust off the picnic basket. Who
put it back on the rack like that?"

"You don't suppose Mrs. Poppy had a twinge of conscience and
dropped in to tidy up?"

"Osbert, you ought to know better than that. Besides, yesterday
was Mrs. Poppy's whist night."

"What about Jane Binkle? She took care of the place while we
were on our honeymoon."

"That was mostly to water the plants. Jane wouldn't come in
without being asked. I didn't even tell her we were going. Come
on, we'd better take a look around."

Even Osbert was convinced when he looked among his papers
and found to his horror that his first draft had got tidily stacked
together with his second draft and now he was faced with the

embarrassment of trying to figure out which was which. As they kept hunting, it became increasingly obvious that some remarkably neat-fingered intruder had gone through every room in the house including the woodshed, the attic, and the bedroom Dittany kept ready for her mother and Bert when they dropped in unannounced, as they were wont to do, on their way from somewhere to somewhere else.

"Whoever it was kept tidying up as he went along because he thought that would keep us from realizing he'd been here," Osbert deduced when he'd got through saying a number of other things about lowdown sneaks and ornery sidewinders. "Little did he know it would be the quickest way to tip us off. Not that you're untidy, darling," he added hastily.

"Nor you, darling," Dittany replied with about equal truth. "We just like to keep the place looking lived-in. But what puzzles me, eh, is that he doesn't seem to have taken anything. Gran's seed pearl brooch and the dining room silver, and my squash blossom necklace and the concho belt Mama and Bert brought you, they're all present and accounted for. So are the typewriters and the television and everything else, as far as I can see. So what was the point?"

"He was looking for something," said Osbert.

"What, for instance?"

"I can't imagine. I think we'd better get hold of Sergeant MacVicar."

To Osbert's surprise, it was Ray who answered the station telephone.

"Hi, Ray. Where is everybody?"

"At the funeral," the deputy answered. "How come you're not?"

Osbert turned to Dittany. "Darling, Ray wants to know how come we're not at the funeral."

"Because we forgot about it, that's why," his wife replied in stricken tone. "Oh, gosh! My name's going to be mud at the museum."

"I expect so," Osbert replied with more truth than tact. "Ray, would you tell Sergeant MacVicar to get in touch with us as soon as he can? We've had a break-in. No, don't you come. Sergeant MacVicar wouldn't want you to leave the station unattended. Besides, nothing's been taken as far as we can make out. I guess I'll have to go out and buy something valuable enough to steal, so Dittany won't be ashamed in front of the neighbors."

Dittany stuck her head under his arm. "I do not feel ashamed. I feel scared, if you want to know. Don't pay any attention to him, Ray. I mean do pay—oh, you know what I mean. Just please get word to Sergeant MacVicar as quickly as you can."

"Sure thing, Dittany. Hey, Osbert, did you locate that roofer?"

"No problem. That's why we were out all night. He's camping up on Little Pussytoes."

Osbert and Ray got into a conversation about camping out on Little Pussytoes. Dittany left them to it and wandered back to put the kettle on. A cup of tea couldn't hurt and might do some good.

By that uncanny sixth sense of hers, Arethusa appeared on the doorstep just as Dittany was setting the bread and butter on the table. She hurled her black kid gloves and purple velvet toque at the sideboard and flung herself into one of the kitchen chairs.

"Damme, wench, where were you? The trustees were planning to go in together. We hung around the vestibule till we well-nigh got trampled underfoot by the pallbearers. Couldn't you have kept that ravening letch at bay long enough to get out of bed and attend to your civic responsibilities?"

"Osbert does not raven," Dittany replied with well-bred hauteur. "We spent the night up at Little Pussytoes on a secret mission for Sergeant MacVicar. When we got back a little while ago, we found the house had been—Arethusa, what were you doing last night?"

"I was entertaining the nephew of the deceased, one Jehosaphat Fairfield, and his wife, Berthilde. They came up for the funeral to see if there was anything in it for them."

"Arethusa, that's unkind."

"Nonsense. Why else would they have come?" Arethusa started eating cheese but did not stop talking. "They can't stand Evangeline and hadn't seen Uncle Peregrine since Jehosaphat's graduation from barber school. Or was it dentistry? He and Berthilde have a great many teeth between them. Big white ones, like those fake china chompers you see getting dipped in blueberry juice on television. I expect Jehosaphat buys them wholesale."

"Where are they now?"

"Therese Boulanger invited the whole gaggle over to her house in a burst of masochism. She's putting on a buffet."

"How come Therese didn't ask you?" said Dittany, eyeing the fast-vanishing cheese with a certain amount of alarm. "Osbert, you'd better come. Your aunt's here."

"Did you ask her why she robbed the house?"

"What?" roared Arethusa. "Why, you vilifying varlet! What do you mean, robbed the house?"

"Somebody broke in last night and ransacked the place," Dittany explained. "Only they straightened up afterward so I knew it wasn't you."

"Stap my garters! They didn't take your grandmother's silver?"

"As far as we can tell so far, they didn't take anything at all."

"Embarrassing for you. And this happened last night? What time?"

"We haven't the faintest idea. We left here about half past seven or maybe eight o'clock and didn't get home till just a little while ago. Whoever did it must have been in the house quite a long time. He went through the place like a dose of salts."

"Egad, it's a good thing I took those quilt pieces home."

"No doubt," said Dittany, stifling a yawn with ill success. "Oh, here comes Sergeant MacVicar, thank goodness. Who's that woman he's got with him? Osbert! Osbert, look. She's wearing a purple dress with chartreuse and turquoise squiggles on it."

"Dash my buttons, so she is," cried Arethusa. "What's he bringing her here for? Why hasn't he dragged her down to the station and started beating her with a rubber hose? Or reciting 'The Cotter's Saturday Night'?"

"Don't be so bloody-minded. You don't suppose that's really the woman who was in the museum?"

"Of course I do. 'Ods bodikins, child, aren't you going to answer the door?"

"You'd better let me," said Osbert, "in case she turns violent."

But she didn't. In fact, the woman looked more amused than alarming as Sergeant MacVicar performed the introductions with his usual punctilio.

"This is Miss Hunding Paffnagel, a former colleague of Peregrine Fairfield. Miss Arethusa Monk and Mr. and Mrs. Osbert Monk, who have kindly offered to put you up, Miss Paffnagel, there being no public hostelry in Lobelia Falls now that Andrew McNaster has seen fit to turn the inn into a restaurant and bar."

"This is tremendously kind of you, Miss Monk," said Miss Paffnagel, making the natural mistake of turning to the older woman.

Arethusa could be gracious enough when she put her mind to it. Right now, though, her mind was elsewhere. She scribbled her autograph on a piece of paper lying handy (which turned out on later inspection to be a recipe for yoghurt pudding with wheat germ and alfalfa sprouts that Zilla Trott had left for Dittany), handed it to Miss Paffnagel with a perfunctory smile, and left the house.

"That was Osbert's aunt," Dittany explained. "She's gone home to 'od somebody's bodikins. How do you do, Miss Paffnagel? Have you had your dinner?"

"Dinner? Oh, you mean my lunch. That is to say, you mean by dinner what I mean by lunch." Miss Paffnagel was obviously a person who liked to get the facts pinned down. "Yes, I have. That's how they nabbed me. After poor old Perry's funeral, I went back to that place where I ate yesterday. Some waitress with the most extraordinary pectoral development I've ever seen recognized me and called the cops."

"Do you mean you attended the funeral in that outfit and nobody spotted you sooner?" Dittany asked incredulously.

"I had a black raincoat in the car and put it on before I went into the church. This is the only dress I brought with me, and it did seem a bit lively for a funeral. Perry was always kind of a fuss-budget about the proprieties, you know. It's drip-dry and I have one of those inflatable hangers with me, so I rinse it out at night and it's ready to go by morning. I hate pants in the hot weather, don't you?"

Miss Paffnagel was awfully lighthearted for a custodee, Dittany thought, if that was the word. She couldn't really be arrested, or on the verge of becoming so. Maybe she was being detained as a witness or something. Dittany thought Sergeant MacVicar had his nerve to foist the woman off so peremptorily on her and Osbert, but she could see Osbert was doing his best not to gloat openly, so she didn't say anything.

She didn't reply to the pants query either, since she was still wearing the Levis she'd put on for their excursion into the wilds. It didn't matter. Miss Paffnagel wasn't waiting for an answer.

"You could have knocked me over with a quetzal yesterday when I walked into that funny old dump and found Perry Fairfield sitting there with an embroidered hot water bottle cover in his hand."

"You hadn't known he was there?" Osbert asked.

"Heavens no. I hadn't seen him since we were at the Bugleheim together. I was curator of Mayan artifacts. Perry was assistant to old Bugleheim's great-nephew, which meant he got to do the dirty work and somebody else hogged the glory as usual. That was the story of Perry's life, poor wimp. At least I'm glad he got to run his own show finally, even if it didn't amount to a row of potsherds."

"We're just getting started," Dittany informed her stiffly.

"I know. Perry told me all about it. The Aralia Polyphema Architrave Museum. Should look good on paper, anyway. I'll send a nice little write-up to the *Curators' Gazette*. That would have pleased Perry. He wanted so desperately to get some recognition one way or another."

"Would you like a cup of tea?" said Dittany, not knowing what else to say.

Miss Paffnagel pulled out a kitchen chair, although Osbert would have been quite willing to do it for her, and sat down. "Sure, why not? Might as well make myself at home. Any idea how long I'm going to be here?"

"Sergeant MacVicar hasn't told us yet."

The sergeant made a point of not noticing the nasty look Dittany threw him. "It's hard to say just the noo. Having Miss Paffnagel turn up at the funeral was a serendipitous occurrence, ye ken. I can only reiterate my gratitude for her willingness to disrupt her holiday by remaining here as a material witness."

"I still can't believe it." Miss Paffnagel accepted the tea Dittany poured out for her and put in a great deal of sugar. "I must have been talking to Perry less than an hour before he died. It makes you stop and think." She added more sugar with an all-flesh-is-as-grass look on her face.

It wasn't an unpleasing face, Dittany thought. Surely not what one might think of as a sinister face. That didn't signify. She'd known another face that hadn't looked sinister, either, until Sergeant MacVicar arrested the murderer it belonged to.

"How long had it been since you'd seen Mr. Fairfield?" she asked, passing the cookies and not being surprised when Miss Paffnagel took three.

"Perry? Oh, six months or so. I was at his retirement party. Wouldn't have missed it for a trip to Machu Picchu. It was oodles of fun once we'd managed to get Evangeline accidentally locked in the ladies' loo. Whoops, I shouldn't have said that. How's she bearing up, or need I ask?"

"Mrs. Fairfield seems to be coping," Dittany replied warily. "How did you happen to be in Lobelia Falls, Miss Paffnagel? Did you come specially to see Mr. Fairfield?"

"Lord no. I'd no idea this was where he'd come to roost. I'm rather out of touch with the old gang these days. Been down in the Yucatan doing research on human sacrifice for a book I'm writing. Popular stuff, you know. My working title is "Disembowelment Through the Ages," but I'm not sure that's got enough punch for the mass market."

"How about 'Evisceration for Everyman'?" Osbert suggested.

"M'not bad. I'll have to give it careful thought. But anyway, there I was and here I am. I buzzed up to attend a conference in Ottawa and thought I might as well go on to British Columbia and take a *shufti* at a few totem poles while I'm in this neck of the world. Happened to stop for lunch in this quaint little backwater and heard somebody mention a museum next door, so I popped over to see what it was all about, and there was Perry. We were having a real old home week till he told me Evangeline was around the place somewhere. That was when I picked up my heels and lippity-lipped out of there."

"Then how did you find out Mr. Fairfield was dead?" Dittany asked.

"Eh? Oh, I heard it on the car radio. Trying to catch a weather forecast, as it happened, and got the news thrown in. It mentioned the Architrave and said the curator had been killed. I knew that meant she'd finally managed it, so I came whizzing back to find out how. I still can't believe her modus operandi though. Perry was totally paralytic about heights. He'd get queasy if a woman walked past him wearing high-heeled shoes."

"This she you mentioned," Osbert began.

Miss Paffnagel favored him with a stare of wide-eyed innocence. "Did I absentmindedly employ the feminine pronoun? Merely a rhetorical device. Far be it from me to lay myself open for a lawsuit. I know that old hairpin too well. Mind you, I'm not saying which old hairpin."

She ate her third cookie, then shook her head. "Anyway, it's no go. Perry's pension from the Bugleheim stopped when he died, and I don't suppose there'll be anything coming from the Architrave. The hypothetical female I may or may not have had in mind would never be fool enough to kill the goose that laid her golden eggs, pullet-sized though they might be. Not that Perry was a goose, mind you. We used to call him the worm that never turned."

Having by now finished her tea, Miss Paffnagel began scraping wet sugar from the bottom of the cup and licking it off her spoon. "Sergeant MacVicar tells me you and Evangeline were together all that afternoon, Mrs. Monk."

"That's right," said Dittany. "We were doing some research in the attic." She thought "research" sounded more scholarly than "mucking around."

Miss Paffnagel looked amused again. "Mucking around, eh? You didn't find any pre-Colombian artifacts, I don't suppose?"

"Not that I can recall."

"Or anything else of value, I don't suppose. Poor Perry. He never gave up hope, though, I'll say that for him."

"Hope of what, Miss Paffnagel?"

"Fame and fortune, what else? Perry was always going to strike it big. You know, make some great discovery that would astound the whole museum field. We all are, of course, when we're young and enthusiastic, but most of us get a bit more realistic as the years go by. Perry kept right on dreaming the impossible dream. He tottered on the brink a few times, or thought he did, but in the long run his golden apples always came up lemons. Even when I talked to him day before yesterday, he was bubbling about an old letter that he said contained a clue to a cipher."

"What was the cipher supposed to be about?"

"Hidden treasure, of course. 'Right here in Lobelia Falls,' he told me. 'Can you believe it?'"

She lapped up the last of the sugar. "Well, needless to say, I couldn't, but I wasn't about to break Perry's heart by saying so. I just smiled and nodded and said wasn't that nice."

"He didn't say what the treasure was?" Osbert asked her.

"Uh-uh."

"Did he tell you how he'd recognize this cipher when he found it, assuming it does in fact exist?"

"Not a yip. Mind you, I wasn't exactly pressing him for information. I'd been through all that with Perry before, and so had everybody else he'd ever worked with. We all knew his dream was not so much of winning fame for himself as of boosting Evangeline's status to the point where she'd decide he wasn't classy enough for her and find herself another victim."

"Then you in fact placed no credence whatsoever in this alleged find of Peregrine Fairfield?" asked Sergeant MacVicar.

"I wouldn't say no credence whatsoever," Miss Paffnagel demurred. "I'm sure Perry'd got hold of something. He wasn't incompetent, you know. He wouldn't have been fooled by a faked-up modern letter or a totally implausible yarn. The thing of it was, he wanted so desperately to fulfill that great ambition of his, and he must have realized if it didn't happen here, it never would. Poor old coot, in a way I'm glad he didn't live to see another of his bubbles burst. Mrs. Monk, would you mind steering me in the general direction of my room? I think I'd like to lie down a while."

# CHAPTER 16

Dittany set out the company towels with mixed feelings. It must be galling for a hunter of pre-Columbian artifacts to find herself being held in protective custody, or whatever the proper term might be, in connection with an old friend's sudden death. On the other hand, if Hunding Paffnagel saw Lobelia Falls merely as a quaint little backwater, she must be so lacking in perception that she wouldn't notice or care what Sergeant MacVicar wanted her there for, provided the food held out.

Dittany herself had a few things to say to the sergeant, however. She made sure there was a fresh cake of pink soap to go with the towels and went downstairs. Before she'd had a chance to unload the words that were hovering upon her lips, though, Sergeant MacVicar began what her stepfather Bert would describe as a snow job.

"Ah, Dittany lass. I was just telling Deputy Monk how greatly Mrs. MacVicar and I appreciate your kindness in offering lodging to Miss Paffnagel."

Dittany snorted. "In a pig's eye you were, with all respect. Osbert and I both know the only reason you brought her here was so that you could con us into keeping her under house arrest, so let's cut the cackle and get to the hosses. Have you caught our burglar yet?"

"Burglar?"

"Certainly burglar. Didn't Ray tell you?"

"I have not yet checked in at the station."

For the first time in Dittany's life, she detected a faint note of uncertainty in Sergeant MacVicar's voice. She leaped on that note like a terrier on a bug. "A fine thing, when our senior law enforcement officer falls down on his job."

"Dittany!" cried Osbert, scandalized.

"Well, darling, you must admit it's a bit much, dumping another probable malefactor on us without so much as offering a word of sympathy about the one we've already had. Being a literary man yourself, maybe you can straighten Sergeant MacVicar out on the relationship between *quid* and *quo*."

"Are we the *quid* or the *quo*?"

"Both, darn it. What about last night, when we paddled our own canoe out into the middle of nowhere at peril of life and limb just to grill Fred Churtle for him?"

"It was only up Little Pussytoes, darling, and it was partly to heal Ethel's broken heart."

"And a fat lot of good that did. She's down in Cat Alley right now, making goo-goo eyes at another woodchuck."

"*La donna è mobile,*" said Sergeant MacVicar. "That minds me, Deputy Monk, I have not yet heard your report on yon Churtle."

"You haven't heard about our burglary, either," Osbert retorted, for he was no wimp and never had been, his aunt to the contrary notwithstanding. "But anyway," he went on, for neither was Osbert a contumacious young man except when goaded by Arethusa, "we did have a long talk with Fred Churtle, in fact we spent the night at his camp. He seems like a nice guy. He told us all about Peregrine Fairfield."

Osbert proceeded to tell what Churtle had told. As any of his multitudinous readers would have expected, he told it well. Sergeant MacVicar hung upon his words, nodding sagely from time to time, pursing his lips when pursing seemed called for, finally delivering the deserved accolade.

"Well done, Deputy Monk. My compliments to you, and to your lady wife as well. As you have doubtless noted, Churtle's explanation of that alleged five thousand dollar loan ties in neatly with what Miss Paffnagel has told us of Peregrine Fairfield's eternally futile quest. Yon swindle must have been the first in a long series of disappointments."

"Second," Dittany contradicted. "He'd already married Evangeline."

Sergeant MacVicar rubbed his chin to conceal the smile that rose unbidden to his lips. "Lass, lass, did I not ken ye so weel, I might suspect you of harboring thoughts less than kind toward her who is e'en now suffering the effects of her tragic bereavement."

"Well, I am sorry about the pension's getting stopped."

Dittany could have added, "because that makes it stickier for us to get rid of her," but forbore partly out of decorum and partly because Sergeant MacVicar doubtless knew what she was thinking anyway, the pious old fraud. Right now he was favoring her with one of those indulgent smiles she'd been getting ever since her fourth birthday, when she'd stormed the police station demanding he arrest a robin that had committed an indecent assault on her brand-new party dress.

"Aye, Dittany, we must consider all practical aspects of the case. From a practical point of view, eh, we may eliminate Frederick Churtle as your burglar, since you had him under surveillance all night at a distance of some twenty miles from here."

"Not exactly," said Osbert. "Fred insisted Dittany and I use the lean-to because we were company. He took his sleeping bag off to the other side of the campfire, allegedly to give us more privacy. What's to say he didn't sneak downstream in his dinghy, or in our canoe, for that matter, while we were asleep?"

"He would have been taking a parlous risk, would he not, to have absented himself for a period long enough to have accomplished his felonious mission?"

"Not if he got somebody else to do the felonizing. He had an outboard motor on his dinghy and a CB radio in his van, which was parked about five miles back at the portage. As soon as he was out of earshot of the camp, he could have started the motor, beetled on down to the van, and radioed to a henchman. Or henchwoman. His wife, most likely. She'd only have had to drive over from Scottsbeck."

"Or what about Andy McNasty?" said Dittany. "Churtle works for him, and he lives in Scottsbeck, too."

"Ah," said MacVicar. "And what would this alleged confederate be told to look for?"

"As a guess," Osbert replied, "that cipher Peregrine Fairfield mentioned to Miss Paffnagel. Fred might think we had it because Dittany'd been at the museum shortly before Mr. Fairfield died. We have only Fred's word, you know, that he hadn't got together with his old pal Perry after the Fairfields moved to Lobelia Falls."

"He admitted he'd seen the piece in the paper about them," Dittany added. "Osbert wrote the publicity release. It was lovely."

"Thank you, darling. Maybe Fred was lying to us. In any case, if he and Perry did get together, they wouldn't have dared let Mrs. Fairfield know or she'd start telling everybody what a skunk Fred was. The only way they could have stopped her would have been for her husband to tell her the truth and get his ear chewed off for the rest of his life. Then most likely she'd force him to get off that trail Miss Paffnagel says he thought he was on, for fear he'd wind up suckered out of another five thousand dollars."

"Astutely reasoned, Deputy Monk," said Sergeant MacVicar. "You assume, then, that since Mr. Fairfield confided his new quest to Miss Paffnagel, he would also have told Churtle about it."

"I don't see why not."

"Nor do I. This plot is thickening like a haggis on the hob. And I must say at this juncture I see no practical way of dishing it up. Did you ascertain whether Churtle's two-way radio was in working order?"

Osbert flushed. "No, I didn't."

"Darling, why should you have?" cried Dittany. "How could you have known it might be important?"

"I should have guessed. Maybe it's not too late."

"I misdoubt it would do us no good to investigate the radio at this time," said Sergeant MacVicar. "If it is working, Churtle could say he just fixed it. If it is not, that may be because Churtle saw his peril and put the contraption out of commission after you left him. On the other hand, Churtle may be innocent as a newborn lamb and we have still to search elsewhere for our malefactor. Unless in fact we have already caught her."

"But if Miss Paffnagel's guilty, why did she come back for the funeral?" said Dittany.

"She may be studying burial rites," Osbert suggested.

Sergeant MacVicar gave them both another of his tolerant smiles. "Miss Paffnagel is a learned woman. Let us assume for the purpose of discussion that she told the truth about not knowing Peregrine Fairfield had settled in Lobelia Falls, and that her choice of a caravansary was indeed serendipitous. Evidence to support this assumption might include her appearing at the inn in conspicuous clothing and lingering over her meal. She then went to the museum in broad daylight, a natural enough action for one of her profession to take, and let herself be seen by both Dave Munson and Mrs. Fairfield."

"But neither of them saw her face," Dittany pointed out.

"Miss Paffnagel was not to know that. She could not but have known there were workmen around the place, and she herself states she was told Mrs. Fairfield was also on the premises. She claims she left to avoid a meeting with Mrs. Fairfield, but she would have to reckon with the possibility that Mrs. Fairfield was also aware of her presence and endeavoring to stay out of her way."

"Because Miss Paffnagel locked her in the loo at the retirement party," said Dittany.

"A cogent reason, to be sure."

"I see what you're getting at," said Osbert. "It does look as if Miss Paffnagel came upon Mr. Fairfield by accident, as she claims. That doesn't mean she couldn't have killed him, but it does explain why she came back. She'd learned from the news broadcast that she must have been among the last to see him alive and that the police would be looking for her in any case. Innocent or guilty, the smartest move she could make would be to show up voluntarily and brazen it out."

"But why would she have killed Mr. Fairfield, darling?" asked his wife. "It could hardly have been on account of any dark secret from their past, I shouldn't think. If it was, she'd have done better to bump him off at the retirement party and get it over with."

"Maybe I'm being fanciful, eh, but I wonder if it could have had anything to do with that letter he showed her. Suppose for once in his life he'd actually happened on something big, and she saw her chance to grab it away from him?"

"Then why did she mention the letter to us?"

"More bluff, possibly. You know what Fred Churtle said last night about old Perry always being about to make some big discovery and always being disappointed in the end. Miss Paffnagel said the same thing just now, so it looks as if Mr. Fairfield's treasure hunts were kind of a standing joke with everybody who knew him. That means he must have gone around shooting his mouth off about them to anybody who'd listen, instead of keeping quiet till he'd got what he was looking for, not that he ever did. She'd be forced to act on the assumption that Perry had already spread the word, and try to make us believe he was only chasing another wild goose."

"Now, Dittany, you see why I have entrusted Miss Paffnagel to you and Deputy Monk," said Sergeant MacVicar. "I will leave you, in your guidman's parlance, to ride herd on her until we learn whether we have any grounds to institute sterner measures."

# CHAPTER 17

The sergeant made a soldierly figure as he marched smartly away in the blue uniform Mrs. MacVicar kept spruce and pressed for him, but Dittany viewed his tall, straight rear elevation with no favor.

"This is a fine kettle of fish!"

"Darling, you're not sorry I let him deputize me again, are you?" Osbert inquired somewhat ruefully.

"Of course not, darling." Dittany gave him a kiss to prove it. "You know perfectly well he'd have brought her here anyway. Remember how it was before we got married: Hazel Munson keeping those forty heads of lettuce in the bathtub, Ellie Despard filling the dining room with gold paper butterflies, and one who shall be nameless trying to rip out the pantry."

"Not to mention those trash cans full of broken beer bottles in the cellar," Osbert agreed.

"Exactly. This house was officially designated the town dump long before you ever showed up. Besides, if we've got to have murders around, it's better to be in on the action than diddling around the sidelines waiting for somebody else to tell us what's happening. Are you going to detect something this afternoon, dear, or do you have to get back to the yaks? Because I'd better take the truck and go grocery shopping or we shan't have anything to feed Miss Paffnagel."

Osbert said he thought he'd finish rounding up the yaks, so Dittany drove over to Scottsbeck by herself and stocked up on food, adding a ten-kilo sack of sugar in case they got stuck with Miss Paffnagel for the rest of the week. As she was trundling her laden shopping cart back to the truck, a large man with shiny black hair stepped in her way.

"Afternoon, Mrs. Monk. Doing your shopping?"

Now was the time for a devastatingly cutting reply. Dittany gulped and wished she could think of one. She would, no doubt, in a few hours. At the moment, she could only stand goggling at Andrew McNaster and utter an inane, "Yes."

"Got to keep'em eating, eh?"

McNaster wasn't so hot on repartee, either. Dittany responded wittily, "That's right."

"Come over here often?"

What the heck did he think he was driving at? Of course she came over here often. Where else was she supposed to buy the family grub, now that Pop Gubbins had rented the general store to Charlene's Chic Coiffures, picked up his jug and his musical saw, and gone on tour with a country music band? She said so. McNaster responded with what must surely be a hypocritical nod.

"That's right, you don't have a convenience store in Lobelia Falls these days, do you? We'll have to see what we can do about that. Can't have you drive all the way to Scottsbeck every time you need a package of frozen meatballs, eh."

"I don't buy frozen meatballs," Dittany told him with what dignity she could muster.

"I wish I didn't have to."

Dittany was so startled by the agony in Andrew McNaster's voice that she forgot to be uncivil. "I thought you ate at the inn."

"Well, sure I do, only sometimes I just don't feel like it. I mean, don't get me wrong, we serve great food over there. Real haute cuisine. Little paper petticoats on the lamb chops and everything. Say, how come I never see you in there?"

"Perhaps because I never go."

"You don't know what you're missing. Say, how about me standing you a meal on the house some night? You and your aunt."

"She's not my aunt. She's my husband's aunt."

"Oh yeah, that's right. Funny, she doesn't look like anybody's aunt. I mean, not like what you'd think somebody's aunt would look like, if you get what I mean."

Dittany had to concede that she got what he meant. It was true, Arethusa Monk did not look like an aunt. Arethusa looked like a Gainsborough portrait of Mrs. Sarah Siddons in her celebrated role as Lady Macbeth. However, it was not seemly to be standing around a supermarket parking lot discussing her aunt-in-law's looks with a man who until recently had been their joint sworn enemy and probably still was, if the truth were known. What the heck was he up to?

Well, if he wanted conversation, she might as well give him
some. "I understand your plumber's been hauled off to the steel
chateau."

"Oh, Cedric Fawcett? Yeah, Ceddie gets a bit hot under the
collar now and then. Funny, isn't it, when he's so quiet most of
time. That's how it is with people, I guess. Who's to say what wild
passions may be seething and fermenting beneath the mildest
exterior? How about me buying you a cup of tea at the Cozy
Corner?"

Had Dittany Henbit Monk been Eliza Doolittle, she would probably have retorted, "Not bloody likely!" Especially after all that
seething and fermenting. Was it possible—no, it couldn't be possible. But it might be possible, and Dittany wasn't going to run any
risk of finding out. She said she had to get home with the groceries
because they had a house guest and her husband would be worried.

"Gee, that's right," said McNaster in a tone of deep contrition.
"His aunt might be worrying, too. Can't let that happen, can we?
Here, let me lift the bags for you."

After that, there wasn't much Dittany could say except, "Thank
you." She said it and left as quickly as she could manage among the
welter of shopping carts, baby carriages, and drivers who couldn't
make up their minds whether they were coming or going. When
she sneaked a look in the rearview mirror, she saw Andrew
McNaster standing next to his baby-blue Lincoln, gazing after the
pickup truck with an expression on his face she could only describe
as enigmatical.

At least that was how she described it when she got home and
told Osbert about this strange encounter. His reaction was ad-
verse.

"Enigmatical, eh? The low-down sidewinder! Darling, I don't
think I care for having large, handsome older men with less than
dubious reputations giving you enigmatical looks in parking lots."

"I wasn't all that ecstatic about it myself, darling."

"And trying to lure you into dens of vice."

"The Cozy Corner Tea Shop isn't exactly a den of vice, darling."
Now that it was too late, Dittany was wondering if perhaps she
should have accepted. "If I'd gone, I might have been able to find
out what he's up to."

"Huh, and have him slip knockout drops in your Lapsang

souchong and shanghai you. Dittany, promise me faithfully you won't try any more detecting on your own. At least not with Andy McNasty. I couldn't stand to have you abducted."

"Don't worry, darling, I'd hate it myself. Samantha Burberry says there's absolutely nothing more horrible than being tied up in a filthy cellar and not being able to get to the bathroom."

"It's even worse if the cellar's got fleas in it." That was the cheery boom of Miss Hunding Paffnagel, bouncing downstairs fresh and raring to go after her nap in the spare bedroom. "Happened to me once in Cuzco, I never did figure out why. My abductors set me free after a while and we all went out to a café for a tequila. Me scratching my head off, of course, but so were they. Speaking of which, how about stepping over to the inn? I'd like to buy you folks a drink."

"We don't patronize the inn," Osbert told her stiffly.

"Oh, sorry. Religion?"

"No, McNaster." The word came savagely grated through his teeth.

"Who's McNaster?"

"The ornery cayuse who owns it. He just tried to seduce my wife at the supermarket."

"Do tell," said Miss Paffnagel. "Then where do we go for a drink?"

"There's beer in the fridge," Dittany told her, "and whiskey in the pantry next to the cookie jar. The wine's down cellar on the shelf with the green tomato relish and I think that funny-tasting liqueur Bert brought on his last visit's on the dining room buffet behind the cruet. Bert's my stepfather. He travels in fashion eyewear."

"How chic. Do I help myself or wait to be served?"

"Whichever you prefer. Osbert makes lovely marmalade old-fashioneds."

"I think I'll settle for a cold beer. Unless you happen to have any *chicha co-pah* or *pulchu* in the house?"

"Sorry. I could step next door and borrow a cupful of Jane Binkle's homemade damson gin, if you like."

"Thanks, beer will be fine. You folks going to join me?"

Since it was, after all, their beer, they thought they might as well. Dittany was getting out some tumblers when the phone rang. Arethusa was on the line.

"That's odd," said Osbert. "What's she calling for? Usually she just barges in."

This time, to their astonishment, Arethusa wanted them to go to her house. *"Pour l'amour de Dieu,"* she entreated, "come and have supper with us."

"Whom were you planning to have cook it?" Dittany asked warily.

"Cease the snide innuendo, chit. It's all cooked. Don't expect anything fancy, just *potage au cresson, coulibiac de saumon en croûte,* and a modest *vacherin aux framboises* for dessert."

"Well, I suppose we could eat a sandwich before we come. But, Arethusa, we have a house guest, too. She's the lady with the purple dress."

"Then tell her to put it on and buzz along. The more the merrier. Which is to say, the less otherwise, *si tu comprends.*"

"I comprend. All right, we'll be along. When do you want us?"

*"Maintenant. Toute de suite. Vitesse, vitesse. Je suis au bout de ma* rope."

There was a click, then silence. Dittany hung up, too.

"Arethusa's invited us all to supper."

"What?" cried Osbert. "Is she hallucinating?"

"No, but she's talking a lot of French. I think it's because she can't stand any more of—er—that is, she has the Fairfield's nephew and his wife staying with her, you know, and she—er— thought it would be nice to—er—"

"In other words, she's trying to—er—"

Osbert couldn't manage to come straight out in front of Miss Paffnagel and say Jehosaphat and Berthilde must be driving his aunt nuts and Arethusa was attempting to ease her burden by inflicting her uninvited house guests on them and their uninvited house guest.

Well, why not? Miss Paffnagel could entertain the Fairfields with tales of her adventures among the artifacts with their late uncle, while he and Dittany snuck off to the hammock on the back porch and caught up on their experience-sharing and Aunt Arethusa did the dishes. Besides, Arethusa was a first-class cook when driven to it. There were worse ways of beguiling an evening, and Arethusa would certainly see to it that Dittany and Osbert experienced one of these in the near future if they failed to rally now in her hour of need. Accordingly, they went; although not until after Miss Paffnagel had drunk her beer and eaten a peppermint.

As it turned out, the peppermint was superfluous. Over at Arethusa's, they were well into the aperitifs, sitting in the big, cool living room with the curtains drawn against the late afternoon sun. Jehosaphat Fairfield, a small man who looked in the dim light almost frighteningly like his late uncle, was in fact having a Molson's. His wife was drinking rum and grapefruit juice, though she didn't appear to be in need of the extra vitamins. Berthilde, interestingly enough, was a strapping woman built along much the same lines as Evangeline Fairfield and having a similar breadth of jaw, although Dittany was relieved to note her gums were decently covered by an amplitude of lip.

Arethusa was so glad to see the newcomers that she even kissed her nephew. "Come in, come in. *Soyez les bienvenus.* Have a drink. And what a charming dress you have on, Miss Paffnagel, if I may venture an expert opinion. Reminds me of one I've seen somewhere quite recently."

"On me, I expect." Berthilde snapped on a table lamp beside the chair she was sitting in. "See?"

Her dress was identical to Miss Paffnagel's down to the last chartreuse and turquoise squiggle.

"My stars and garters," gasped Dittany. "What a coincidence. It means you both have lovely taste," she added quickly.

That was a line her mother had once used to good effect in an even more critical situation at a church supper. Everybody laughed politely, especially Miss Paffnagel and Berthilde Fairfield, to show what swell sports they were. Arethusa, who could be a gracious hostess if she kept her mind on what she was doing, fetched Dittany a glass of white wine and invited Osbert to belly up to the bar for a shot of red-eye, but he decided on beer instead.

Miss Paffnagel asked for rum and grapefruit juice because, she always made it her policy to sample the native beverages when on a field trip. She gave them a learned little discourse on how the Inca used to make *chicha mascada*. This involved getting all the old men and women together to chew (or gum) balls of malt, which they then added to the other ingredients while still warm. On occasion, several pounds of raw beef were also thrown in, and the container was buried six or eight feet underground for several years.

Dittany thought this sounded like the right thing to do, until Miss Paffnagel went on to explain that they then dug it up and drank whatever was by that time in the jar. It was with no great appetite that she went to dinner.

Like any housewife sitting down to an inviting meal she hasn't had to cook herself, however, she found her interest piqued by the chilled watercress soup and by the time they got to the elegant coulibiac of salmon and rice in its coffin of puff pastry, accompanied by a first-rate pouilly-fuissé, she wouldn't have called the Queen her cousin.

Arethusa's dining room, like the rest of her house, was furnished in the regency style, running to delicate chinoiserie, spindly-legged chairs, and hints of Brighton Pavilion, notably in the gilded crocodiles holding up the glass-topped table. Diners sometimes found them off-putting, but Berthilde Fairfield was not the nervous type, and the reptilian pedestal merely inspired Hunding Paffnagel to tell an amusing anecdote about her encounter with a man-eating alligator on the upper Amazon.

As for Jehosaphat, he sat saying little and tasting his food in the gingerly fashion of one who ventures alone into strange, dark places. Dittany wondered, odd though the notion might seem, whether he was mourning his departed relative.

"I expect you'll miss your Uncle Peregrine," she said to him kindly.

"Eh? Oh, no. Not particularly, I don't suppose. Not that I wasn't fond of him, you know. It's just that we never got together very often. Still, I suppose I sort of knew he was there, wherever he happened to be at the time. I don't know. Maybe I'll miss him."

"Nonsense, Jehosaphat," said his wife crisply. "Why should you?"

"Yes, Berthilde." He essayed another nibble at his coulibiac. "At least it means we can sell the Reo now."

"Rio as in Rita?" Osbert inquired, his mind flowing naturally in a south-of-the-borderly direction.

"No, Reo as in horseless carriage," Jehosaphat explained. "A 1924 touring sedan, to be precise. It belonged to my father and Uncle Peregrine when they were young fellows. That is to say, it belonged to their father, but he let them drive it sometimes, so they had a sentimental attachment for it, which is only natural, I suppose."

"Don't be silly, Jehosaphat," said Berthilde as the Monks had been rather expecting she would. "What's natural about grown men mooning around after an old automobile? It's no good to anybody taking up space in our garage all these years. If your uncle was so attached to the Reo, why didn't he offer to pay a little rent for it once in a while? If it had been left to me, I'd have sold the miserable thing long ago. Antique cars are bringing good money these days, though don't ask me why for I can't tell."

"But it wasn't ours to sell, Berthilde. Not all of it, anyway."

"Nonsense, Jehosaphat. I never did believe that yarn about your father's bequeathing his half of the Reo to his brother Peregrine. It wasn't in the will."

"But that could have been because father never made a will, Berthilde. I felt bound to honor his wishes in case he meant to if he had, you know that. I had my integrity to think of."

"Humph. I trust your integrity won't extend so far as to give your Aunt Evangeline half of whatever we get for selling the Reo."

"Oh no. I'm sure Dad wouldn't have put Aunt Evangeline in his will. Anyway, she'll have Uncle Perry's pension from the museum."

"No she won't," said Miss Paffnagel with some satisfaction. "It stopped at his death. Vangie will just have to buckle down and scratch for herself like the rest of us lone females."

"But she's got a job here in Lobelia Falls," cried Jehosaphat, sounding as if his integrity was beginning to act up again.

"In point of fact, it was your uncle we hired," said Arethusa. "Your aunt merely came along for the ride, as one might say."

"But you've been working her like a dog ever since she got here," Berthilde argued. "She told us so herself. She said Mrs. Monk here kept her slaving away in a hot, filthy attic all afternoon the very day Uncle Peregrine died, and how he got killed was Mrs. Monk left the windows open. He had to go up and close them later on, which probably gave him a heatstroke, which is why he fell out. Not that I'm holding it against you, Mrs. Monk, but that's what Aunt Evangeline said."

"Nor does it surprise me a jot," Dittany replied. "Want me to help carry out the plates, Arethusa?"

"Yes," said Arethusa. "You might bring in the dessert plates while you're at it. And the dessert. And the tea and the coffee. Also the after-dinner mints. I put them in the fridge because I was afraid they might get dizzy from the heat and hurl themselves off the sides of the bonbonnière."

Hunding Paffnagel snickered. Berthilde and Jehosaphat exchanged uncertain glances. Osbert got up to assist Dittany, but his aunt grabbed hold of his buckskin vest and hauled him back.

"Sit down, you unprincipled rake. Stap me, can't you control your lusts in front of company? You wouldn't believe this, Mrs. Fairfield, but he was a beguiling rogue at the age of four. I have a snapshot of him in his little cowboy suit somewhere or other. Remind me to dig it out and show it to you before you leave here punctually at eight forty-five tomorrow morning so I can get back to work."

Berthilde took the hint, if such it could be called, cheerfully. "I know just how it is. I'm a working gal myself. I travel in needlework supplies, which is how I happen to be here now. Miss Jane Fuzzywuzzy's Yarnery over in Scottsbeck is one of my best customers. When I checked in with Jehosaphat night before last, he told me Aunt Vangie had called about Uncle Perry and he thought he ought to come, so I said all right, I'd join him, and here I am."

"Bet you're on pins and needles, though," Miss Paffnagel quipped. "Must get kind of prickly." She guffawed at her own wit.

Berthilde didn't mind that, either. "Oh, I'm sharp as a needle myself, or so they tell me. You ought to hear my sales talk. When it comes to spinning a good yarn, I've never been worsted. That's what our division manager said at the last sales meeting."

"Cute of him." Arethusa neatly suppressed a yawn. "Do you go in for stitchery yourself, Mrs. Fairfield?"

"Lord, yes. I needlepoint like an absolute fiend sometimes. Don't I, Jehosaphat?"

"Like a fiend," her husband confirmed. "Put a needle in her hand and there's no stopping her."

Arethusa turned to Dittany with a smile of desperation. "Then I expect Mrs. Fairfield would like to see those embroidered quilt pieces you found in the attic at the museum. Let's see, was that before or after her husband's aunt came barging along to see what you were up to?"

"After," said Dittany. "I remember distinctly because that was when the forty-seven mice jumped at me and I was too unmanned to unwrap the box they were in. Or should I say unwomaned? So I really didn't mind her butting in and taking over as usual. Anyway, her hands were clean because she hadn't been doing anything, and mine were filthy. What did you do with them, Arethusa?"

"They're upstairs. I'll get them as soon as we've had our dessert. In the meantime, you can be clearing the table so we'll have a place to spread them out. I haven't had a chance to study them properly, myself."

"Come to think of it, neither have I." Therefore, Dittany obeyed without demur. While she lugged out plates and cups, however, she brooded on the odd coincidence of having shared a vacherin with two women of much the same size and build, wearing identical purple dresses.

She also brooded a bit on Miss Jane Fuzzywuzzy's Yarnery, it being situated right next to the Cozy Corner Tea Shop whence she might or might not have been abducted this afternoon. Now that she'd met Berthilde and Jehosaphat, she wondered if perhaps she'd been oversqueamish in passing up Andy McNasty's invitation to imbibe that hypothetical dose of knockout drops. Of course Osbert would have been dreadfully upset, the cellar very likely would have had fleas in this hot weather, and she'd have missed letting Arethusa do the cooking for a change. Dittany dwelt fondly on those fresh raspberries in the meringue tart for a moment, then dragged her mind back to Berthilde's purple dress.

After Hunding Paffnagel's story of her visit to Peregrine Fairfield, they'd all naturally assumed it had been her back both Dave Munson and the dead man's wife had seen. Maybe it was, but then again, maybe it wasn't. Berthilde had, by her own account, been in the area, and she knew her husband's uncle was working at the Architrave. Maybe there'd been another coincidence.

As to why Berthilde would have wanted to kill Peregrine, Dittany could only conjecture. It seemed unlikely the niece-in-law would have gone to the bother of boosting him through the skylight and chucking him off the roof just to get that old Reo out of her barn, but one never knew. She removed the last dish from the table, wiped the glass top free of crumbs, and remarked to the gilded crocodiles, "Okay. Ready for your next course?"

# CHAPTER 18

"Lovely, lovely, lovely," Arethusa was singing to herself as she laid out the dainty scraps of silk and satin and velvet. She'd switched on the silk-shaded brass sconces around the dining room for better viewing of the charmingly imagined, expertly embroidered motifs, and the gilded crocodiles were grinning up through the glass as though even they were enjoying the sight.

"What a shame the quilt was never made up," said Berthilde. "I don't know when I've come across finer specimens of needlework."

"Maybe the Architrave's lucky it wasn't," Hunding Paffnagel remarked. "As a quilt, it might already have been worn out. This way, you still have it fresh as the day it was put away, though I personally would be awfully careful how I handled those bits of taffeta. Silk's apt to split on you when it gets old."

"True, i' faith," said Arethusa. "They should be backed with cambric or something before we start putting them together. I'll do that."

"Can you, Miss Monk? I'd say it's a job for an expert."

"I am an expert. Stap me, dost think I lack the womanly skills just because I can also execute a faultless lunge, parry, or riposte? Take that bee perched on a thistle, for instance. I can back it so that one would swear the surface was never touched by human hands."

Osbert had a reply for that one, but Dittany gave him a look, so he contented himself with remarking, "The bee's got one purple whisker."

"What are you driveling about now, prithee?" his aunt snapped back. "Most bees have one purple whisker. It's a well-known entomological fact."

Hunding Paffnagel was poring over the scraps with professional interest. "I must say those women who created these artifacts were hipped on bees. Here's one climbing out of a rose."

"It's got a green whisker," Osbert said, but nobody could hear him because the erstwhile silent Jehosaphat was clamoring for the floor.

"My mother had a phonograph record of John McCormack singing, 'When You Look into the Heart of a Rose.' Back when I was a boy soprano, I could do a perfect imitation of him, including the crack in the record. Want to hear how it went?"

It occurred to Dittany that Jehosaphat was more than a trifle whacked. Berthilde must be noticing, too. A few minutes later, when his wife caught him sidling toward the brandy decanter, she decided it was time they stepped out for a breath of fresh air.

"Jehosaphat and I had better walk off that delicious meal," she told Arethusa, "or we'll never be able to get up tomorrow. And I suppose we ought to say good-bye to Aunt Evangeline since we won't be seeing her again. Want to come, anybody?"

Hunding Paffnagel said she wouldn't mind a little stroll. Dittany and Osbert said they'd stay and help Arethusa with the dishes, which seemed the lesser evil. They weren't worried about Hunding's skipping town while under the Fairfields' escort, though perhaps they ought to be concerning themselves with Berthilde and Jehosaphat in view of recent developments. Anyway, it was highly unlikely all three were in a plot together and even more improbable any one of them was sober enough to engineer an escape just now. The Monks waved them off and adjourned to the kitchen sink.

"I don't know whether you two happened to notice how much Berthilde and Hunding resemble each other in those purple dresses," Dittany remarked as she filled the dishpan.

"Egad, how could one miss it?" Arethusa replied. "They look like Mrs. Tweedledee and Mrs. Tweedledum."

"I wonder if I ought to go mention the coincidence to Sergeant MacVicar," said Osbert, not without guile.

"Stay, base varlet," barked his aunt. "You're not weaseling out on the dishes that easily. If Sergeant MacVicar doesn't already know about those duplicate dresses, you can rest assured his wife does. And if she doesn't, she will. Whatever possessed me to vaunt my skill as a needlewoman? There are others—"

"Quit looking at me, Arethusa," cried Dittany, seeing all too clearly which way the ball was about to bounce. "You're a million times better than I am. So's Minerva. Zilla's not bad, either."

"Zilla wouldn't have the patience for such fiddling work, and Minerva has her hands full already. Unless," and Arethusa began to look more and more like Mrs. Siddons doing Lady Macbeth, "we can evolve some wile or ruse to rid her of Evangeline Fairfield."

"Arethusa, how can we?" Dittany protested. "Miss Paffnagel says Evangeline's lost Perry's pension and we darn sure can't give her one from the Architrave. I don't know if she's entitled to anything from the government or not, since he'd been working down in the States for so long."

"Dittany, stop dithering. The man must have had life insurance, and surely they'd managed to save something."

"How, if he was always haring off after artifacts?"

"Natter, natter, natter! Cease and desist, wench. I refuse to accept any suggestion that might lead to our having Evangeline Fairfield dangling albatrossly around our necks for the rest of her life. Damme, I'll pension her off myself, if I have to. I'm sure you realize that last remark was uttered in the heat of the moment and not to be taken literally," Arethusa added hastily. "Surely there's a comfortable rest home somewhere for relicts of deceased curators. With a few well-chosen artifacts displayed on top of the television set to remind them of all that has gone before."

"Never mind what's gone before," snapped Dittany. "We've got troubles enough with the present. Where do I park this fish slice?"

"Leave it on the counter. I'll put it away later. Is that all the silver? Anything left in the dining room?"

"Nothing but Osbert and the quilt pieces. Last time I looked in, he'd found a bee with a baby-blue whisker."

"Gets that from his mother's side of the family, I hope. *Pardieu*, to think what your children will be like! A gaggle of little Osberts chasing after bees to see what color their whiskers are."

"Our children will not be chasing bees. They're going to have their own ponies and ride wild and free down Cat Alley. Osbert always wanted a pony when he was little, and his stuffy old parents wouldn't let him have one."

"That may have been because they lived in a high-rise apartment in the heart of picturesque downtown Toronto, you know. A pony could be a dreadful nuisance in a crowded elevator."

Osbert's father was a somewhat high powered oil company executive and still couldn't figure out how his younger son had turned out to be Lex Laramie. Mr. Monk blamed his sister, of course.

"Getting back to the quilt pieces," said Arethusa, "we've got to have them all fixed up and ready to assemble by the end of the week. We must get cracking on the quilting bee before the galley proofs for *Sir Percy Foils Again* come in."

"Why?"

"Because as soon as I've got them corrected, I have to whiz off to a writers' conference and make a speech."

"Arethusa, how exciting. Where's the conference?"

"I forget. Somebody will remind me, I expect. If not, I'll get out of making the speech. But you do understand the need for haste in either event."

"Not really, but I suppose if we're going to do it, we might as well make a start. I'll take them with me and see whom I can round up to work."

Dittany didn't see why she'd wound up getting stuck again after Arethusa's grandiose talk, but she'd have accepted any excuse to escape before Berthilde and Jehosaphat got back. Minerva must be giving them tea and cake or something. It was scarcely credible that sheer delight in Aunt Evangeline's company could be keeping them out this long.

Maybe Hunding had lured the Fairfields off to the inn for a nightcap, come to think of it. That would be nice, even if it did mean throwing business Andrew McNaster's way. With any luck, the outlanders would make a night of it, and she and Osbert wouldn't have to listen to another of Hunding's travelogues. She collected the quilt pieces and her somewhat bemused spouse, and headed for home.

After they'd gone a little way, she said abruptly, "Osbert, what do you really think he was up to?"

"The bee with the orange whisker?"

"No, darling, Andy McNasty."

"Oh." Osbert pondered for a while. "Well, darling, assuming he wasn't trying to shanghai you into some foul den for nefarious purposes, he might simply have thought it would be pleasant to buy a cup of tea for a beautiful woman."

"Darling, I'm not."

"That," said her husband, "is too silly a remark to dignify with a reply."

Somewhat to Dittany's surprise, Osbert did in fact make no further response. Her patience held out until they were almost to Applewood Avenue, then she said, "What do you say we stroll up to the Enchanted Mountain and see how Ethel's making out with her new boyfriend?"

He shook his head. "Actually, I was thinking I'd like to take another look at those quilt pieces."

"But why? Not that I think it's sissy for a man to show an interest in embroidery, but—"

"I know, sweetheart. I can't explain it, myself. It's just that there's something about all those red and blue and orange feelers on those bees that keeps nagging at me. You say each embroidery was done by a different girl?"

"That was the custom."

"Then how come they all ran out of thread in the same place?"

"You know, Osbert, that's an awfully good question."

Osbert had another one. "Who knew you'd taken the pieces home?"

"Mrs. Fairfield, of course. I expect she told Minerva and Zilla while they were waiting for Mr. Fairfield to come home, and no doubt they told a few more. You know how things get around."

"But do you remember telling anybody that Aunt Arethusa had taken them away from you?"

"Now that you mention it, no. After she left, I didn't see anybody to tell. I housecleaned all afternoon, then I went to Minerva's tea party and it wouldn't have been exactly delicate to talk about them in front of Mrs. Fairfield. And then you and I went off to find Fred Churtle."

"And our house was ransacked while we were gone, and nothing was taken."

"Osbert, you don't mean the burglar was looking for those quilt pieces?"

"Why not? They're the only thing somebody might have thought we had but we didn't. And they did come from the Architrave, and Hunding Paffnagel told us Mr. Fairfield had got hold of a letter that mentioned a secret code. Darn it, I wish I could figure out what a baby-blue whisker on a bumblebee might mean."

"Darling, how could a bee's whisker be a code?"

"Don't ask me, but I think it's funny, that's all. I tell you what, why don't we tell a few people Arethusa's got the quilt pieces instead of us? If she gets burgled, too, then we'll know."

"Osbert Monk, don't you dare. If she gets burgled, she'll be too scared to stay alone, and you know darn well where she'll wind up."

"Dittany, not—not our happy home?"

"You bet your Sunday socks our happy home. She'll pack up her typewriter and her crocodiles and hike herself straight upstairs to the spare bedroom, and you know darn well neither of us would have guts enough to kick her out. Oh, my gosh!"

"Dearest, you've blenched. You're not going to faint?"

"Why not? It's too late for anything else. Osbert, don't you realize the hour of doom is upon us? Hunding, Berthilde, and Jehosaphat all saw those quilt pieces just a while back at Arethusa's, and now they've gone to Minerva's."

"But maybe they'll talk about something else."

"What, for instance? Here's Berthilde, an embroidery expert; here's Hunding, sniffing around after artifacts; here's Evangeline, infesting the Architrave and no doubt taking full credit for discovering the quilt pieces; and here's Jehosaphat, too drunk to shut them up, which I don't suppose he'd see any reason to do anyway. And there's Minerva wanting to hear about the pieces because she hasn't seen them yet herself."

"Could we get Minerva not to spread the word?"

"Hah! If I know Minerva, she's got Dot Coskoff over there helping her ride herd on Mrs. Fairfield because Dot's kids are away at camp and Bill's gone fishing, and Zilla Trott and goodness knows how many more. No doubt they've already formed a delegation to go and borrow Hazel Munson's grandmother's quilting frame. Come on, quick."

They ran into the house, rushed to the phone, and dialed Arethusa. "Has anybody phoned you yet about the quilting bee?" Dittany panted into the mouthpiece.

"What quilting bee?" Arethusa sounded rather annoyed.

"The one they evidently haven't phoned you about yet. Look, if anybody does, tell them—Osbert, what should she say?"

"Good question. She'd better not say anything about us." He took the receiver from Dittany's hand. "Aunt Arethusa, if anybody calls you and says anything about those quilt pieces, why don't you just tell them you're busy with your house guests and you'd rather talk later."

"I'd rather not talk at all. I'm trying to get a little work done. Are you out of what you erroneously refer to as your mind?"

"Look, Aunt Arethusa, this is serious. We think those embroideries may be more important than we thought they were, but we don't yet know why. We need your help, honest. Can't you act glamorous and inscrutable, like one of those seductive foreign spies in the old E. Phillips Oppenheim novels you sneak your plots out of?"

"I do not sneak my plots out of E. Phillips Oppenheim!"

"Well, you know what I mean. Slink around tight-lipped and mumchance, like the twenty-ninth of February. Look enigmatic."

"Over the telephone?"

"Then sound enigmatic. Don't go telling anybody we brought the quilt pieces here with us, if the subject comes up. Say they've been taken to a safe place. If they ask where, say you've got something boiling over on the stove. Got that?"

"What did she say?" Dittany asked him after he'd hung up.

"Mainly a lot of flapdoodle about my mother's side of the family. I expect she'll go along, though. You know how Aunt Arethusa loves to hurl herself into a role. Dad-blang it, I wish I could think what it is that bee with the orange whisker reminds me of!"

"It will come to you, darling. Come on, let's take the pieces in and spread them out on the dining room table, the way we did at Arethusa's."

"But what if Hunding and the others come barging in?"

"Well, darling, they already know we've got them."

"No they don't. They think Aunt Arethusa does."

"Oh, that's right. Maybe I shouldn't have eaten so many raspberries. I can't seem to think straight any more. How about if I take them down cellar and hide them in the washing machine?"

"Suppose Hunding decides to rinse out her purple dress?"

"Behind the pickles, then. No, I've already told her that's where we keep the wine."

"How about under our mattress? We've already been burgled there. Look, darling, I'm sure you'll think of something. I've got to go see Sergeant MacVicar and arrange a stakeout in case somebody tries to dry-gulch Aunt Arethusa tonight. Not that I really think they would with the Fairfields still there, but you never know."

"Be sure and mention the matching dresses, just in case."

"I will. Are you sure you don't mind staying alone? I'll only be gone a few minutes."

"I'll concentrate on dog biscuits. Maybe that will bring Ethel home. I've often suspected she has psychic powers."

"You do that, darling."

# CHAPTER 19

He kissed her and was gone. Dittany took that troublesome box of exotic scraps upstairs, trying to think about milk bones but finding her attention inexorably switched to multicolored bees' antennae.

Were the truth but known, they were probably some silly whim the girls in the sewing circle had cooked up one rainy afternoon over a pan of fudge. Red for Beatrice, orange for Bessie, purple for Berthilde—drat! Whichever way she turned, those two purple dresses kept poking themselves forward. Backward, actually, and the odds were they didn't mean a darned thing. Gram Henbit's friend Agnes used to complain about how hard it was to find pretty clothes in half sizes. Here was an attractive style in a flattering color; no doubt it had been selling like hotcakes all over North America. South America, too, for all Dittany knew. Why look for new complications when they had plenty already?

What she ought to be doing was what people did in mystery stories: sit down and make a timetable of who'd been where around the time Peregrine Fairfield met his doom. And what would it tell her? That Fred Churtle had been at the Architrave, that Cedric Fawcett had been there, that Hunding Paffnagel might or might not still have been there, that Berthilde Fairfield also might or might not have been there and might or might not have been mistaken for Hunding Paffnagel, not that anybody appeared to have paid much attention to either one of them.

Suppose Berthilde had happened to drop in for a chat with Uncle Perry on her way to sell Miss Jane Fuzzywuzzy a few binfuls of yarn. Suppose she'd seen someone who looked much like herself chatting with Perry up among the artifacts. Might she not have decided now was as good a time as any to rid herself of an uncherished in-law because she could put the blame on that other woman?

It might seem a trifle outré to commit a murder just because the chance seemed too good to miss, but stranger things had happened. Conversely, Dittany supposed, Hunding could have done the fell deed intending to blame Berthilde, again assuming Berthilde had been there to blame. In that case, though, why hadn't Hunding dropped some incriminating remark when they met, such as, "Oh, yes, I saw you at the museum. You were sneaking in just as I went out leaving my old friend Perry sound in wind and limb. I didn't speak because I assumed at the time you were merely my doppelgänger."

She shared her thoughts with Osbert when he got back from the police station, but he shook his head. "Miss Paffnagel wouldn't have said doppelgänger, darling. She'd have employed some Mayan equivalent. Anyway, I don't think we ought to bother the MacVicars again just now. Their son Alex and his wife and baby are visiting. The kid's cut a new tooth. They were all sitting around gazing into its mouth and I could hardly get a word in edgewise."

"But what about the stakeout at Arethusa's?"

"Oh, that. Sergeant MacVicar deems it unnecessary in view of the fact that (a) Arethusa has house guests to protect her, and (b) he hasn't anybody to stake. Bob and Ray have the night off and Ormerod's still away. So if anybody's going to guard Aunt Arethusa, it'll have to be me."

"And leave me here alone with Hunding Paffnagel? Not on your life, hombre. You did promise to love, honor, and cherish me, you know."

"Darling, I do. I am. I will. All right, let's forget the stakeout. I had something else in mind for this evening, anyway. Why do you always have to wear blouses that button up the back?"

"Osbert, stop that. We can't."

"But we can, darling. We do, quite often. Remember?"

"I mean we mustn't, till we get Miss Paffnagel tucked away for the night. I don't want her strolling in here and finding an excuse to give us a lecture on pre-Columbian fertility rites. Let's go back downstairs and have a glass of lemonade. I'm thirsty after all that wine at Arethusa's."

"Yes, dear, if we must. What did you do with the quilt pieces?"

"Wrapped them up in Gramp's old doughboy tunic and locked them in the cedar chest with the slop jar from the night stand on top. If anybody tries to open the chest, at least we'll hear the crash."

"Good thinking. Come on, then. Maybe the lemonade will damp down my inner fires."

"Not for long, I hope."

They took the plate and pitcher and went to sit out on the porch like a proper old married couple. Jane and Henry Binkle sauntered over to share their genteel refreshment and chat about books. After a while, the Binkles drifted back home and the bats started coming out. Along about the seventh bat, Hunding Paffnagel showed up.

"Have a nice time?" Dittany asked her sociably.

"To the besht of my recollection, yesh," Miss Paffnagel replied. "Been shampling the native beverages. Dandelion wine and camomile tea. Intereshting combination."

"Was that by any chance Zilla Trott's dandelion wine you were drinking?"

"No, it was mine," Hunding responded, being extremely careful with her sibilants but not quite careful enough. "She sherved it to me. In a glash. They don't sheem to ushe botas around theshe partsh. You know, thoshe wineshkinsh with the nozzlesh that you shquirt into your moush."

"Oh, yesh," said Osbert. "I tried it once. The wine went into my left ear and I kept hearing gurgling noises for about a week. Have some lemonade?"

"No thanksh. I'm alwaysh careful not to mix my drinksh. Perhapsh I should have refushed the camomile tea. It sheemsh to be affecting my shenshe of balanshe."

"Perhaps you ought to go straight up to bed," Dittany suggested in rather a forceful tone. "You've had a long day."

"Have I? Then perhapsh you're right. Whish way ish the shtaircashe?"

"I'll show you."

Osbert took Miss Paffnagel's arm and led her up to her room, Dittany tagging along in case of emergencies. Minerva should have known better than to let Miss Paffnagel drink Zilla's dandelion wine on top of rum and grapefruit juice. Zilla could get more kick out of a dandelion than anybody else in the history of Lobelia Falls. Grandsire Coskoff said so, and it was generally conceded that he ought to know if anybody did.

Anyway, the wine's effect on Hunding Paffnagel appeared to be mostly soporific. She went to sleep and stayed asleep. They knew, because her steady, resonant snores echoed through the house all night long like the rhythmical beat of a ceremonial drum on the purple peak of Popocatepetl. Dittany and Osbert didn't mind so much because they were used to Ethel, but they did think it a bit much when half past eleven rolled around the next morning and Miss Paffnagel was still snoring.

"Darn it," said Osbert, ripping a sheet out of his typewriter and wadding it up in disgust, "isn't she ever going to wake up? She makes more noise than a herd of yaks."

"Do you want me to go and try to rouse her?" Dittany asked him.

"No, let sleeping Paffnagels lie. At least this way we don't have to keep an eye on her."

"I wonder if the Fairfields got off all right," Dittany mused. "They were pretty rory-eyed themselves by the time we finished supper, especially Jehosaphat. Honestly, I do think Minerva might have known better. What would you like for lunch? We could take it out on the table in the back yard."

"Her bedroom's right above."

"I know, but the noise might be sort of dissipated by the fresh air."

"There's plenty of fresh air in the house, and I can't say I notice it helping any."

"Then why don't we drop in on Arethusa and see if she has any of that coulibiac left over?"

Dittany spoke too late. Arethusa was already heaving into view, a green silk caftan billowing behind her like a spinnaker in reverse and a good many strings of Venetian glass beads tinkling pleasantly around her neck. She looked a trifle wan, but that might have been the reflected green of the caftan. Her lustrous dark eyes were sparkling, and there was excitement in the flare of her patrician nostrils.

"I've had a visitation," she announced.

"We know," said Dittany. "Did you get rid of them on schedule?"

"What? Oh, the Fairfields. Yes, they dragged themselves off about half an hour ago. That was shortly after I'd put the *1812 Overture* on the stereo and turned it up full blast when it got to the part where the cannons are shot off."

"Darn, why didn't we think of that? How about lending us the record? We may need it if Hunding Paffnagel doesn't wake up pretty soon."

"Oh, let her alone. She's probably dreaming about obsidian knives and steaming entrails." Arethusa flopped into her usual chair and arranged her shimmering draperies about her. "What's for lunch?"

"Good question. Chicken salad sandwiches, I guess."

"Uninspired but acceptable. Leave the pickle out of mine."

"What for? Don't tell me you're dieting."

"Why should I? I never gain an ounce. You know that." She took a plum out of the dish on the table and bit into it. "It's just that pickles strike one as being somewhat unspiritual."

"I suppose they are, now that you mention it," Dittany conceded. "What difference should that make? To the pure, all things are pure."

"How beautifully true." Arethusa waved what was left of the plum in a graceful parabola. "One does have to be mindful of these things, though, when one moves on the higher planes."

"Tell you what, Arethusa, I'll just set the pickles on the table and you can take them or leave them as the spirit moves you. What's all this about the higher planes?"

"I told you. I've had a visitation. From a spirit."

"What's all this about spirits?" said Osbert. "Would that be as in *spiritus frumenti?* Miss Paffnagel's was brought on by mixing Zilla Trott's dandelion wine with that rum and grapefruit juice you gave her."

"I wish I'd let your parents name you Ralph," Arethusa retorted viciously.

"Careful," Dittany warned. "You're sliding off your plane. Do try to be a trifle less enigmatic about this visitation, Arethusa. Do you mean you've seen a spook?"

"Don't be crass. It was no spook. It was a being."

"What makes you so sure?"

"One is either attuned to these things or one is not."

"Oh, yeah? Was it a he-being or a she-being?"

"How do I know? Anyway, what difference does it make? They don't go in for that sort of thing on the higher levels."

"That's what you say," said her nephew. "All right then, could you give us a general idea of what this being looked like? Did it appear in human form?"

"Of course. Don't they always? It's part of their mystique."

"Well, was its mystique tall or short? Fat or skinny? Did it have clothes on, or was its androgyny open to view?"

"Osbert, you are disgusting. It was," Arethusa hesitated, "majestic, that's the word. Tall and of imposing build. The face was serene."

"You actually saw the face?"

"Not precisely, but one could feel the serenity. At least, I could. You wouldn't have, because you're a clod. It, or he, or she was clad in what appeared to be a simple garment of some soft, drapey material. Like this." She gazed down complacently at her sea-green caftan.

"Aha, that accounts for the getup. You're impersonating a higher being. Why don't you try Calamity Jane? That would be more in character."

"Darling, let Arethusa go on about the visitation," said Dittany, not so much to pour oil on the waters as because she was beginning to see something, too. "What did it do?"

"Just stood there sending out emanations," said Arethusa. "To raise the vibrations, you know."

Hunding Paffnagel chose that moment to emit a particularly reverberative snort with a hideous gurgle at the end. They all glanced upward.

"So that's what the racket's all about," Osbert remarked. "We thought she was sleeping it off, but she's merely raising the vibrations."

"Sounds to me as if she's choking to death," said Dittany. "I'd better go see."

She ran upstairs, to find Perry Fairfield's erstwhile colleague sitting on the edge of the bed clutching the sides of her head.

"What's the matter, Miss Paffnagel? Don't you feel well?"

"I am dying, Egypt, dying. Ebbs the crimson lifetide fast. If I weren't of so abstemious a habit, I'd swear I had the father and mother of all hangovers. I haven't felt like this since that night in Cotopaxi when—excuse me."

Miss Paffnagel made a beeline for the bathroom. Dittany decided the best thing for a hostess to do at a time like this was to go away. She went back downstairs and reported her finding.

"She says she's dying, Egypt, dying. It must have been the camomile tea. What sort of shape were the Fairfields in this morning?"

"In a word, dire. Berthilde appeared to think it was all my fault. She kept asking me what I'd put in that *potage au cresson*. Idiotic woman! At any rate, I didn't have to cook breakfast for them. Let's get back to my visitation."

"Yes, let's," said Dittany. "What happened when you saw it? Weren't you scared stiff?"

"*Moi?* Play the poltroon? *Jamais de la vie!* I merely gathered the draperies of my couch about me and cried, 'Speak!' I think I said 'Speak.' On the other hand, in the confusion of the moment, I may have said, 'Aroint.' "

"Well, which did it do while you were hiding under the bed-clothes? Speak or aroint?"

"I was not hiding under the bedclothes. I was merely straighten-ing my nightgown in order to appear before it in a more seemly guise. In point of fact, by the time I looked up again, it was gone. But ne'er shall I forget the exaltation of that moment. You wouldn't happen to have the address of the Psychical Research Society handy?"

"Not just at the moment. Arethusa, have you thought of count-ing the—"

"What Dittany means is, had you ever counted on seeing an apparition?" Osbert interrupted in an unusually loud pitch. "That must have been quite an experience, Aunt Arethusa. Don't you think so, too, Dittany? Wasn't it quite an experience for my aunt to have seen an apparition in her own lovely home where she has spent so many happy and productive years and will, God willing, spend so many more?"

"Oh, yes! Yes, it certainly must have been quite an experience," Dittany babbled, aghast to realize how close she'd come to sug-gesting Arethusa go back and inventory the teaspoons. "I believe apparitions are experienced mostly by very spiritually inclined people, such as those who spend a lot of time meditating lofty thoughts in their own lovely homes, where there are a lot of Grade A vibrations floating around and bouncing off the woodwork. Look, why don't I see about those chicken salad sandwiches? Maybe you should lay off the pickles, though, Arethusa. Just in case, you know. Osbert, why don't you holler up the stairs and ask Hunding if she'd like a drink of plain soda water?"

"Let her alone," said Arethusa. "You'd only set her off again. I'll send her mental healing."

"That's very nice of you, Aunt Arethusa," said Osbert. "About this visitation. You didn't hear it making noises of any kind?"

"Higher beings don't go around falling over the furniture, you know," his aunt replied frostily.

"Some of them do, I believe. Poltergeists, for instance. They chuck plates at people."

"And ring bells and blow trumpets," Dittany added. "Mama and Bert went to a séance once and they said there were bells jangling and horns tooting all over the place. They said it sounded like New Year's Eve at the Owls' Club. Think hard, Arethusa. Can't you remember even the tiniest little sound?"

Thus prompted, Arethusa said, well, she'd heard that loose board in the upstairs hallway squeak. She'd thought at the time it must have been one of the Fairfields getting up to go to the bathroom, but come to think of it, they'd both been snoring like pigs so perhaps it was the exalted visitor, after all.

"Sending you a message of reassurance and affirmation, I shouldn't be surprised," said Dittany.

"Just to let you know it was thinking of you," Osbert added. "As a friend, of course."

"How sweet of it." Arethusa's vast, unfathomable dark eyes grew moist with unshed tears. "I must go tell Reverend Pennyfeather."

Her nephew shook his head. "I shouldn't if I were you, Aunt Arethusa. The clergy tend to be somewhat narrow-minded about this sort of thing, you know. I realize we've had our little differences from time to time, but I'd really hate to watch you get burned at the stake as a heretic."

"Darling, I rather doubt whether Reverend Pennyfeather would go quite that far," Dittany objected. "I expect he'd settle for denouncing her from the pulpit. Of course I don't suppose that would be any too pleasant, either, with the whole congregation pointing the finger of scorn and opprobrium at one who has hitherto been admired and respected throughout the length and breadth of Lobelia Falls. Why don't you eat your lunch and think it over, Arethusa?"

"Oh, all right, if you say so. At least now I know what Joan of Arc went through."

# CHAPTER 20

Arethusa was halfway through her second sandwich and casting wistful eyes at the pickle jar when Hunding Paffnagel staggered down to the kitchen, clutching a red nylon jersey bathrobe about her and looking like something left over from a brisk session at the sacrificial altar.

"You wouldn't happen to have any black coffee, Mrs. Monk?"

"Coming right up. Take a chair."

"Next to all that food? Ugh!"

Hunding went over to the walnut rocker Gram Henbit had set next to the black iron stove when she'd come to the house as a bride, and plunked herself down like a sack of scratch feed. "God, why did I drink that camomile tea?"

"You'll know better next time. Here, try this."

Dittany put a full mug into the palsied hand Miss Paffnagel had stretched out in mute appeal. Arethusa leaned over and whispered to Osbert.

"I don't think I'd better tell her about my visitation."

"Perish the thought," he replied earnestly. "Her vibrations are in no shape to cope with the higher level. Well, I must get back to work. You, too, eh?"

"Not now. I think I'd better go see what's happening at the museum, if anything. Are you coming, Dittany?"

"Why not? You'll be all right, won't you, Miss Paffnagel?"

"Some day, perhaps. Whatever happened to Berthilde and Jehosaphat?"

"They left," Arethusa told her.

"God, what fortitude. I think perhaps I'll go back to bed for a while."

"That's an excellent idea," said Dittany. "Osbert will be downstairs if you need anything. I'll be back in a while."

She put the last cup in the dishwasher, set the pickles in the refrigerator, and announced she was ready to travel. Arethusa rearranged her silken robes, untangled her strings of beads, and said, "So am I. Wherefore lookst thou so glum, prithee?"

"I'm just wondering if we're having a visitation over there."

They were. They'd no sooner set foot in the Architrave's door than those bright pink gums were flashing at them.

"Ah, there you are. I'd been wondering whether anybody was going to show up today. The plumber hasn't come."

Arethusa turned to Dittany. "Henchperson, why hasn't the plumber come?"

"Because he's in jail."

"Ah."

"Then have you ladies given any further thought as to how I'm going to get my sink fixed?" demanded Mrs. Fairfield.

"Not I," said Arethusa.

"Miss Monk, I hate to complain, but really, how do you expect me to get anything accomplished around here unless I get a little cooperation from the trustees?"

"We don't."

That stopped her, but only for a moment. The gums flashed again. "I don't believe I quite understand. What do you mean, you don't?"

"I mean," Arethusa replied, speaking slowly and enunciating with all her might and main, "We don't. Do not. Have not. Shall not. Our expectations with regard to your performance are nil."

"Oh."

Mrs. Fairfield stood absolutely still for perhaps half a second, then shook her head and essayed a pathetic attempt at another smile, with hardly a vestige of gum showing. "I see. You think I ought to be in a darkened room with a smelling bottle and a cologne-soaked handkerchief, sobbing my poor, tired eyes out. I know you mean to be kind, Miss Monk, but that's not what Peregrine would have wanted."

"No?"

"Not at all. Carry on, Evangeline, that's what he'd have said to me. I can almost hear him now. We were always such close partners, you know. Side by side through thick and thin, through joy and sorrow, sickness and health, till death—but I mustn't dwell on my personal tragedy when there's so much to be done, must I?"

"Why not, in sooth?"

"Miss Monk, I thought I'd just got through explaining."

"So did I. It appears we have some kind of communication gap here."

"Then perhaps we ought to change the subject and see if we can do better," said Mrs. Fairfield with a jarring laugh. "You may be pleased to know I've just finished authenticating those seventeenth-century Dutch brass candle sconces Mrs. Burberry's mother-in-law sent us."

"How remarkable. What did you authenticate them as?"

"Seventeenth-century Dutch, of course."

"*Vraiment?* And had you some particular reason for doing so?"

"Certainly. Reference books, my personal expertise."

"Along with the letter from the elder Mrs. Burberry's cousin Georgina which she'd enclosed with them when she wished them off on Mrs. Burberry, perchance?"

"Family records are always helpful, naturally."

"Georgina?" said Dittany. "Oh, yes, the brass molder's widow. Wasn't she the one Samantha was telling us about, who tried to institute a breach of promise suit against Lord Tweedsmuir while he was off at a Presbyterian conference?"

"Egad, yes," said Arethusa. "Also the Duke of York, if memory serves me, and the Archbishop of Canterbury. How Samantha happened to mention her was that the last time they visited her at the Eventide Home, they saw a steel engraving of the Prince Regent on her dressing table. In his earlier, handsomer, and slimmer days, *naturellement.* It had 'To Georgy Girl with love from Georgy-Porgy' written on it."

"That's right. Samantha said Georgina was having a heck of a time trying to get a lawyer to take on the case. The thing of it is, eh, Georgina's always been addicted to what you might call romantic embroidery."

"Ah, like that bridal quilt." You really had to hand it to the old trout. "My niece-in-law mentioned last evening that you'd been showing her the pieces. I must say I was a little surprised at that, when poor Peregrine didn't even get to see them before he died. I've been hoping to get a peek at them myself. They're not still spread out on your dining room table, by any chance?"

"*Pas du tout,*" said Arethusa. "They're all safely—*mon Dieu!*"

*Mon Dieu,* Dittany thought, hardly covered it. Over the threshold came, first, a box of tools and second, a foot wearing a cutaway shoe revealing the pink and white striped sock of Cedric Fawcett.

These were followed in rapid succession by the rest of Fawcett and by Andrew McNaster.

Mrs. Fairfield stepped right up to them, ready for battle. "Well, this is a pleasant surprise. I was led to believe you weren't coming back at all. Now, you get this and get it straight, Fawcett. I want that sink fixed. I want it fixed right, and I want it fixed now. I'm not shelling out good money—"

"That is quite correct, Mrs. Fairfield." Arethusa could be the grandest of grandes dames when she chose, and she chose now. "Any disbursement of museum funds is handled by our treasurer, Mrs. Coskoff, under my personal direction. In any case, we are obtaining Mr. Fawcett's services through the disinterested generosity, or so we perhaps naïvely believe, of Mr. McNaster. Is that not correct, Mr. McNaster?"

Andrew McNaster laid a large, beefy hand on that region of his waistcoat where his heart might be presumed to reside, assuming he had one after all.

"That is wholly and entirely correct, Miss Monk. And may I take this opportunity of saying I deem it an honor and a privilege to be associated, however distantly and humbly, with a lady whom I—I —aw, shucks."

McNaster turned as pink as Cedric Fawcett's sock and floundered himself into silence. Arethusa bowed her gleaming freight of jetty tresses in gracious acknowledgment. Dittany gaped in wild surmise. What the heck was going on here? She essayed a tactful inquiry.

"How come you're on the loose, Mr. Fawcett? My husband said you'd had one Labatt's too many and wound up in the slammer."

Fawcett jerked his head toward McNaster. "He sprung me."

"How come?"

"For her."

"Her who? Mrs. Fairfield?"

Fawcett gave her a cold look. "Not her. Her."

"You mean Arethusa? Miss Monk? My husband's aunt?"

Fawcett grunted, picked up his tool box, and disappeared sink-ward. Arethusa was left face to face, or vis-à-vis as she herself would perhaps have expressed it, with Andrew McNaster.

"Mr. McNaster, am I to place any credence in the word of that man with the bunion?"

"Jailbird though he may be," McNaster replied in a voice choked with emotion, "Cedric Fawcett does not lie."

"He says you got him out," Dittany protested. "Last I heard, you were determined to press charges."

"I was, but I didn't."

"Why not? He crowned you with a plunger."

McNaster winced at the recollection. "He did. He offered me the supreme insult. Nevertheless, I dropped the charge. It was a far, far better thing I did than ever I have done before. I know, Miss Monk. I have been a reprobate. I have indulged in chicanery and malfeasance. I have schemed. I have dallied with the truth. I have looked upon the wine when it was red. I have consorted with loose women. I have risked my all at the gaming tables."

"You have?" Arethusa was looking at him with a strange dawning of interest.

"I have. Just like Sir Percy, before he fell under the redeeming influence of Lady Ermintrude. Well, maybe not quite like Sir Percy, but I used to play the slot machines a lot."

He turned his eyes bashfully floorward. "You scowl, Miss Monk, and I am powerless before your glance. Your very frowns are fairer far than smiles of other maiden ladies are. Even as I stood there with that plunger crammed down over my ear, something inside me kept saying, 'Miss Monk wants that sink fixed.' Even as those two deputies of Sergeant MacVicar were putting the collar on old Ceddie and I was yelling for his head as any red-blooded member of the landed gentry would naturally do, that little voice kept saying, 'How the heck is Miss Monk going to get that sink fixed if I allow my baser nature to prevail and exact my petty revenge on old Ceddie?' It was like there were two Andrew McNasters, each clamoring for supremacy over the other one. You know what I mean?"

"You might think of them as self A and self B," Dittany suggested.

"I never heard such drivel in my life," said Evangeline Fairfield.

It was the most injudicious remark she'd ever made. Arethusa turned on her like a wounded tigress.

"Madam, I *write* such drivel!"

"Hear, hear," Dittany murmured, but nobody was paying any attention to her. Andrew McNaster was goggling at Arethusa much as Sir Percy might have goggled at Lady Ermintrude in a similar instance. So was Mrs. Fairfield, only hers was a goggle of consternation. It must be dawning upon her that she had finally and irrevocably cooked her goose with the Aralia Polyphema Architrave Museum. If it hadn't, Arethusa's next utterance left no room for doubt.

"Mrs. Fairfield, go away."

"I beg your pardon?"

"Granted. Now go away."

"Very well," said Mrs. Fairfield haughtily. "If you wish to continue this conversation in private, I shall be in my office."

"Mrs. Fairfield, you do not have an office. You do not have a position at the Architrave."

"What do you mean, I have no position? You can't just fire me out of hand."

"Correct. I can't fire you because you were never hired. The only contract we had was with your husband, and that was terminated on his death."

"And what, pray, does a writer of trashy romances know about contracts?"

"A great deal more than you do about antiques. I sign one about every three months. Now go away."

Mrs. Fairfield, without another word or so much as a backward glance, went. Arethusa raised a shapely hand to toy idly with her Venetian glass beads.

"Please forgive the interruption, Mr. McNaster. You were explaining the supreme soul-searching struggle that led you to discover the essential nobility of your character beneath the false veneer of the hardened rake."

"Yeah, that was it. Somehow when Ceddie zonked me with that plunger, it sort of made everything come into focus. Miss Monk, I will confess all. Ever since the day when you walked past the parking lot wearing your Spanish shawl with a rose between your teeth, I have—maybe your little niece here better stop unde."

"Heck, no," said Dittany. "I'm a married woman. You mean you lusted after her flesh?"

"Well, I was going to put it more genteel, but that was the general idea. But you snooted me, Miss Monk. I was desperate. I even thought of—well, you know in *Vilest Villainy in Velvet* where the wicked baronet comes along in his barouche landau and puts the snatch on Lady Ermintrude while she's taking a bucket of soup to the poor widow lady?"

"An abduction?" Arethusa's bosom was heaving much as Lady Ermintrude's would have done in a similar circumstance, making the Venetian beads rattle like castanets.

"Devil-may-care rogue that I was, I entertained that notion, Miss Monk. I thought of using your little niece here as a decoy, even called up a car-hire place and found out how much it would cost me to rent a Rolls Royce limousine. What the heck, I might be a villain and a rotter, but I wouldn't have wanted you thinking I was a chintzy cad."

"Why, you swashbuckling scoundrel." Arethusa was still trying to look haughty, but a hint of a smile was playing about her rosaceous lips. "But your better nature prevailed," she said with the merest tinge of regret.

"I saw the light just in time, Miss Monk. What happened was, I picked up a copy of *Saving a Swine* at the drugstore. Then I realized I must not aspire to capture your favor but rest content to worship you from afar, like a moth trying to get inside a light bulb but it can't on account of the glass is in the way. That was me, beating my wings in vain against the cold disdain of which my rotten ways had made me so contemptibly deserving. But I can still serve you, Miss Monk. I ask no greater boon than to fork out union wages to Ceddie Fawcett to sit out there under your sink trying to figure out which end of the wrench is up."

"Nobly spoken, Mr. McNaster. I will confess that I am not insensible of the esteem in which you appear to hold me, but you must give me time. Time to think. Time to study my heart. Time to ponder whether there might be a usable plot in this. Excuse me, I have to find a pencil."

McNaster gazed after her, his heart bulging out of his eyes. "What a woman!"

"She's all that and then some," Dittany agreed. "Excuse me, Mr. McNaster. I'd better go after her in case she needs her smelling salts or anything."

"I could get them for her!"

"It's not the done thing. Why don't you find a quiet corner somewhere and memorize some poetry?"

"Great idea. I'll go read the greeting cards at Gumpert's. The mushy ones, I mean. Not those other kind."

Well, it was a start. Not that it was likely to get him far. First Ethel and the woodchuck, now Andy McNasty and Arethusa Monk. What was the world coming to?

# CHAPTER 21

"Whoa there, gal," said Osbert. "Back up and come at me again. I thought I heard you say Andy McNasty's in love with my aunt."

"That was the impression he conveyed," Dittany insisted. "He claims to have worshipped her from afar ever since he saw her sashay past the inn parking lot doing her impersonation of Carmen."

"Does that strike you as a plausible tale?"

"Darling, your aunt Arethusa is a stunning woman, with all that black hair and those great big flashing eyes."

"And that tiny little brain flashing on and off. What was her reaction to this astounding news?"

"She burbled something about a plot and ran to get a pencil."

"Good old auntie. I knew there must be a vestige of intelligence in there somewhere. Of course it's a plot, darling. Don't you see what's happened? First Andy gets Fawcett mad at him, knowing Fawcett's tendency to have at it with snake and plunger when his dander's up. Then Andy gets Fawcett jugged for assault, as is only natural under the circumstances. Then Andy says no, he won't press charges after all because his nobler nature—"

"Self B," Dittany interjected.

"Thank you, darling. Self B has been stirred to action by the rose between Aunt Arethusa's teeth, so he gets Fawcett sprung. What in fact happened was that underhanded old self A whom we know so well and detest so heartily was conniving to put Fawcett in a position where he'd have to do self A's dirty work for him or else self B would cancel his cancellation of charges and Fawcett would be back in the jug."

"Then it was Cedric Fawcett who burgled us?"

"Isn't it obvious, darling? You know that uncanny ability plumbers have to appear and disappear when you least expect them to. And they're always hunting for things."

"Darling, hunting for a leak in a gas pipe isn't quite the same thing as rifling Gram Henbit's cedar chest."

"I grant you that, darling. It's an infinitely more subtle process. Therefore, by a simple process of deduction, to a plumber rifling a cedar chest ought to be easy as pie."

"But what about Arethusa's visitation? Do you honestly believe Cedric Fawcett could have gone padding into her bedroom in his pink and white socks and stood there looking majestic long enough to fool her? Long enough to fool anybody?"

"Arethusa isn't just anybody, darling. If there's a cockeyed way of looking at anything, you know perfectly well she'll find it. Besides, she admits herself she only caught the merest glimpse of him before she ducked under the bedclothes."

"That's true. And I suppose if she had realized who it was and challenged him, Fawcett could always say he'd had an emergency call about a leak in the gas pipe."

"And got into the wrong house by mistake," Osbert finished. "You see, dear, it all hangs together. And we wouldn't have thought of Fawcett because we'd have assumed he was safely tucked up in the hoosegow."

"But that scheme didn't work, so now McNaster's trying to lure Arethusa with lying heart and flattering tongue. The blackguard! Now who's that coming up the walk? Oh, Zilla. Look, darling, don't say anything about McNaster to her. She'd go after him with a tomahawk. She looks as if she's on the warpath about something already."

She was. Zilla Trott was no sooner in the door than she had Dittany pinned against the wall, demanding, "What's all this about Arethusa attacking poor Mrs. Fairfield?"

"Attacking Mrs. Fairfield? What's that supposed to mean?"

"Well, abusing her. Telling her she wasn't wanted."

"She isn't. You said so yourself a few days ago. You said Mrs. Fairfield was a pest and a know-it-all and you wished she'd go fly her kite."

"That was before her husband got killed."

"Since which time she's been flapping around the museum proving that she is in fact a pest and a know-it-all. She apparently thought if she stepped right in and started throwing her weight around, we'd be deceived into thinking she was capable of taking her husband's job."

"Well, he was no human dynamo. At least she's got a little get up and git to her. Anyway, what's this got to do with the museum? As I understand it, Arethusa flew off the handle because Mrs. Fairfield happened to intrude upon a scandalous scene between her and some man. He was described as Andrew McNaster but of course that's ridiculous. Arethusa's done some pretty outrageous things in her day, but even she draws the line somewhere."

"Zilla, you've been the victim of misinformation. In the first place, Arethusa didn't fly off the handle. She remained icily calm as she pointed out to Mrs. Fairfield the error of her ways, and no more than graciously attentive when Andy was baring his soul on the side porch."

"He wasn't!"

"He sure as heck was, eh. Andy's been panting like a hart on the mountain ever since she slunk past him one day wearing her Spanish shawl. He's even reading her books. He says they've made him a far, far better man."

"Hogwash!"

"Quite possibly, but that's what he was saying when Mrs. Fairfield was so rude as to interrupt. How it happened was, Mrs. Fairfield started bawling out the plumber."

"What plumber? Cedric Fawcett's in jail. For beaning Andy with a plunger, as who wouldn't, given the opportunity."

"No he isn't. Andy refused to press charges for love of Arethusa."

"Well, I'll be gum-swizzled! He told her that?"

"Cedric Fawcett did."

Not, come to think of it, that Dittany had any special reason to assume Fawcett had been telling the truth. A man who'd go prowling into people's bedrooms impersonating a higher being was perhaps not the most reliable of informants. Perhaps he hadn't meant to impersonate a higher being. More likely, he'd simply meant to rifle the room while Arethusa slept.

But why should he have been so bold in assuming Arethusa was going to be asleep? Because her house guests had gone reeling around the village stewed to the gills and it would be assumed they'd left their hostess in similar condition? At least that might be assumed by somebody to whom Arethusa was either only a distant dream or a proposed gull or catspaw, as the case might be. In point of fact, Arethusa never got even marginally sozzled. Only the other day Osbert had remarked, watching her lap up their best sherry as if it had been weak tea, that his aunt had inherited her father's hardness of head along with his softness of brain.

The case against the McNaster/Fawcett contingent was looking stronger by the minute. However, Dittany wasn't about to tell Zilla that. Instead, she gave her a carefully edited account of just how outrageously Mrs. Fairfield had been behaving since her husband's death. By the time she got to the part about authenticating Cousin Georgina's brass sconces, the well-defined planes of Zilla's face were shifting like the San Andreas Fault.

"Mrs. Fairfield actually fell for one of Cousin Georgina's fairy stories?"

"Zilla, would I lie to you?"

"Probably not," Zilla conceded. "You're surprisingly truthful, all things considered. But I still think Arethusa could have been a little more tactful. What if Mrs. Fairfield decides to slap the museum with a suit for negligence in the death of her husband? Even if she doesn't know beans, we'd have done better to jolly her along till she could get her feet back under her and find a place to go."

"Zilla, if we gave that woman a chance to dig herself in, you know darn well the devil and all his angels wouldn't be able to dig her out again. The way I see it, we'd have had a fight on our hands sooner or later anyway, so it might as well have been sooner."

"Huh. That may be the way you see it, eh, but you can bet your boots a lot of other people are going to see it differently. Arethusa's made us look like a bunch of skunks irregardless of whether she was in the right or in the wrong. If she's taken up with Andy McNasty, that will put the capsheaf on it. It looks to me as if we're going to have to ask for her resignation from the board, Dittany."

"Zilla, you can't do that. Arethusa's done more than all the rest of us put together to get that museum going. Besides, she's the only one in the club who really knows anything about antiques. And furthermore, if she got kicked off the board she'd feel obliged to resign from the club. If she did that she might as well leave Lobelia Falls and be done with it. She'd be a dead duck around here and you know it as well as I do. This is her home, darn it. You can't run a person out of town just for pointing out a few home truths to a pushy ignoramus we hardly know from a hole in the ground."

"Well, I'll see what Minerva has to say," Zilla sighed. "But I warn you, she's pretty hot under the collar right now."

"So am I," Dittany snarled. "Send her over to me, I'll straighten her out in a hurry."

"Now, you lay off Minerva. She's got her hands full already."

"I'll say she has. She'll probably have to set fire to the mattress to get that incubus out of her spare room. Sorry if I've wounded your sensibilities, Zilla, but you might as well realize I'm one hundred percent on Arethusa's side in this wrangle. If she has to go, then I'll have to go with her. You might bear that in mind before you start putting on the war paint. How about a cup of tea, since I haven't a peace pipe to offer you?"

"Peppermint tea?"

"Why not?"

They drank the cup of amity, but before it was drained Therese Boulanger was already on the phone wanting to know the ins and outs of Arethusa's cruel persecution of Mrs. Fairfield. By the time Dittany had got Therese silenced if not entirely placated, Hazel Munson was at the door, allegedly to return a ladder Roger had borrowed from the toolshed but in fact to find out whether Arethusa had really visited Mrs. Fairfield with bodily violence before eloping with Andy McNasty or if the story had somehow got blown out of proportion. Dittany brewed up another pot of peppermint tea and settled herself for a long, hot afternoon.

She'd grown thoroughly fed up with repeating what really happened when she hit upon the happy thought of switching her evergrowing circle of listeners to plans for the quilting bee. This entailed laying the pieces out on the dining room table and started a good deal of wrangling over which piece looked better next to what. By the time they all said well they guessed they'd better go home and start thinking about supper, Arethusa's alleged outrage had simmered down to a mere tempest in a teapot—although it was doubtless growing in magnitude outside their own little circle —and Dittany was too exhausted even to think about putting the pieces away. When Osbert emerged from his office, where he'd barricaded himself and his typewriter during the invasion, he spied them and made, not surprisingly, a beeline for the table.

"Ah, there they are, the intriguing little rascals."

Dittany came in from the kitchen. "Hi, darling. Had a rough afternoon among the yaks?"

"Yaks? Oh, they're out to pasture. I averted a train wreck."

"Good for you. How did you manage that?"

"Well, you see, the rustlers had got to fiddling around with the semaphore signals—leaping lariats, Dittany, I'll bet that's it! Was any of the Architraves ever involved with the railroad, do you know?"

"I'd be surprised if they weren't. Western Canada would never have been hatched if it weren't for the railroads, you know that. I could call Minerva. She'd know, I expect."

"Never mind. Have you got an old Girl Guides' manual around here anywhere?"

"Sure. You mean that stuff with the flags? We never learned codes because somehow or other we always wound up practicing archery instead. Just a second."

Dittany ran up to the small bedroom that had always been hers till she'd moved into the big one with Osbert and fished in the bookcase Gramp had made to hold her personal library. There was the manual, right between *Alice in Wonderland* and *The Wizard of Oz.* She flipped the pages and found the little diagram figures with their arms waving in twenty-six different positions. "Here you are, darling."

"Great." Osbert began comparing the diagrams with those hitherto puzzling multicolored antennae. "Yep, pardner, I think we've struck pay dirt. Here's a B. And this one's definitely an F. Could you find a paper and pencil?"

"Sure, just a second. That was a B and an F." Dittany scribbled them down. "And there's another B, only the first one was yellow and this is green. Any more green whiskers?"

"Yes, but it's signaling an F. I think it's an F. They're so darn little. Put down an F anyway. And a third F, only it's purple. Does BFBFF mean anything?"

"Sounds Welsh to me. Are there any L's? Welsh words always ▨▨▨ to have scads of L's and Y's."

"L, L—ah, here we are. One L, red. Second L, blue. And a third L, by gad, orange. We're getting somewhere, but I'm danged if I know where."

"I spy a Y, a fat yellow Y. And a blue P. See, that one thumbing its nose at the daisy."

"I wish we'd get some vowels for a change," Osbert fretted. "We're almost out of bees. Any A's?"

"Would you settle for a U?"

"It might help. Aha, and here's an E."

"BLUE," cried Dittany. "That's a word. But it doesn't explain all those other colors. What about that scrawny-looking little bee over there on the scrap of pink velvet?"

"It's a C."

"Marvelous! CLUE. Clue, not blue. Now we're getting somewhere."

"Maybe so, darling, but don't ask me where. So far we've got—what?" Osbert scanned Dittany's list. "BFBFFLLLYPUEC. And that's it, as far as I can see. No more bees."

"Maybe some of the pieces fell out when we opened the box," Dittany fretted. "With all those mice hurling themselves at me, I might have been a wee bit jittery."

"Did you actually open the box yourself?"

"Come to think of it, no. Mrs. Fairfield did. But I was right there watching, and she was very careful. I suppose I could ask her. No, I guess I couldn't, in view of that hairtangle we got into this afternoon. Not that I blame Arethusa, darling. I just wish everything hadn't blown up all of a sudden like that. I suppose it does look pretty rotten to throw a middle-aged woman out on her ear right after she's lost her meal ticket, even if she did bring it on herself. We'll have to manage some kind of going-away present, I expect, just so nobody can say we sent her off penniless. Could we squeeze another few dollars out of the egg money, do you think?"

"I expect likely," said Osbert. "We'll make Aunt Arethusa cough up, too. And there must have been a little something coming to Mr. Fairfield in the way of salary, wasn't there?"

"Darn little. Maybe we ought to get Dot Coskoff out on the street corner passing the hat while the tide of public sympathy's still running in Mrs. Fairfield's favor. Let's ask Miss Paffnagel if she'd like to kick in for auld lang syne."

# CHAPTER 22

"Kick into what?" That was Hunding herself, looking somewhat less bedraggled than she had a few hours ago.

"Oh, hello," said Dittany. "How are you feeling?"

"Better, I think. Were you planning to offer me anything to eat?"

"If you like. It's about time you got something into your stomach. How about a cup of weak tea and a piece of toast for starters? I'll be getting supper in a while."

Miss Paffnagel said tea and toast would be acceptable and expressed wholehearted enthusiasm at the prospect of supper. Once she'd got her mouth comfortably full, she asked again, "What was that you said about kicking in?"

"Oh. Well, you see, Osbert's aunt gave Evangeline Fairfield the boot this afternoon, and we've been thinking we ought to get up some kind of retirement fund for her."

"Vangie? Don't fret yourself about her. She'll manage one way or another. Flap in through people's bedroom windows and suck the blood from their throats, I expect. Getting back to the subject of supper, you did say you were planning to serve it fairly soon? Something on the hearty and substantial side, perhaps?"

"We could grill a steak outdoors," Osbert volunteered.

"Let's. If you happen to have a polished bronze mirror ready to hand, I could show you a neat little trick for kindling the sacrificial fire."

Osbert said he didn't have a polished bronze mirror and thought he'd just use a match. He went off to find the charcoal while Dittany started putting a salad together and Hunding began excavations on a plate of molasses cookies that hadn't got put away after the impromptu tea party.

"Now what's the poop on Vangie?" the latter asked as Dittany picked up a cucumber to peel. "Not to criticize the native customs, but one might almost have thought a lady so imbued with the social graces as Miss Monk could have waited till Perry was cold in his coffin before plunging the knife."

"Arethusa would have preferred to wait, I'm sure," Dittany replied, "but Mrs. Fairfield wouldn't let her."

"How so?"

"Well, it would have been all right if Mrs. Fairfield had been content to settle down under her weight of woe for a while and let us rally round with cups of tea and words of cheer. Instead, she insisted on galloping over to the museum."

"Which she's about as well equipped to handle as a good-sized wombat," Hunding remarked. "Vangie's the type who picks up a few catchwords and applies them without regard to context in a frequently vain attempt to make you think she knows what she's talking about. With all respect to Miss Monk, however, one might almost have thought some small temporary job could have been found for her instead of the summary coup de grace."

"Mrs. Fairfield didn't want some small temporary job," Dittany objected. "She wanted to run the whole show, and she'd been pretty offensive about letting everybody know it. You can't boss volunteers around as if they were galley slaves. She tried that on me the very morning after Mr. Fairfield died, which wasn't very judicious considering I'm one of the trustees. She also gassed a good bit about her expertise while making it obvious she didn't know which end was up. What really put the frosting on the bun, though, was when she bawled out the plumber."

"But why shouldn't Vangie bawl out a plumber? I've bawled out plumbers myself."

"In the first place, she had no real cause to, as far as I could see. In the second, she threatened not to pay him when she wouldn't have had any authority to pay him anyway. In the third, she did all this chewing out right in front of the man who's been coughing up the plumber's wages out of his own pocket as a donation to the museum and a token of his personal regard for Arethusa."

"A patron? Gorblimey! Didn't Vangie know who he was?"

Dittany stopped short in the act of slicing her cucumber. "You've asked a mighty interesting question, Miss Paffnagel. Mrs. Fairfield must have known. She's heard enough talk about Andrew McNaster ever since she came here. The thing of it is, the Fairfields were supposed to live in the museum as part of the deal.

We've been fixing up an apartment for them fast as we could. Not having any money to speak of, we've had to rely on free help a lot."

" 'Twas ever thus at museums."

"So it was a break for us when Andy—that is, Mr. McNaster, who's a contractor, began sending his workmen over to give us a hand during their spare time. That meant we never knew when they'd show up, but of course that's apt to happen regardless. Mrs. Fairfield understood the situation, or should have. She's done a little mild bitching from time to time, as who hasn't, but I'd never seen her so downright belligerent before."

"No, it's not like Evangeline to fly off the handle," Miss Paffnagel conceded, thoughtfully considering the last cookie and deciding in the affirmative. "Especially in front of a patron. Her customary procedure would be to give you one of those crocodile grins and make some catty remark cunningly disguised to pass for sweetness and light."

She finished the cookie and began dabbing up crumbs from the plate. "Ah, well, these things happen. I've seen it often enough on digs. Some meek little mouse who hasn't said boo for twenty years suddenly grabs the first obsidian dagger that comes to hand and begins hacking out the entrails of casual lookers-on. Vangie will calm down sooner or later, I expect. The main thing is to lock up the knives and cater to her every whim for a few years. Otherwise, I expect Berthilde will be back here socking your aunt with a whopping lawsuit for driving Vangie over the edge."

"But she didn't!"

"Oh, no doubt it's been festering for years, but you know how lawyers for penniless widows get when they spy a rich defendant in the offing. I suppose what they'll do is ask for some nice, round sum like five million dollars, then dicker for an out-of-court settlement. Wouldn't you think it must be almost time to put that steak on the grill?"

"I'll go see."

If Dittany's voice sounded a trifle dim and far away, it was not without reason. Could they actually be faced with the equally dire alternatives of having to put up with Evangeline Fairfield forever and a day, or else seeing Arethusa stripped of her money, her jewels, and even her gilded crocodiles, landing destitute on their doorstep some wild and stormy night when they'd absolutely have to take her in? She asked Osbert. To her dismay, he didn't know.

"I'd have to ask my agent" was his uncomforting reply. "Archie handles all that legal stuff. Try not to worry, darling. There must be a rainbow shining somewhere."

"Yes, darling. I'll bring the steak."

"Maybe you should bring us a few cold beers, too, eh."

Osbert wasn't all that much of a beer drinker as a rule. Perhaps he was feeling that if malt does more than Milton can to justify God's ways to man, then maybe it could cast some light on the whys and wherefores of Evangeline Fairfield and Hunding Paffnagel, not to mention a swarm of bees that spelled BFBFFLL- LYPUEC.

# CHAPTER 23

"Did you actually get a look at that letter Mr. Fairfield told you about?"

Osbert, who was a dab hand at a grill on account of all those camping trips, carved Hunding Paffnagel another strip of perfectly broiled steak and handed her a third beer. She helped herself abundantly to more salad and chips, chewed a while, then nodded.

"Yes, I did. He had it right there in his desk drawer. Typical of Perry. Woolly as a newborn lamb."

"And what did the letter say?" Dittany prompted.

Hunding shrugged. "Don't ask me. It was written in French, a language I never got around to learning."

"Couldn't you have asked him to read it to you?"

"I was infinitely more interested in persuading him not to read it to me. You must remember I'd been through this buried treasure delusion with Perry on various other occasions."

"But you did at least get a close look at the letter?" Osbert persisted. "Other than its being in French, could you describe it in any way?"

"Well, needless to say, it was handwritten. With a steel nib, I should say, instead of a quill. The paper was yellowed with age and torn in a couple of places. The ink was somewhat faded and brownish. The handwriting was rather pretty, as I recall, in a spiky sort of way, even and well-spaced. Oh, and the signature was Henriette. I do remember that, because it was the only word I could decipher."

"In French and signed Henriette," said Dittany. "That surprises me. I never heard of any Architrave marrying a Frenchwoman. Then again, I never heard of any Architrave not marrying a Frenchwoman. Minerva would be the one to know."

"Ask her," said Osbert. "Anyway, I think we ought to stroll

down to the museum and collar that letter as soon as we've finished eating. More steak, darling?"

"No, you finish it. I was thinking maybe I could con you into buying us an ice cream later at the drugstore. We don't have any dessert, unless anybody would like a plum."

"What happened to all those cookies?" Hunding asked brazenly.

"Guess."

"Oh. Well, take it as a compliment to your cooking. Isn't anybody going to eat that last piece of steak?"

"Feel free."

Osbert loaded the meat on Hunding's plate. Dittany had had vague thoughts of saving it for Ethel, but she supposed she ought to have known better. How long were they to keep shoveling groceries into this human disposal unit, anyway?

"What's new with Sergeant MacVicar?" she asked Osbert, knowing he'd understand what she really meant.

He shook his head. "I haven't heard a yip out of him all day. I suppose I ought to have checked in with the station."

"What for? He'd have hollered fast enough if he'd wanted you."

"That's true. The sergeant wouldn't interrupt my work for idle chatter. He knows I have a wife and dog to support. Not to mention freeloading droppers-in. Like my aunt, I mean," he added hastily, for Osbert wouldn't have wanted to offend Miss Paffnagel even if she did eat up every last one of his molasses cookies. "Mighty mavericks, Dittany, do you realize Aunt Arethusa isn't here? We've actually got through a whole meal without her. Do you suppose she's sick?"

"Maybe she's eating up the leftovers from last night," said Dittany, but she didn't believe it. Considering that Hunding Paffnagel had been of the party, it seemed unlikely there'd been any leftovers. More likely, Arethusa had by now heard so much flak about her alleged mistreatment of Evangeline Fairfield that she was afraid to step outside her own door for fear of being stoned to death by some misinformed hothead. Dittany ventured that hypothesis and added that perhaps they'd better stop by on their way to the museum and see if Arethusa was all right.

Osbert vetoed the suggestion. "I'd back Aunt Arethusa against a howling lynch mob any day. Let's do the museum first. I want to get my hands on that letter."

But the letter was not to be got. They searched the desk and found several other letters, none of them of any great interest. They found a crocheted chamber pot cover, a bunch of old photographs of men in hunting garb with dead deer strung up on poles between them, of boys swimming unselfconsciously naked at the old swimming hole, of ladies looking proud in new Sunday bonnets, and of tots looking miserable in corkscrew curls and starched dresses. They found a half bushel or so of notes in Mr. Fairfield's fussy handwriting and the usual odds and ends that accumulate in desk drawers. Nowhere did they find a piece of paper written on in French with faded brownish ink and signed Henriette. Dittany picked up the telephone and called Minerva.

"Hi, *c'est moi.* Is Mrs. Fairfield there? No, I don't want to talk to her. I want you to ask her what she did with a letter written in French and signed Henriette. The paper's yellowed with age and slightly foxed. Yes, foxed. No, that doesn't mean drunk. It means those brown spots old paper gets. Mrs. Fairfield will know, if she knows anything whatsoever, which I—all right, Minerva, we won't go into that now. Look, I don't care if she's prostrate. Go unprostrate her. She had no business taking anything from the museum in the first place. No, go ahead. I'll wait."

Minerva must have gone but was back in a minute or so to say Mrs. Fairfield didn't know anything about any foxed letter signed Henriette and wished to inquire whether this cruel persecution would ever cease.

"Horsefeathers," said Dittany, "and tell her I said so. You might also tell her she'd better rack her brain about that letter because Sergeant MacVicar can persecute a lot more effectively than I can."

She listened to a few more sputters, then said, "Good night," and hung up.

"Sounds as if Minerva's a bit upset, eh," Osbert remarked.

"You might say that. So am I, Darling, if Mrs. Fairfield hasn't got that letter, who has?"

"Don't look at me," cried Hunding. "If I'd taken it, would I have told you about it in the first place?"

Maybe, Dittany told herself, if Miss Paffnagel thought old Perry had already been showing the letter around to other people. Osbert, however, seemed to accept Hunding's protest.

"Let's just make sure it's not still here. The fact that Miss

Paffnagel saw him take it out of his desk drawer doesn't necessarily mean he put it back there."

"I know, darling," Dittany argued, "but he was an orderly sort of man. I can't see him stuffing it in his pocket or dropping it behind the radiator."

"No, but mightn't he have put it away somewhere for safekeeping?"

"Where, for instance?"

"Is there a filing cabinet with a lock on it?"

"Nope, just these old oak ones that came out of Dr. Busch's office after he died. Hazel had them in her cellar."

Osbert wasn't interested in Hazel's cellar. He was combing the files. Since the museum hadn't been operating long enough to accumulate much in the way of archives, that didn't take him long. The letter definitely was not in one of the folders. It wasn't anywhere. After a while, Dittany phoned Minerva again.

"I know you're mad at me, but we've looked absolutely everywhere, and that letter hasn't turned up. Give Mrs. Fairfield a slug of corpse reviver and tell her to look through her husband's things. Sergeant MacVicar's going to have a fit."

It occurred to Dittany they'd better tip the sergeant off about the letter so he'd know what to have his fit about in case Minerva happened to bring up the subject in his presence. She called down to the station. Mrs. MacVicar told her the sergeant was off investigating a daring robbery of six pocket computers and a leather briefcase to carry them off in from Ye Village Stationer. Bob and Ray were down at the ball field directing traffic. Ormerod was still on holiday. Mrs. MacVicar promised to give her husband a message. By then it was getting late, so they skipped the ice cream and went home without calling on Arethusa. It was best, they decided, to let sleeping aunts lie.

Events, however, proved them wrong. It was at half past eight the next morning that they got the call. Arethusa had been slugged into unconsciousness, bound and gagged, and her house ransacked. Mrs. Poppy, coming to work early for the first time in her life, had got a dazzling reward by becoming the heroine of the hour. She wanted to tell them all about it, knot by knot and bruise by bruise, but Dittany and Osbert were both pounding at Arethusa's door before Mrs. Poppy realized she was talking to an empty line.

A crowd had already gathered around the house, and there were scoffers among them wondering loudly whether Arethusa hadn't staged the whole thing herself to take people's minds off the rotten way she'd treated poor Mrs. Fairfield. Perhaps they would be somewhat chastened a bit later when they'd see Doc Somervell come out of the house looking grave and shaking his head. Dittany and Osbert didn't go down to find out.

Sergeant MacVicar was already there at the bedside, shaking his own head and telling them sternly that this was a verra bad business. Arethusa was stretched out looking like the Lily Maid of Astolat on her barge. Mrs. Poppy was dithering in the doorway, bursting to talk and being instructed to "Whist, wumman" by the sergeant every time she opened her mouth except to gape. Dittany, who in spite of everything was extremely fond of Arethusa, went over to the bed, kissed Arethusa's pale cheek, and began to cry. Osbert was whispering to the doctor in a strangely hoarse whisper, "Is she going to be all right?"

"I hope so" was the answer. "She got an awful whack."

"Aye, a sair dunt," Sergeant MacVicar confirmed.

"But nothing seems to be broken," Dr. Somervell went on, "and she's breathing normally enough. I think that heavy hair must have saved her from the worst of it. I don't want to lug her off to the hospital till I see what happens. If it's just a concussion, she's better off in her own bed. Don't go pestering her to talk. She'll come around. She's semiconscious now."

"Conscious," muttered a feeble voice from the depths of grogginess. "Hit me."

"Who?" Osbert couldn't keep himself from asking.

"The visitation."

Sergeant MacVicar nodded. "Aye, she's havering, puir leddy."

"No she's not," said Osbert.

"Oot of the room if you're going to talk," snapped Dr. Somervell with his fingers on Arethusa's pulse. "And leave the door open. There's a god-awful stink of perfume in here."

"It's Romaunt de la Rose," Mrs. Poppy put in eagerly. "The visitation must of knocked it off the dresser. I picked up the bottle, but it was empty. She'll be sick about that."

"So am I," Osbert groaned, thinking of fingerprints that might have been.

"Git," said Dr. Somervell, and they got.

Mrs. Poppy tagged along, avid to tell again what she'd already told because she'd thought up a few more embellishments, but Sergeant MacVicar said, "Whist, wumman," again so she didn't. It was Osbert who got to hold the floor.

"She told us yesterday she'd seen somebody in her room the night before. She assumed it was a visitor from a higher plane. Aunt Arethusa would, you know."

"Aye, and what did this visitation look like?"

"Like a person, only she didn't get to see the face. She described it as majestic, which probably means tall and stout. Not little and skinny, anyway. She said it was wearing a dark drapery."

"Not exactly a drapery, darling," said Dittany. "She said a garment. That could mean a dress or a bathrobe or just that it was so dark she couldn't see anything at all but a blob. Anyway, she ducked under the bedclothes and when she peeked out again, it was gone."

"She said there wasn't any sound, except that the board in the hall creaked when the apparition stepped on it," Osbert added.

Sergeant MacVicar nodded. "Ah, a supernatural creak. And nothing was disturbed?"

"Not that she noticed," said Dittany. "And I think she would. Arethusa's awfully choice of her possessions, you know."

"Anyway," said Osbert, "we had the quilt pieces at our house."

"Er—Mrs. Poppy, hadn't you better go down to the kitchen and put the kettle on? Dr. Somervell will be asking for hot water any minute now," Dittany interjected. She couldn't think why offhand, since Arethusa wasn't having a baby, but knowing Mrs. Poppy's penchant for telling a story and getting it wrong, she thought they'd better get the woman out of earshot. "Make a pot of tea while you're about it," she added. After all, one could always use a cup of tea, as Osbert's cousin Rosemary was wont to remark.

"Um ah," said Sergeant MacVicar in appreciation of this stratagem. "Now, Deputy Monk, what is this about quilt pieces?"

Osbert explained. "You see, when we were burgled we were assumed to have had them, but we didn't. When Arethusa was burgled, she was assumed to have them, but we did."

"I see. That is perfectly clear. And the pieces, you believe, are the clue that was referred to in this letter Miss Paffnagel claims Mr. Fairfield showed her shortly before he was foully done to death."

"That's what Dittany and I think," said Osbert. "We haven't

figured out the code yet, but maybe I got some of the letters wrong. It's the bees, you know, waving their feelers. I'm not much up on semaphore code. I was going to take another crack at it today."

"I suggest you do so. First, however, I wish you two would look around this house and try to ascertain whether anything of value has been abstracted. Oh, and one other question. This apparition, or visitation, did Mr. or Mrs. Jehosaphat Fairfield see it also?"

"No, Arethusa said they were both sawing wood like a house afire," said Dittany in a fine concatenation of metaphor and simile. "In fact they both overslept and were late getting off. They'd been whooping it up on Zilla Trott's dandelion wine when they went to visit Mrs. Fairfield at Minerva's. That was after we'd had supper here together. They drank a fair amount then, too. You know, Osbert, I can't imagine Minerva getting them drunk, now that I think of it. She must have seen they were already half loaded, and you know she's always inclined toward temperance."

"Well, Miss Paffnagel had the father of all hangovers yesterday or I'm a coyote's uncle," Osbert insisted. "You know something? I'm going to call up Minerva right now and ask her what shape they were in when they left there."

"I think you may have a point, Deputy Monk," said Sergeant MacVicar.

But the point was not taken, because nobody answered at Minerva's. Dittany phoned the museum, thinking Mrs. Fairfield might have been taken there under escort to pick up her personal effects, but got no answer. Then she called Zilla, because if Minerva wasn't at home Zilla was sure to know where she'd be. But Zilla didn't.

"She wasn't going anywhere that I know of. Mrs. Fairfield was pretty cut up, thanks to your dear Aunt Arethusa, and Minerva was just going to try to get her to spend the day quietly around the house."

"Then why doesn't somebody answer the phone?" Dittany demanded.

"Don't ask me. Maybe they're out in the back yard. Did you let it ring?"

"Of course I did. Look, maybe you'd better take a run over there, if you don't mind. I'm at Arethusa's. She got knocked out and burgled last night, in case you hadn't heard."

"She what? Dittany, are you sure?"

"Doc Somervell is, and so's Sergeant MacVicar. Arethusa still isn't fully conscious, and we don't know if she ever will be. The doctor says it's probably only on account of her thick hair she wasn't killed outright. Now will you go check on Minerva?"

"Yup."

That was what was so great about Zilla. Dittany hung up and went to make sure the dining room still had its full quota of crocodiles. A few minutes later, Zilla called back.

"Dittany, is the doctor still there?"

"No, why? Don't tell me they've—"

"They're still asleep and I can't wake them up. They're snoring like pigs. Minerva doesn't snore. At least I've never heard her. And don't start in on my dandelion wine, because she didn't have any. It looks to me as if they've both been drugged."

"Drugged? Then that's what was wrong with Hunding Paffnagel and the Jehosaphat Fairfields the night before. Try not to worry Zilla. They'll wake up sooner or later with awful hangovers. Stay with them. I'll send somebody."

Dittany gave Zilla's news to Sergeant MacVicar, heard him utter a word she'd never thought would pass his lips, and saw him leave the house at what could best be described as a stately gallop. Then she went back to searching. It took a long time, because the house was large and Arethusa was acquisitive. As far as they could tell, nothing was missing. At intervals, she or Osbert checked in on Arethusa. At last Osbert was rewarded by finding his aunt awake and aware.

"What are you doing here?" was her fond greeting.

"It's all right, Aunt Arethusa," he told her in a gentler tone than he had perhaps ever used before. "Don't try to thrash around. You've been hurt, but you're going to be all right."

"Who hurt me?"

"You said it was the visitation. Don't you remember?"

"No. Ridiculous. Visitations don't go around bashing people on the head. I want some tea."

"I'll get it. You lie still." Dittany ran down to the kitchen, wondering what had happened to the tea Mrs. Poppy was supposed to have made and, for that matter, to Mrs. Poppy.

That little mystery, at least, was solved when she found the kettle boiling dry on the stove and the woman out by the back fence in excited confabulation with Grandsire Coskoff's new wife. Dittany left her there, refilled the kettle, and made up a tray for Arethusa. Surely a piece of toast and a little orange juice wouldn't hurt. When she got back upstairs she was met by Osbert assisting his aunt back from the bathroom.

"Up and about already? Wonderful! Just don't get too frisky. Here, let me fix your pillows. How's that?"

"Ugh," Arethusa groaned. "Would you mind holding the cup for me? My hands don't seem to have any strength in them."

"It's just the shock. You'll be all right." Dittany hoped she was telling the truth. "Here, take a sip."

Arethusa's alimentary system appeared to be working at any rate. She drank the tea, sipped the juice, and even managed a corner of the toast. Then she said, "Too tired," and closed her eyes again.

"Do you think she's all right?" Osbert whispered to Dittany.

The lids flew up. The great eyes flashed. "Idiot," snarled Arethusa.

Dittany's own eyes filled with happy tears. "Yes, darling," she whispered back, "she's going to be just fine."

# CHAPTER 24

Therese Boulanger showed up a little later with a bowl of blanc-mange, a bunch of snapdragons from her garden, and a plea to be useful. Dittany and Osbert left Therese babysitting the convalescent and went to see what was up at Minerva's. There, they found Sergeant MacVicar and Zilla Trott in earnest conference with Dr. Somervell.

"Aye, they've been drugged, nae doot about it," the sergeant told them. "The sair question is, how?"

"Camomile tea," Dittany told him promptly. "Hunding Paffnagel and the Jehosaphat Fairfields had some here the night before, and the same thing happened to them. Miss Paffnagel thought she was hung over. So did we, considering. But then we got to thinking. Zilla's dandelion wine is potent stuff all right, but people don't get drunk on those little thimblefuls Minerva serves them. You know her folks were all blue-ribbon. Go look in that canister, Zilla. I'll bet you find something besides camomile."

Mrs. Trott ran to get the painted tin box she herself kept filled with the soothing herb for Minerva and spilled its contents out on a clean cup towel. "You're right, Dittany. Look at those little specks." She picked up a few on her fingertip, sniffed, and tasted. "Valium or some such muck, I'll bet. Who could pull a rotten trick like that?"

"Anybody who took a notion," said Dittany. "You know Minerva never thinks to lock her doors, and I suppose half the town's been through here, what with the funeral and all. Well, I expect they'll sleep it off sooner or later. The others did."

"I don't know as I'm going to take a chance on that," said the doctor. "We'll try rousing them first. If that doesn't work, I'll use the stomach pump. Zilla, you can help me. The rest of you clear out of here. You'd only be in the way."

"Then let's go home," said Osbert. "I want another whack at

that code. Sergeant, maybe you could check those bees over and
see if we made any mistakes."

Sergeant MacVicar could and did, but had to concede he agreed
with them and the Girl Guides' manual. "Maybe yon colors mean
something," he offered, "though I'm sair fuddled as to what."

"I know," cried Dittany. "Don't you see? It's the rainbow. Red,
orange, green, blue, purple. Try them in that order."

Osbert began to scribble. "LUBFYPE . . . that's not getting us
anywhere. CLYBLU . . . Nope. FLY . . ."

"Fly," shouted Dittany. "At least it's a word. Then FP. And look,
here comes FLUB."

"Flub's rather modern slang, I think," Osbert objected.

"FLU, then. The fly flew. That makes sense, sort of."

"But what's so—hey, wait a second. FP, that could be fireplace.
Fly fireplace flue, which leaves BBLEC left over."

"BBL is the abbreviation for barrel," Sergeant MacVicar
pointed out. "Could it be a barrel of something beginning with
EC?"

"Eclairs?" Dittany wondered. "Embroidered corset?"

Osbert shook his head. "I must be wrong about fireplace. Wasn't
the house built after airtight stoves came in?"

"That's right," said Dittany. "The mantelpieces are all fakes. But
how about FP standing for front parlor? There's that monstrous
great round stove with the cast-iron roses on top. I suppose you
could call it barrel shaped."

"Fly front parlor flue," Osbert nodded. "That sounds more like a
direction. Kind of a risky place to hide something, though. Tin
stovepipes get awfully hot."

"Not that one," Dittany insisted. "The front parlor was the one
room the Architraves hardly ever used. I'll bet there hasn't been a
fire in that stove for the past eighty years. Come on, let's go take a
look."

"But darling, we haven't finished working out the code."

"Maybe it'll work itself out when we take the stovepipe down.
Oh gosh, and we just paid for having that Axminster carpet sham
pooed."

"Take some newspapers." The blood of the MacVicars was up.
The sergeant grabbed yesterday's *Lobelia Leader* which the
Monks hadn't even got around to reading yet and led the charge
on the museum.

Again they had the place to themselves. That was a good thing. After all the hard work that had been put into redding up the parlor, the act of vandalism they were bent on committing might have evoked strong protest. But commit it they did, with Dittany holding the ladder while Osbert took down the pipe and Sergeant MacVicar barked out instructions in words no doubt learned from his father and mostly unintelligible to his hearers.

"All right," Osbert panted at last. "The flue's open. Now what?"

"BBLEC," said Dittany.

"Daft," said Sergeant MacVicar.

"Not if B stands for brick," Osbert retorted. "The flue's all lined with them, right up to the—aha! C. Chimney. Behind the brick. Entering chimney. And the L must be for left-hand side. Got something sharp I can poke with?"

Sergeant MacVicar passed up his jackknife. Osbert prodded, yelled, "Wahoo!" pulled out a loose brick and then a small tin box, somewhat kippered, with Mail Pouch Chewing Tobacco painted on the lid.

"Here, darling, take this till I—"

"Ooh!"

Dittany hadn't meant to open the box till Osbert got down, but she couldn't help it. The overcooked hinges gave way. Something heavy and glittering fell smack into her hand.

"It's the fly," she gasped. "Look!"

It was indeed a fly, a huge one, almost two inches long. The body was an emerald the size of an almond, the wings were carved crystal. The head was a single, blazing ruby and the eyes were glittering diamonds.

"And I'll eat my badge if they're not genuine," murmured Sergeant MacVicar in awe and reverence. "Yon bauble must be worth a wee fortune."

"Wee, my eyeball," said Dittany. "Have you priced any rubies and emeralds lately? Where on earth do you suppose it came from?"

"Was any of the Architrave ladies ever the mistress of a foreign potentate?" Osbert wondered.

Dittany shook her head. "We don't get many foreign potentates in Lobelia Falls. He could have been an admiral of the fleet, I suppose. That would account for the semaphore code. But why hide it in the chimney? I should have thought she'd want to wear it."

"I misdoubt she'd have found sic a gaudy breastpin somewhat dressy for Wednesday night prayer meeting," Sergeant MacVicar replied. "Though so light a leddy might have been nae muckle churchgoer. Guid losh! John Architrave left you a far greater inheritance than he knew, Dittany lass."

"Me? Oh, you mean us. The club."

"Aye. The house and all it contained was how the will read, if memory serves me. What would a thing like this fetch now?"

"I couldn't even begin to guess." Dittany turned the fly this way and that, watching the stones flash. "Poor Mr. Fairfield! What a thrill this would have been for him. Osbert, you don't suppose he actually had found its hiding place, and somebody knew?"

"I doubt that, darling. Why would they have put it back and called attention to themselves bashing around after the code? I just wish to heck I could get my hands on that letter so we'd know what this is all about. Darn, why couldn't Miss Paffnagel have learned French?"

"Mayhap she had," said Sergeant MacVicar drily.

"That's right," cried Dittany. "Nothing went wrong till old Hunding blew into town, did it? Why don't you pinch her, Sergeant? Give her the third degree and make her squeal. Or shut her up without any food. That should make her confess quick enough."

"Noo, lass, let us refrain from hasty judgment. True, Miss Paffnagel is the only person so far who admits to having been shown that hypothetical letter. Her frankness in this regard may indeed be a ruse to disarm suspicion. Knowing Mr. Fairfield of old, she would have assumed he also showed it to others. Indeed he may have done so. Its being in French would present no great bar to any Canadian. There are enough French-speaking pairsons aboot. Even Cedric Fawcett could have easily found someone to read it to him. Churdie also, needless to say, had ample opportunity to abstract the letter from Mr. Fairfield's dook, even as you and I. The field appears wide open still."

Osbert shook his head. "Not exactly, Sergeant. There's that question of why Mr. Fairfield was taken up to the roof and thrown off. We know he wouldn't have gone under his own steam because of his acrophobia. We also know from the sweater fuzz we found on the railing that he'd been there, unless somebody else went up wearing his sweater, then went back and put it on him, which is silly. What I think is, somebody whopped him with something heavy, then hoisted him up through the skylight by means of Fred Churtle's ropes, and dumped him off. I think we'd better get Fred back here, *tout de suite.*"

# CHAPTER 25

"Fred," demanded Osbert, "what did you lie to us for?"

"Huh?"

It was half an hour or so later. They were in, of all places, Minerva Oakes's dining room. Sergeant MacVicar had gone to collect the roofer while Osbert and Dittany went back to see how Arethusa was doing. They'd found her sipping beef tea made by Hazel Munson from a cup held by Dot Coskoff while Therese Boulanger swathed her head in a gauzy silken scarf to hide the bandages and Ellie Jackson tiptoed in with a bunch of black-eyed Susans picked by her angelic little son Petey, no doubt from somebody else's yard. Sensing they were not needed here, they'd gone on to their appointed rendezvous, although Dittany still wasn't quite sure why.

"Come on, Fred," Osbert insisted. "Night before last up at Little Pussytoes, you told Dittany and me you'd gone over to the museum to pick up your tackle, looked at the place and figured there was nobody around. You led us to believe you didn't even try the door. You claimed you'd merely taken a stroll around the yard, looking up at the roof from force of habit, and stumbled over Peregrine Fairfield's body by accident. That's a lot of garbage, right?"

"Now look," Churtle began.

Sergeant MacVicar stopped him. "We have looked. That is why we now request your cooperation."

"Colle cooperation," Churtle snorted. "Dragging me off the church steeple in full sight of Reverend Pennyfeather. The Lord giveth a job and the cops taketh it away."

"Blasphemy will get you nowhere, Mr. Churtle," said Sergeant MacVicar severely. "I suggest you answer Deputy Monk's question."

"All right," said the roofer sulkily. "It's a lot of garbage. See, what really happened was, I hadn't gone back for my gear because

I was what you might call ambivalent about meeting up with Perry again. I mean, I wouldn't have minded seeing him, but I sure as heck didn't want to tangle with Vangie. On the other hand, I didn't much give a hoot one way or the other because it was all so long ago and far away, if you get what I mean."

"We follow your drift, Mr. Churtle. Go on."

"But see, the thing of it was, I needed my gear because I've got a big job coming up on the new curling rink over in East Scottsbeck that Andy's building. So I figured if I went to the museum just at suppertime, eh, I might be able to sneak in and get my stuff and sneak out again without meeting anybody. So that's what I did."

"Continue your narrative," said Sergeant MacVicar relentlessly.

"Well, to make a long story short," which Churtle clearly had no intention of doing, "I tried the door. It was unlocked, so I peeked in and didn't see anybody. So I said was anybody around, you know how you do, and nobody answered, so I went on in. So there was my gear only somebody'd been fiddling around with the ropes which I might have known they would be. So I go to straighten 'em out so's I can haul 'em down. But no sooner do I give a tweak to see if the pulleys are jammed than I hear this noise. Kind of a mixture of a heavy thud and a muted slam, only mostly thud. So I think to myself, what the heck? I mean, what would you think?"

"Any conjecture of mine would not be germane to the issue, Mr. Churtle."

"Okay, so anyway there I am, analyzing the situation as you might say. I didn't know whether to give the rope another pull or what. To tweak or not to tweak, that was the question. What if it was a hunk of the chimney that fell off? That was another question, see. So I said to myself, Fred, I said, you better go out there and see what it was made that thud you just heard."

"A reasonable conclusion," Sergeant MacVicar conceded. "So in short and without wishing to put words in a witness's mouth, you went."

"I went. And there was Perry, dead as a proverbial mackerel. It took an awful hike out of me, I can tell you."

Churtle fell silent, perhaps in mourning for the departed, perhaps in retrospective horror at his gruesome discovery. Whichever it was, Sergeant MacVicar wanted none of it. "And how, Mr. Churtle, did you know he was dead?"

"Well, heck, how wouldn't I? I knelt down beside him and said,

'Hey, Perry, old buddy, it's me, Fred,' and he never answered. And his hand was cold and there wasn't any pulse and he just sort of flopped when I turned him over."

"Turned him over?" yelped Osbert. "Holy tumbleweeds, Sergeant—"

"Aye, Deputy Monk. Mr. Churtle, are we to gather that when you found Mr. Fairfield, he was lying face down?"

"Why else would I have had to turn him over? See, I wasn't really sure it was Perry. I mean, here's this gray-haired geezer hunched up in a heap among the bee balm. Mostly what I could see was the seat of his pants and the back of his sweater and naturally they wasn't the same ones he'd had on when I'd last set eyes on him some thirty-eight years previous."

"But how could you be immediately sure he was dead? Did it not occur to you there might still be a spark of life that you might extinguish by turning him over?"

"Nope. Not with the back of his head bashed in."

"Dang it, Fred," howled Osbert, "why couldn't you have told me that before?"

"Because I had this natural aversion to getting pinched for a murder I didn't do," Churtle replied without hesitation. "That's why I dropped him like a hot potato and hightailed it out of there, being darn careful not to crush the bee balm. Then I realized somebody might have noticed my van, so I went back the next morning so's I could act the part of the innocent bystander, added to which I still needed and shall continue to need my tackle and buckets, assuming you're not going to shove me in the slammer despite the fact that I stand before you purified and shriven by a full confession of my involvement, such as it was, in this mysterious and sinister happening."

"Sinister but hardly mysterious," said Osbert, "now that we know for sure Mr. Fairfield was dead by the time he was put on the roof, and that the rope had been arranged so all you had to do was give a tweak and he'd fall to the ground and the skylight would slam shut. Let's go see how Minerva's doing."

To Dittany's ineffable relief, they found their unwitting hostess sitting up in bed, sipping orange juice. "How do you feel?" she asked.

"Like my Uncle Abednego after he'd been on one of his toots. Used to beg us to put slippers on the cat so's its toenails wouldn't click. Zilla here tells me I've been doped. In the camomile tea. Can you imagine? Poor Evangeline's still asleep. She must have got a worse dose than I did."

"How so?" Sergeant MacVicar wanted to know. "Did you give her a bigger cup?"

"Why no. We both had the same. My nice bone china with the rosebud pattern. But maybe she—"

"Maybe me no maybes, wumman. This is a desperate crime we're investigating. Did you watch Mrs. Fairfield sup her tea?"

"Come to think of it, no. She took the cup to her room. She wanted to read her Bible before she dropped off, poor soul."

"Umph. Minerva Oakes, I want your offeecial pairmission for Deputy Monk and myself to search her room in the public interest."

"Quit gargling your r's at me, Sergeant. My head can't stand it. Of course, if you must. Only don't wake Evangeline if you can help it. She's been through enough already. Maybe I'd better go with you. Hand me my bathrobe, Zilla."

"You're not going without me," Zilla insisted.

"Or me." Dittany wasn't going to be left out.

The three women clustered in the doorway like Clotho, Lachesis, and Atropos while Osbert and the sergeant made their search. It didn't take long. They found the letter tucked in between Amos and Obadiah, and Sergeant MacVicar waxed grim over the use of Holy Writ for so base a purpose. They found a drapey dark nylon dress with a thread from Arethusa's rose-colored bedspread clinging to the skirt. They found sensible black walking shoes with rose-colored fuzz from Arethusa's deep-piled bedroom carpeting caught on the crepe soles. They found the scent of Romaunt de la Rose emanating from a pair of hastily washed black panty hose hanging over the doorknob.

When Zilla, at Sergeant MacVicar's request, drew back the covers and sniffed, she found the identical scent arising from the sleeper's left leg as well as from the badly chipped plaster cast on her broken wrist. Sergeant MacVicar drew up a chair to the bedside and sat himself down to maintain grim vigilance until Evangeline Fairfield should awaken and be duly and properly taken into custody.

# CHAPTER 26

"It wasn't much of a mystery, really," Osbert half apologized. "The only one who'd have had any special reason to haul Mr. Fairfield up through the skylight and dump him off the roof was his wife. She was handicapped by that bum wrist, and didn't dare let the body be found before she could get away and establish herself an alibi. So what she did was bop him over the head with her cast while he was sitting at his desk, drag his body out into the hall still in that office chair—it's got casters on it, remember—and hitch him to Fred Churtle's hoist. Then all she had to do was haul him up to the skylight, go back upstairs, and climb the ladder."

"Just as you and Sergeant MacVicar did later on," cried Dittany.

"That's right, darling. From the ladder, she could boost him through the skylight and swing him outside by means of the hoist. The body must have caught on that ornamental railing and snagged the sweater. I expect Mrs. Fairfield had some trouble juggling him into position, but she's a pretty hefty woman and he was a little runt of a guy. Anyway, she must have got him out on the slope of the roof with the rope looped across his body and caught under the skylight so he wouldn't start to roll until she gave it a yank from below to turn him loose and shut the skylight. Then she went off to show Minerva how dirty she'd got grubbing around the attic."

"With me cracking the whip over her," Dittany interjected.

"Yes, darling. So she cleaned herself up in case anybody noticed she had the wrong kind of smudges on her, went through her act of getting worried when Mr. Fairfield didn't show up and got Minerva to walk back to the museum with her. Once they were inside, all Mrs. Fairfield had to do was make sure she steered Minerva away from the stairwell and pull on the rope. Fred Churtle had already pulled it, of course, but that didn't matter. For a spur-of-the-moment murder it was pretty ingenious, you have to admit."

"But why kill him at all?" Zilla demanded.

"Because Dittany'd just found the bees, and Mrs. Fairfield knew they were the clue to the jeweled fly. It's right there in the letter she stole. Read it, darling. Your French is better than mine."

Dittany took the yellowed page from him and read aloud, translating as she went. "You know, Aralia chérie, how my great-grandmother got the fly. She was lady's maid to the Empress Josephine and delighted to deck her mistress in the wonderful jewels Her Majesty loved so well. You know how extravagant the Empress was, how impulsive, how generous. She could refuse nothing to anyone—except the Emperor, poor man! At the end she proved his loyal friend, so who is to judge? But to the fly. To honor the Emperor, Josephine ordered a ruby and emerald brooch in the form of the imperial bee. The jeweler, a Bourbonniste enraged at this Bonaparte's pretensions, made a common fly of the jewels instead. Another in her place would have had him guillotined; Josephine only laughed. 'Here, Mouche,' she said. That was her pet name for my great-grandmother, who was so tiny and always flitting about like a fly. 'Take your namesake for a wedding present when you join your new husband in Canada, and keep it always to remember me.'

"So I entreat you, my darling, to keep the fly safe and secret as I have done, in memory of the Empress and of me. That new husband of yours is funny about money, I think. Your loving Grand'mère, Henriette."

Dittany cleared her throat. "There's a footnote in a different writing, Aralia's, I suppose. 'To my daughter, when I have one: The bees know the hiding place. Grand'mère and I worked them together after we hid the fly. We thought the Empress should have her bees at last. Discover their message for yourself and keep the secret as I mean to do. Your loving mother-to-be.' She spelled it 'bee.' I suppose she couldn't resist."

"But Aralia never had a daughter," said Minerva, "and John didn't know a word of French. I wonder where she hid the letter all those years."

"I suppose Evangeline won't tell us, just for spite," Zilla sniffed. "Too bad her husband couldn't have kept his mouth shut like Aralia. And they say women are the blabbermouths. Huh! Struck lucky for once in his life, and it killed him."

"Mrs. Fairfield must have known what that bee meant as soon as she opened the box and saw it stuck inside the lid," said Dittany. "I'm surprised she let me get away with the pieces."

"She expected to have no trouble getting them back," Sergeant MacVicar replied. "She assumed that without the letter you would never guess they had any hidden meaning."

"She didn't know Osbert," Dittany rejoined proudly.

Zilla was still fretting. "I still can't see why she beaned old Perry. He wanted the fly as much as she did."

"Aye," the sergeant answered, "but he wanted it to display at the museum and enhance his professional reputation. I misdoubt she had other notions."

"Darn right," said Dittany. "She'd have sold it and lived the life of Riley on her ill-gotten gains. She must have realized that the brazen theft of an important artifact was the one thing she'd never bully Peregrine into going along with. In spite of the fuss she put up, I expect Mrs. Fairfield was tickled silly when I took the bees away. If her husband had seen them, he'd have shown me Henriette's letter. Then she'd either have had to kill us both on the spot or miss her chance at the fly. But whatever possessed her to burgle our house the very next night, do you suppose? Couldn't she wait? I'm sure she'd bagged the letter as soon as she clobbered old Perry."

Osbert shrugged. "How've you been sleeping lately, Minerva?"

"Like a rock. My stars, you don't mean she drugged me twice?"

"I make it thrice. No doubt Mrs. Fairfield had some painkiller for that broken wrist and bungod it into your camomile the night after she killed Peregrine. I think her big rush was because she'd recognized Miss Paffnagel at the museum, even though she said she hadn't. She knew Hunding and Perry must have been having an old home week, which meant Hunding had seen the letter."

"As in fact she had," Dittany put in.

"Yes, dear. Mrs. Fairfield didn't know if Miss Paffnagel was still around town and didn't get a chance to find out because Aunt Arethusa strong-armed her into going to your tea party. I expect the quilt pieces were mentioned over the crumpets and Mrs. Fairfield found out they hadn't yet been shown around, so she figured she still had a chance to get to them before Miss Paffnagel did. But she struck out because we didn't have them. And then that next night, after the funeral, Miss Paffnagel and the Jehosaphats barged in here telling how they'd just seen the pieces at Aunt Arethusa's.

She must have been frantic at that. So she made sure you all had a slug of camomile tea, counting on the liquor they'd drunk to give the sedative an extra kick, which it certainly did, and burgled Aunt Arethusa."

"Only of course that didn't work, either," said Dittany, "because by then we'd taken them back. And Arethusa woke up and thought she was a higher being, so she had to scram. Then yesterday they had that big row and Mrs. Fairfield must have figured this was her last chance, so she went back and conked Arethusa so hard she—she—I must say she doesn't handle frustration in a very adult way. And Miss Paffnagel hadn't even read the letter Perry showed her, so it was all for nothing. There's irony for you."

Minerva shook her head, wincing at the pain. "Not for me it isn't. I'll tell you one thing, this is positively the last time I let a stranger set foot in my spare bedroom."

"Huh! I've heard that one before."

Zilla's snort must have roused the woman in the bed. Mrs. Fairfield stirred, groaned, and opened her eyes. "What are you all doing here?"

"We came to tell you we've found the fly," Dittany chirped.

"The fly! No, you couldn't!" She recollected herself. "I don't know what you're talking about."

"Nonsense, wumman," said Sergeant MacVicar. "We have the letter you stole from the museum and concealed in this verra room after you killed your husband and disposed of his body by means of Frederick Churtle's rigging in a vain attempt to pull the wool over our eyes. We have further evidence of your heinous crime, and I have the offeecial duty to place you under arrest for murder in the first degree as well as breaking and entering in the nighttime with aggravated assault on the person of Miss Arethusa Monk. I will now proceed to read the formal charge in accordance with the laws of Lobelia Falls and the Government of Canada and in the presence of these witnesses. You will then dress yourself under the surveillance of Mesdames Oakes, Trott, and Monk while I guard the door and Deputy Monk nips over to get the official police vehicle in which we shall convey you to the lockup."

"You can't do that. I'm a sick woman."

"You are not. You are merely feeling the aftereffects of the drugged camomile tea you drank in order to give yourself an alibi after you got back from pounding Miss Arethusa Monk over the head with your plaster cast. She is now conscious and will no doubt take pleasure in identifying you as her assailant."

"She couldn't have seen—I mean, I wasn't there."

"Do not trifle with the law, Mrs. Fairfield. You reek of her spilled perfume and there is pink fuzz from her carpet all over your shoes."

"And to think I used to wish Mrs. Poppy would vacuum under the beds," Dittany marveled. "My gosh, Minerva, I just remembered. You're the last of the Architraves. What are you going to do about the fly?"

"I'll think about the fly when my head clears. The main thing now is to start piecing that quilt before the excitement dies down. You'd better—oh, there's the phone now."

"I'll get it."

Dittany ran downstairs but was back in a jiffy. "That was Therese, yelling for reinforcements. She says Andy McNaster's baying at the door with a mushy get-well card and an armload of red, red roses. Sorry to break up the pinching party, folks, but I've got to go."

"Oh well," said Osbert philosophically, "at least he's not a woodchuck. Give Andy a nephew's blessing for me, darling. Only for Pete's sake don't invite him to supper."